THE CUTTER

CHARLOTTE BARNES

First published in 2021 by Bloodhound Books.

www.bloodhoundbooks.com

Print ISBN 978-1-913942-34-2

ALSO BY CHARLOTTE BARNES

PSYCHOLOGICAL THRILLER

Intention

CRIME THRILLERS

The Copycat

The Watcher

Dear Beth,
thank you for being there chapter by chapter –

NOW

PROLOGUE

Melanie watched the sea crash against the shore with an anger she'd only ever seen in humans. She timed her walks to catch each high tide; whether it was before the crack of dawn or hours after. She did the normal things as best as she could. She'd make trips to the small town shops to buy her bread and milk, always in cash. During each trip she made idle conversation with the ice cream and souvenir shop owners, who complained religiously about the perils of closed season. Melanie smiled knowingly, as though she could understand their plight somehow.

'Feeling settled now?' one of them asked as she tried to walk away.

'Oh, you know, things still feel new.'

'You'll be a regular before you know it.'

'I'm hoping so,' Melanie replied, thinking, *I'm hoping not*. 'I better get going if I'm going to catch that sea drawing in.'

'Yep, you go ahead and get your fins wet, Kelly. Be seeing you.'

'Take care now,' Melanie shouted back.

The sea was furious and there was something comforting in

its madness. Melanie imagined her own feelings being channelled through it somehow. She walked along the beach for as long as she could before froth and cold water began to lap at her feet, then she climbed the steps to the seafront. The wind was vicious too, and she was glad she'd brought a scarf. She was midway through her walk to the boats when she decided to call him.

The seafront was dotted with benches, some of them were out in the open but some were tucked away inside small brick structures. The front of the building was open, but the shelters around the sides and the back would give Melanie the quiet she needed to make a phone call. She keyed in the right speed dial number and waited.

'DS Carter speaking.'

The sound of his voice was more of a comfort than Melanie had expected it to be. She smiled, but the sensation of sea salt cracking on her lips brought home the situation. 'It's me.'

She heard him sigh before he answered. 'Christ, boss, is it good to hear you.'

'Is everything okay?'

There was a long spill of silence before Carter replied. She pressed the phone hard against her ear in case the wind had snatched his reply away.

'Everything's fine,' he said after a few seconds. 'It's just been... It's been a day.'

'You can't say?' Melanie knew the answer before she'd even asked the question. It was an ongoing investigation; of course Carter couldn't say. But she was desperate to know all the same.

'I shouldn't say.'

Yet, from his tone, Melanie had a feeling he would...

BEFORE

1

DS Edd Carter walked in ahead of his daughter to make sure there was nothing damaging on the evidence board. He'd managed to give Emily a tour of the station without her seeing anything she shouldn't; he didn't want his own office space to be the spot that ruined it. He felt a pang of relief when he stepped in and saw the board was blank, presumably waiting for fresh material. But whatever the reason, it made this room a safe space. Emily had never been to the office and it was one of the many things he'd promised her to soften the blow of a boring half-term.

'And this is where I work,' he said, by way of alerting his colleagues to their arrival.

Emily looked around the room with awe. 'So, you hunt bad guys down from here?'

'Well, your dad doesn't do much of that, but we do,' DC David Read replied, crossing the room with a smile. He crouched to be eye-to-eye with Emily, held out a hand and said, 'I'm David, that's Brian.' He nodded behind him to his partner, who waved.

Emily took his hand with a confidence that looked strange

on a child. 'It's nice to meet you, David and Brian. Who's everyone else?' She scoured the office then, her eyes soon landing on DC Chris Burton. 'Chris!'

Burton joined the huddle forming in the centre of the room. 'Young lady. How are we?'

Emily shrugged. 'Okay, I guess. But I wish Dad didn't have to work.'

'But I have to catch bad guys, right?' He knelt to speak to his daughter directly. 'I have to be here, and you have to be with Mum, but I'll get you as soon as work is over. Deal?'

'Spit deal?' she said, looking from her hand to his.

'No, Em, we talked about that.'

The door jolted open with a force that grabbed everyone's attention, and in walked DI Melanie Watton. She was juggling her phone against her ear, a full file of paperwork in one hand, and a to-go coffee mug in the other.

'It's good that you've called us, really,' she said, walking past the group. 'It doesn't sound like your basic robbery to me either.'

'Melanie,' Emily whispered.

'I think it's best if I get a couple of officers down there...'

Melanie headed towards her office without a word, and Emily's disappointment was clear. Carter was still level with his daughter, and he placed a finger under her chin to guide her face to his, and away from the closed office door. He kissed her nose lightly. 'Mel is always happy to have visitors, but she's a really busy lady.'

Emily's lips were downturned at the edges. 'I do understand, Dad.'

'Shall we go and see if Mum's here?' he asked, and Emily nodded in reply. He stood up and tried to straighten out the beginnings of creases in his trousers. 'Trish is coming to pick her up from the main office, so we'll head down. If it's anything especially interesting will you ask her to hang fire for a second?' Carter said, his eyes shifting from one colleague to another.

Read rubbed at the back of his neck. 'Sure, I'll be the one to ask her.'

'Good man.' Burton punched his arm gently. 'Nice to see you, Emily.'

'Nice to see you all,' she spoke to the group as Carter guided her towards the exit.

Melanie stepped out of her office to find the shared space in a state of calm. Read and Fairer were talking among themselves, a splay of paperwork taking up their desks, while Burton was furiously tapping at her keyboard. Melanie looked around again for the missing officers and noted that DC Lucy Morris' desk looked untouched, though it was well into her morning shift. Melanie crossed the room to check the calendar to find out whatever it was that she'd forgotten this week.

'Everything all right, boss?' Burton took a pause from her typing.

Melanie turned. 'Morris?'

'Half day.'

'On a course?'

'With the tech team.'

Melanie frowned. 'Do you think they're going to pinch her?' The question was only half-serious, but it was a thought that had crossed Melanie's mind frequently since their last murder investigation. Morris had been integral to identifying their killer, and Melanie knew that people much higher up had noticed the DC's performance.

'Would you let them?'

'Would I hell.' Melanie closed the gap between them. 'Carter?'

'Taken Emily downstairs.'

'Bugger.' Melanie breathed the word out in a harsh puff. 'I wanted to say hello.'

'Cute kid, isn't she?'

'They all are at that age; give it time. We'll wait for Carter to get back and then–'

There was a clatter somewhere behind her and when she turned for the door she spotted Carter, leaning over with his hands on his knees. He looked to be out of breath but trying to gain some composure.

'I'm here.' He panted. 'I'm here and I'm ready for robbery and– Christ, I'm unfit.'

'We'll get started,' Melanie addressed the team from the centre of the room. 'We had a call come in this morning to report a murder-robbery on the outskirts of town. It looks as though whoever did this went all out on both the victim and the crime scene, quite a nasty one. Thousands of pounds-worth of artwork has gone missing.' She took out a small sheet of paper from her trouser pocket, with the essentials scribbled on. Before she could introduce any further details, Carter took three strides across the room and nabbed the sheet.

'Burton and I will take that.'

'You've recovered,' Burton snapped.

'The victim's name was Norman Halloway and he was a celebrated taxidermist,' Melanie continued. She spotted the sudden change in Carter's expression. 'His home had a studio attached which is where he was found, and this is also where the artwork was taken from. Taxidermy is a pricey but particular business by all accounts so we're looking for someone who knows their exotic animals, but also knows how to store them.'

Carter held the sheet of paper out as though it were also a dead thing. 'Taxidermy?'

'Yes. Problem?'

He offered the sheet back to Melanie. 'Hard pass, actually, Burton and I are swamped.'

'You called it,' Melanie replied, her smile set in a smirk.

'But when I called it–'

'Carter, let the woman speak,' Burton interrupted. 'You called it.'

Melanie cocked an eyebrow at Carter and continued. 'The artwork on site has to be stored and cleaned in a very specific way apparently. Halloway has, had, a cleaner who would come in every day to sort out the house, the studio and intermittently the pieces themselves. She turned up to work this morning to find the door to the studio wide open, went in to see that everything was okay, and that's when she found her employer.'

'Definitely a murder?' Fairer asked.

'Hunting knife.'

Read whistled. 'Yep, definitely a murder.'

'How much has been taken?' Burton asked, her pen hovering over a fresh sheet of paper.

'We're not entirely sure yet,' Melanie replied. 'The cleaner is in a bad way, although she's trying to be co-operative. Part of that co-operation is identifying the empty spots in the studio. When I spoke to the call-out officers earlier she'd spotted around ten missing items but that could have changed by now.'

'It's a lot of trouble just for ten,' Read said.

'I think we need to be prepared for that number to rise over the next few hours, as she notices more changes around the place. We also need to be especially vigilant with out-the-back deals going on right now. There's a lot of money in taxidermy, but it isn't going to be any old Joe on the street who's looking to buy it. We'll be dealing with some specialists along the way, I should think.' Melanie turned to Carter. 'Anything you need before you get going?'

'I mean, if there are already officers on site and investigating, what do we even need–'

'Anything you need before you get going?' Melanie cut across Carter and craned around him, directing the question at Burton instead.

'I'll take a less squeamish partner if there's one kicking around.'

Carter looked offended. 'I am not squeamish.'

'So why don't you want to go?'

'Because.' He hesitated. 'Okay, fine, because dead animals.'

Burton stood from her desk and shrugged on her blazer. 'Squeamish.'

Carter held the sheet out for Burton to take and then stepped towards his own desk to grab his coat and his ID badge. 'Burton, you'd be stuffed without me.' There was a beat of silence while he looked from one colleague to another. 'Come on, stuffed?'

'Very clever of you, Carter,' Melanie said, her tone flat but her expression playful.

'Bloody wasted in this office,' he said, following his partner to the door. 'Wasted…'

2

Carter and Burton pulled up at the scene to find it dotted with flashing lights. There were three marked police cars and a cordon around the building. Uniformed officers were contending with nosy neighbours in an orderly fashion. The most disruption seemed to be coming from an older woman, in the inner sanctum of the crime scene, who was being gently shushed by a male officer. He looked uncomfortable with the responsibility and kept looking round at few-second intervals as though waiting for a shift change.

'Do you think that's the cleaner?' Carter asked, following Burton's stare.

'There wasn't a mention of a wife, was there?' She turned to face him. 'Plus, that amount of distress, she certainly looks like she might have just found a body.'

'But they're around them all the time.'

Burton snorted. 'I mean, animals are one thing...'

'Fair point. Do you want to take lead in there, and I'll take crowd control?'

'Officers have already got crowd control,' Burton replied, nodding at their colleagues ahead of them. Carter looked as though he were feeling around for a reply, but Burton beat him to it. 'You still don't want to see the animals, do you?'

'It's not that–'

Burton cut him off by opening the passenger door and clambering out of the vehicle.

'Oi,' Carter continued. 'I said it's not–'

She slammed the door behind her and headed towards the only uniformed officer who didn't look to be juggling anyone, a young woman who was frantically scribbling something down. Burton waited for a pause in the officer's writing before she spoke.

'Excuse me, sorry, I'm DC Burton,' she said, catching the officer's attention. 'I'm here with DS Carter from the major incident team.' The other officer was visibly relieved at the announcement. 'Any chance you could walk us through what's happening around here?'

The officer tucked her notebook into a pocket. 'Everyone will be glad to know you're here. I'm PC Izzy Peters, I was one of the first officers on the scene. We arrived to find this lady,' she paused to gesture to the woman who Burton had guessed was the cleaner, 'outside the property in a state of distress. My partner and I determined that she's the housekeeper of the home and the accompanying studio where the crime looks to have taken place. Middle-aged white male stabbed with what appears to be a hunting knife of some kind. We didn't touch the scene, just called it in and got the witness out of the building.'

'Okay, good work,' Carter replied.

Burton cast a glance over one shoulder; she hadn't realised he'd joined her.

'They sent additional officers because we seemed to be attracting some attention. Like I said, the housekeeper was in quite a state of distress when we got here,' PC Peters clarified.

Burton could understand it: if she'd found a body out of the blue, she thought she'd cause a scene as well.

'Has anyone else been called?' Carter asked.

'We've since been informed that your DI has arranged for forensics, and for the medical examiner to visit the scene, but we haven't heard more than that. We've been instructed to offer whatever support you might need though.'

'Burton, shall we?' Carter stepped around his partner. 'We can't do much until forensics arrive, but it'll be worth looking around to get a feel for the scene.'

'Oh, will it now?' Burton said, her tone jovial. 'And what about all the–'

'Nothing wrong with a bit of blood and guts,' Carter cut her off, saving himself the embarrassment of his real fear – that was, the mass amount of taxidermy waiting on the other side of the wall – from being outed in front of another officer. 'Come on, let's get it over with.'

'Thanks for your help. If you could keep the witness calm and keep these people at bay for the time being, that's about all we need,' Burton instructed PC Peters before following Carter.

The officers stepped into the studio one after the other and took in their surroundings. Neither said a word as they eyed up steel tools and instruments pinned to a back wall, and mounted animal heads hung on the surrounding ones. There was a snarling fox, a solemn deer and, loitering beneath the more recognisable creatures, there was what looked to be the head of a hare with antlers fixed to it. In such a room full of oddities, it took both officers a beat in time to notice their real reason for being there.

Carter was the first to spot the victim. 'Jesus.'

Norman Halloway lay towards the back of the room, near a workbench and preparation area. There were obvious stab wounds at various points in his abdomen, some of which had bled out across the light floorboards. A knife had been discarded near the body, blood caked around the blade and handle. However, the weapon wasn't the only thing that had been left close to their victim.

Burton took a step back and tilted her head to one side. 'Carter, are you seeing this?'

'Seeing what?' He moved to stand alongside her.

It was only from an angle that the scene fell into a more disturbing focus. There were neat flowers causing a polka dot effect through the spilled blood, accompanied by what looked to be small tufts of grass – or at the very least some kind of greenery. The small clots of blood that had formed made it hard to discern the fine details of everything left behind. But the longer the officers looked, the more they saw, including the stance of their victim. Halloway was lying on his side and, close up, he appeared to have died in a position of self-defence, his hands raised half-towards his face as though about to shield himself from something. But from a short distance away, the fingers looked more like–

'Claws. Do you see it? It's like his fingers have been splayed to look like claws.'

Carter looked from one angle then another. 'How has he been fixed like that?'

The man's eyes were partly open which added to his uncanny appearance; there was something deer-in-the-headlights about the way he'd been left. His knees were bent at strange angles in a way that could have been accidental, but also could have been designed to give him the appearance of running – or, more likely, fleeing. It would be impossible to say one way or another how deliberate the positioning was, but there was certainly something action-like about the legs, down to the feet, one of which looked as though it were flat and the other pushing away from imagined ground.

'Carter?' Burton stood at another workbench on the other side of the crime scene. There were fewer tools near this one, replaced instead with books, scraps of paper, and artistry materials. 'Look at this.'

Carter crossed the room to meet his partner. There on the flat surface of the table lay a collage of discarded illustrations showing different animals, anatomically labelled, but each one in a different position to the other. There were some that had been embellished with further details: a trunk of tree for the animal to sit on; a squat bark with branches big enough to hold a bird; a small stretch of greenery, dotted with plain flowers.

'Is that our crime scene?' Carter pointed at the final illustration in the sequence but was mindful not to touch.

'It looks a lot like it to me.'

'And I thought the taxidermy was going to be the weirdest part of this case.'

'How are we, kids?' George Waller's booming voice infiltrated the space as he stood centred in the doorway. 'DI Watton tells me you've got something a little peculiar for...' he petered out as he laid eyes on the body, rigid and decorated at the back of the room. Waller sighed. 'Not that I'd expect anything different from Watton.' He turned to face the officers. 'Forensics are suiting up outside. We'll get started, shall we?'

3

Melanie pushed the door to her office closed as Carter's name appeared on her mobile. There were PCs reporting back to Read and Fairer in the shared office, and Melanie had a feeling that whatever this call was, it wasn't something that should be overheard. She connected the line and pressed the phone to her ear. Before Carter spoke, she could hear a commotion in the background, and what she thought was Waller's voice.

'Carter, what's going on there?'

'A bloody busy crime scene, sorry, boss. Let me try over here, hang on.' The sounds faded slightly as Carter moved. 'This might not be much better. I wanted to let you know that I'm sending Burton back with the witness, the cleaning lady. She's a bit of a state; the woman, not Burton.'

Melanie held back a sigh. 'Okay, and what about everything else?'

'The uniformed officers are doing a grand job of keeping out nosy neighbours, but we've upgraded to nosy passers-by and I think I need to be here. Forensics have stepped in already to start sweeping the scene. Waller is waiting for their go ahead to move the body, but he's managed to do a preliminary spot-check of it already.'

'And?'

'The victim was definitely stabbed, boss, there's no doubting that. But he was staged.'

'Staged?'

Carter lowered his voice. 'Like, taxidermy staged. There's flowers and greenery dotted about him that match the designs of some rough sketches the victim had on one of his workbenches. It's like someone killed him and tried to – Christ, I don't know, copy his design.'

Melanie tried to quickly process the news, but this was a blow she hadn't been expecting. She paced the room while she tried to gather her thoughts. 'First thing, where's Burton now?'

'She's outside helping uniforms, but only while I'm on the phone to you. We wanted to forewarn you to get an interview room ready for the witness.'

'Right. Have forensics said how long the sweep is going to take?'

'We're in for a late one, that's as much as I know. Waller and his helping hand are sticking around until the scene's been picked apart for samples and the rest of it, but he's said they won't be able to get an autopsy done straight away.'

'What kind of delay is there?'

'He didn't say, boss.' There was a pause and shuffle as though Carter were readjusting the phone. 'He also said not to bother calling because it won't make a difference.'

'Well that's scuppered that plan.' She set a hand on her forehead and took a deep breath. 'Okay, send Burton on her way and I'll make sure there's an interview room ready. I'll get Fairer and Read onto looking into the victim, and the cleaning lady. Can you text her name over?'

'As soon as we're done.'

'I'll let Morris know what she's walking into, and Archer.' Another sigh. She was beginning to feel like the only time she went to Superintendent Beverly Archer was with a blow of bad news. 'Will you keep me posted on everything there? If things are running too late, let me know and I can take over.'

Since Carter's custody arrangements had been finalised, the entire team had tried to help where they could to get him in and out of the office on time. Although Melanie sensed there were a few all-nighters ahead of them. She finished her conversation with Carter and waited for his text to come through with the name of their incoming witness: *Stela Ionescu*.

Outside her office, Melanie was pleased to find the shared space empty of all visitors. Read and Fairer looked up at her entrance. 'I need you to start background checks, lads. One on the victim, and one on the woman who found him, as a matter of urgency.'

Read straightened up and hit a series of keys on his computer. 'Hit me.'

'Stela Ionescu, that's I-O-N-E-S-C-U. Fairer, you'll take the victim. Norman Halloway.'

'On it.'

'Burton's bringing in Ionescu for an initial interview, so I'll be downstairs if you need me.' The two detectives grunted their understanding, already fixed on the first flitters of information on their screens. She stepped out, letting the door bang closed behind her, and went to secure her and Burton their interview space.

Stela Ionescu was a short and slim brunette, with her hair pinned back efficiently, and a few wisps of grey escaping the large grip. When Burton had brought her into the station reception, Ionescu had smiled timidly at being introduced to Melanie, and had remained quiet on the walk to the interview room too. Sitting opposite the woman, Melanie could see her face was streaked with what little make-up was left, and there were small blotches of red blended in with her natural complexion. Melanie guessed there had been more tears on the journey to the station.

'For the benefit of the recording, I'm DI Melanie Watton and this is my colleague DC Chris Burton. Could you please confirm your name for us to start?'

The woman hesitated. 'Stela Ionsecu. Miss.'

Melanie recognised the name as foreign, but the woman's accent seemed neutral; it gave nothing away of her mother tongue. 'Where are you from originally, Miss Ionsecu?'

'Romania, but I moved here when I was young. Eighteen or so.'

'And how long have you been working with Mr Halloway?'

The witness bobbed her head, once, twice, a few times again; it looked as though she were literally totting up notches. 'I'm not sure, it's been so long now. Ten years or so, I think.'

'Is he a good man to work for, would you say?' Melanie said, throwing out an early hook.

Ionsecu shifted her gaze then. She stared at a fixed point on the table, and her face dropped into a sad sort of smile. 'Mr Halloway was always kind to me. We had a good relationship, at work, that is, and we would always have a cup of tea and a talk when I had finished. He would tell me about his latest...' she hesitated and gestured with her hand. 'Well, you know.'

'Do you feel able to walk us through what happened this morning?'

The woman flashed a quick look at Burton.

'I know you've already been through this at least once,' Burton said, her tone apologetic. 'But we need to make sure we have everything formally documented, so we can start a thorough investigation into what's happened here.'

Ionsecu seemed to soften then. 'I arrived at work at the normal time, about half past nine. I usually start with the house, because by the time I'm finished in there Mr Halloway is ready for his morning break, which means I don't disturb his work when I go to the studio, you see.'

Melanie nodded her understanding and urged the woman to continue.

'But I walked down the pathway along the side of the house, and the studio door was open. He was so protective of his projects. Anything from outside could have been detrimental to some of them,' she explained. 'I knocked on the door, just in case, but there was no answer, so I went inside then.' Her breathing became laboured and bulbous tears formed in each eye. A hard blink sent them rolling down her cheeks.

'Take your time,' Melanie reassured her.

The woman took a deep breath. 'That's when I found him. It's dark in there; he doesn't like bright lighting; it can be damaging to the projects. So I didn't see him to begin with, because of the darkness. But then I looked at the back of the room, because there's another door, into his storage space, and I thought that he might–' Her sentence broke off without an interruption. She raised her hand to her mouth as though trying to catch a sob. 'I thought he might have been working in there. That's when I saw him, though, and I called you. I called you and I waited outside.'

'And there wasn't anyone at all suspicious that you saw on your walk into work?'

She shook her head absent-mindedly, as though her thoughts were somewhere else, then said, 'There was no one. There hadn't been anyone either. I'm there every day. I would have seen someone, if they'd been loitering or trouble making.'

Melanie was prepared to launch into her follow-up questions when her mobile began to hum in her jacket pocket. She glanced at the time – it had been hours since her last call with Carter – and she guessed this would be him trying to arrange cover. She checked the name on the screen of her phone and excused herself. 'I'll be right outside for just one minute. I'm sorry about this,' she said, already out of her seat and stepping backwards to the door. 'Carter, can you hang fire for like, thirty minutes, and I can take over? We're still with the witness.'

'Boss, it's not that. I don't need...' he paused, hesitated. 'I don't need cover, but I do need you to come down here when you can.'

'What's going on?'

'Forensics are still working here but they cleared Waller to move the body. The thing is, when they moved him, there was something else there, something the killer had left underneath...'

4

Melanie arrived at the scene to find Carter outside with Graham Williams, a member of the forensics team who Melanie had spent far too much time with over the last couple of years, thanks to their major cases. Both men looked perplexed, concerned even, and they were so engrossed in their conversation that they didn't notice Melanie's crunching footfalls on the gravel.

'How bad is it?' she said, coming to a stop behind them. The men turned to greet her. During the short drive over, Melanie had imagined all sorts and she'd arrived at a point where what she was expecting must surely be worse than the reality of the situation. 'Are we talking specialists, a technology team, what?' Even though it had been a year, the memories of their last murder investigation had stuck well in Melanie's mind.

'Some people say hello,' Graham said, his tone jovial.

Melanie cracked a thin smile. 'I'm sorry. Hi, Graham, how are you?'

'I'm well, DI Watton, thanks for asking. I won't ask back; I can see from your face,' he joked, but Melanie thought he was likely telling the truth. 'In terms of a specialist, you might need to call on a taxidermist at some point, but that's nothing to do with what's under the body.'

'It's best if you just look,' Carter added. He was notably sterner than Graham.

'Right, lead the way then.'

Graham stepped towards the open doorway, but Carter dropped back a step to be in line with Melanie. 'There's something written on the floor,' he said. Melanie's head twitched as though she might turn towards him but her eyeline remained ahead. 'Like, a message on the floor,' he spoke again and from his tone it was clear he was shaken.

'Of course. Naturally. Perish the thought we get a normal one.' Melanie stopped and turned, and Carter matched her. 'Do you need to wait out here?'

'No, boss, I'm fine, it's just–' he broke off. 'It's a weird space, that's all.'

They walked the rest of the driveway in silence. Williams was already in the room when they arrived at the door. He stood, hands on hips, his plastic suit crackling like a wrapper as he looked from one member of his team to another, as though assessing them. He nodded.

'We're making good headway in here,' he shouted back to Melanie and Carter.

'Well, let's see what all the fuss is about, then,' Melanie replied. She inhaled hard and stepped into the space. It was dark, dimly lit by the small lights that each member of the forensics team had fixed into rubber bands around their heads; they looked as though they might be going mining when their shift was done. But as each member of the team went about their business, small segments of the space were thrown under spotlights for Melanie: the knives lined according to size; the pictures, showing pelts and hides and who knows what; then, with a sharp shift of the head from a member of Williams' team, a mounted deer head that was fixed to the wall next to Melanie lit up in her peripheral vision. She sharply stepped away.

'I told you it was weird, boss.'

'Where's this message?'

'Over here,' Williams answered, stepping further into the space. Melanie followed but Carter stayed by the door. 'We'll need to run some tests to be certain but from the way the wood was carved I'd say it's the same knife the victim was stabbed with.'

Melanie looked down at the bloodied mess. It took her eyes a moment to adjust but she soon spotted the light angled towards a cordoned patch of floor, and there the message was: NOT EVERYTHING CAN BE BROUGHT BACK.

She read it through three times, then a fourth before she nodded. 'Brilliant. Are you good to head back?' She turned to face Carter as she spoke. Her colleague looked startled by the tone she'd taken. 'We can hang around with forensics if you'd prefer,' she said, trying to sound more jovial but there was an undercurrent of something else. 'Graham, pleasure as always. You'll be in touch when...' she petered out as she noticed Williams' tired nod, accompanied by a thin smile. 'Of course, not your first rodeo.'

Melanie stalked out of the room with Carter trailing behind. When they reached the edge of the property Melanie slowed down for her colleague to come up level with her. 'You should pick Emily up.'

'I can call Trish, it's fine.'

'Carter, I'm telling you to pick Emily up.'

Her colleague hesitated before saying, 'Boss, are you all right?'

'I'm fine,' she replied, thrown by the question. 'Why do you ask?'

He nodded to the building behind them. 'You took that – well.'

Melanie shrugged. 'Activist with a grudge, isn't it?' She tapped him lightly on the shoulder. 'Get in your car, get your girl, go home. There's nothing we can do until we get background checks pulled on the victim. Burton will have wrapped up the last of the witness' details by now. Seriously, go home.' She flashed him a tight smile before she turned to her car. Speaking over the top of the vehicle, she added, 'This is old hat for us now. It'll be over within a week or two, mark my words.' She thought about winking but couldn't bring herself to; it would be too much, she decided.

Melanie keyed *Norman Halloway* into the search bar of her browser. The results were slow to load, and she couldn't be sure whether it was the ageing work computer or the overloaded internet connection. Although at this time it shouldn't be the latter. Melanie was the last of her team left in the office. Burton had trailed out just over an hour ago – 'Sure I can't tempt you to a quick drink with the rest of us?' – and since then, silence. Melanie had thought about making a move herself, but she was in a state of mind where she needed to be doing something – anything, to get the case started.

The web browser unfolded in front of her and brought with it a string of digitised newspaper articles. Some of them looked to be several years old whereas others were published as recently as last month. She skimmed through an older one – 'Local artist turned taxidermist' – *Christ, was that news*? she thought as she worked her way to something more recent. There was a report dated from four and a half weeks back claiming that Halloway was putting taxidermy on the local map.

'It's a very underappreciated art,' he was quoted as having said. 'I think especially with alternative artists' markets popping up elsewhere, it's only right that we look to make something more local and homegrown.'

The progressive attitude didn't quite sit with the suit-and-tie gentleman pictured alongside the piece. But something about the lop-sided smile that Halloway had flashed at the camera made Melanie warm to him.

She scrolled further down and found there had been objections to Halloway's hopes for local artistry though. 'Some sources have claimed that adding taxidermy to the blend of oil paintings and pottery won't fit with the town aesthetic,' the writer claimed, without having clarified exactly who those sources were. Melanie scanned through the rest of the article looking for a name but couldn't find anything. She noted down the author instead. He'd be one of the first people she'd look to track down in the morning to see if she could find out exactly who'd made these comments. Whoever had said such things, they obviously hadn't kept track of the news in the last few years. *The odd piece of tasteful taxidermy should be the least of their concerns*, Melanie thought as she closed the window.

She clicked into another article and as she waited for the piece to load her desk phone kicked into life. The loud chirp was disconcerting in the quiet of the office space and Melanie couldn't help but answer with an abruptness.

'Watton.'

'Addair.'

'Shit.' Melanie exhaled the word.

'Oh, that's the reaction I was going for.' Thankfully, Hilda Addair, the forensic linguist who Melanie had been sort-of-seeing-on-and-off for several months now, wasn't the type of woman to take offence.

'Hilda, I'm so sorry–'

'For being an hour late, or for not calling?' Melanie opened her mouth to answer but Hilda cut her off too soon. 'Oh, or for having your phone switched off.'

Melanie pressed the home screen once, twice on her mobile and then exhaled another expletive. 'My battery must have died. I didn't even think to check my phone,' she admitted, not knowing whether that made the situation better or worse.

Hilda laughed lightly. 'Shall we give it a miss tonight?'

'No, no really, I can leave work in the next...' Melanie hesitated, not knowing how to end the sentence.

'But you never really leave work, do you?' Her tone was jovial but the comment itself was too cutting for Melanie not to feel irked by it. 'It's no bother. You can owe me dinner another night. Deal?'

'I have to eat tonight though,' Melanie replied, as though this were a weighty protest.

'I'll order food to yours. Take your work home with you at least, would you? I know you'll be at it for hours.'

Melanie hated the truth of what Hilda was saying. But she also loved that Hilda knew this about her. 'Thank you,' she replied. 'Not many other women would be quite so calm with me at this point, I shouldn't think.'

'No, I shouldn't think so either,' Hilda replied, as though really thinking the idea through. 'But I'm a big lass and I know full well I can't compete with a murder...'

5

Humans have a strange relationship with animals, don't they? When I was a kid, Mam always seemed to think the dogs we had were more important than the lot of us. I never got it though; never understood how they took pride of place over us all. I remember when Alf died. A German Shepherd who she'd had and loved for as long as I'd been alive. She mourned like one of the kids had passed. Cried for weeks and wouldn't come out the house, only looked through the back windows wistfully as though the mutt might come dashing across out of nowhere to surprise her with sprightly limbs and a 'Gotcha.' On her worst days she'd look at us with shifty eyes and shame. It crossed my mind she might have thought one of us had done away with the dog. Then she must've felt a quick burst of embarrassment at suspecting such a thing of her own children.

That was the first time I took another dog. I wasn't bothered about having one about the place, only bothered about keeping her quiet, making her happy, keeping the family going. It often felt like my job, despite not being the parent – and shit, if there weren't enough parents knocking about the house at one time or another. Or adults, at least. Uncles. Mam's friends. The problem being that because I'd taken the bloody thing, it always came sniffing around me. I didn't like that to begin with. Mam didn't either, I remember.

'It's more your dog than mine,' she moaned and groaned and fucking griped.

'I've never wanted a dog.'

'Well, you've got a good one now. Look at how he listens to you!'

He did listen to me too. Whatever I told him, he just seemed to pay good attention. Even if I was telling him to do something he shouldn't have been doing.

'You can't let him go snapping at people,' Mam warned me. But I could. Who'd tell me otherwise? I let the little git run riot and I finally started to see his worth when we got into the fights together. He was the first I'd taken but he turned into the first of many. He was a right bloody mess after a few months and the others told me that was normal, that they all go that way after a time.

'You shouldn't train him so hard, mind,' one bloke said, so we set the dogs on each other to see who the real winner was. It was the first time we'd lost, and I cut the hound loose after that. There was a chap on the circuit who dealt with dogs who'd had their day. It seemed like the fairest thing to do. But I did miss him, mind you. It made me understand Mam and how she'd gone to pieces over Alf. It almost made me feel guilty for doing away with him. But she'd never know, and I'd take that to grave.

You can't bring them back though. It's a blasphemy to think otherwise. Blokes like him – artist, they called him – can play at doctor with their nips and cuts and stitches. But once a dog's gone they're gone. Like humans in that way. If you don't do things while people are around to see them you lose the chance altogether, don't you.

6

Melanie was the last into the office the following day, thanks to a hungry journalist who caught her outside the station. Her team were positioned around their monitors, engrossed in their workloads, and Carter looked to be the only one who'd heard her arrive. He flashed a quick glance from behind his monitor but then went back to his phone call. 'That's great, thank you. We'd really appreciate getting in contact with her...'

Melanie half-heard his conversation as she made a beeline for Morris. 'How much do you know?' Melanie asked, leaning on the edge of her colleague's desk.

Morris finished up the sentence she was typing before she answered. 'Dead taxidermist, eerie office space, weird message.'

'Brilliant. You're up to speed.' She heard Carter drop his desk phone down behind her and she turned sharply. 'Who do we need to get into contact with?'

'The ex-wife,' Read answered from across the room. Melanie swung her head round to face him. 'When Fairer and I started our background checks we found out that Halloway had got a recent ex-wife kicking around.'

'How recent?'

'Hard to pin down exactly but maybe about three years.'

'Suspect?'

'Out of the country,' Carter answered. 'I'm trying to get contact details from Spanish police but there's only so much they can do without putting a bulletin out on the woman, which seems extreme.'

'Can we get travel arrangements?'

'I can,' Morris interrupted. 'I mean, you'll need to give me a minute or two.'

The quick update had turned into a tennis match between her detectives and Melanie's neck cricked from keeping up with the moves. 'Okay. Morris, take a whole five minutes, go wild. Everyone else, gather up anything you want shared and we'll set up camp at the evidence board at half past. Deal?' she asked but didn't wait for an answer before heading straight to her office and shutting the door behind her. She'd spent too much of the night before doing online searches of their victim. She knew a lot about the man, but she didn't know for certain how much sleep she'd managed, and it was already starting to tell on her.

She rubbed at the back of her aching neck and hit the blinking voicemail button on her phone. While the automated voice talked her through the formalities, she sat down and rested her head on the desk. Seconds later George Waller arrived through the speakerphone.

'Hi, Mel, it's George – Waller,' he added his surname as though it were an afterthought and Melanie smiled. 'I'm unlikely to get around to the post-mortem today. I wanted to let you know because...' he hesitated and then said, 'well, because I know how you like to rush these things. I'll give you a call when everything is dealt with. Take care now.'

The line went dead, and Melanie exhaled hard against the

veneer of her desk. Despite her cocksureness yesterday, there were so many things about this case that she already didn't like.

After three minutes – Melanie was sure it couldn't have been a whole five – there was a knock on the office door. 'Come on in,' she shouted.

Burton remained just outside the doorway. 'We're about ready to start when you are.'

'Does anything feel weird about this to you, Burton?'

She smirked. 'You mean, apart from the dead animals?'

Melanie tried to match her colleague's ease. 'Yes, apart from the dead animals.' She shook away the misgivings and stood from her desk. 'Come on then, let's be having you all.'

The two officers stepped out into the shared space where the rest of the team had already gathered. There were smiles and elbow nudges to suggest one of two things: they'd either struck lucky with the information they'd found; or they weren't worrying about the case yet. Whichever option it was, their gentle amusement passed a cheer on to Melanie. *No one ever solved a case based on misgivings*, she thought, although she wasn't sure of the truth in it.

'Right, who's going first?' she asked, coming to a stop at the front of the group. Carter and Read's hands shot up in synchronicity like schoolboys readying to impress a teacher. 'Go on, Read,' Melanie encouraged, and Carter let out a heavy sigh.

'Fairer found an ex-wife and I found a squeaky-clean housekeeper. Stela Ionescu has been in this country for thirty-one years. She's never been in trouble with the police or any other official government body. I found evidence to suggest that she's been working for Halloway for the best part of a decade, which I think supports what she told you?' he asked and when Melanie nodded, he continued. 'Nothing we've got against her suggests there's foul play here.'

'Might money have been a motive for her, though, or

anyone?' Morris asked. 'There's a lot of money in taxidermy, especially stuff that you can't get above board in this country.'

'It seems a leap at this stage, but we can't rule it out.' Melanie looked at Fairer then. 'You're the one that tracked down the wife?'

'Penelope Halloway, who doesn't look to have changed her name since the divorce.'

'Good sign,' Carter interrupted.

'You'd know.' Read kicked gently at Carter's leg as he joked but the comment didn't look to have been well-received. Fairer ignored the jibe entirely and continued.

'She's out of the country at the moment and it looks as though she's a bit of a jet-setter but that's more from an internet search than anything official I've found.'

'What kind of an internet search?' Melanie asked as she grabbed a pen and turned to the blank board behind her. She wrote Penelope's name in large letters in the top left corner.

'Social media, mostly. I started with a basic search engine nosey which is how I found her Instagram, which is completely open. She's really active on there, especially for a woman of her age.' Fairer paused and when Melanie turned she caught him wincing at his own phrasing. 'I just mean – you know, for someone, from an older generation.'

'Do we know how old she is?' Melanie asked, still facing the board.

'Fifty-eight, same as a Halloway,' he answered. 'So I found her through Instagram primarily which is how I found the jet-set lifestyle. Her Facebook supports that too. I wondered whether the Spain pictures might be old photos being re-used but she was doing check-ins at Spanish bars as recently as yesterday evening. I know that's not definitive proof or anything, but it near as damn it rules her out, I should think.'

Morris gently punched her colleague on the arm. 'I'm proud of you, Brian.'

'Carter, what was it you wanted to add?' Melanie asked.

'Oh, nothing, I was just winding Read up.' He nudged his colleague back and the earlier jibe looked to be forgotten by them both.

Melanie rolled her eyes and turned back to the board. 'Okay, so, wife, suspect, maybe but unlikely. Housekeeper, suspect, maybe but also unlikely. I can't see why she'd benefit from it unless it's the money element. Where are we in working out what's actually missing from the victim's studio?'

'Ionescu is drawing up a list of things and she's bringing it in later today,' Burton answered. 'She cleans the pieces so often she thinks with a little time she should be able to tell us what's gone. But she also said that when we empty out the place, we should find a ledger.'

'Finances?' Carter asked.

'No, a ledger of all the pieces. She said whenever Halloway finished a new piece he'd add details of it to a ledger, only she called it "a special book". Apparently there are descriptions of the items in detail plus dates for when they were finished and whether they were sold.'

'Okay, who fancies a trip to evidence?' Melanie asked the room and Read and Fairer were the first to volunteer. 'Burton, did she give you any idea what this book looks like?'

Burton shrugged. '"Special book" was about as much as I got.'

'Right, that'll have to be enough for you chaps to go on. Get down there, raid whatever you can and bring back anything that might be useful. It should all be in there by now anyway.' She paused while the two officers grabbed their jackets and cleared out of the room. 'Morris, can you pull financial records? We need as much behind the scenes stuff as we can find on the victim to get us started with the money motive angle.'

'Do you have suspicions on something?' Morris replied.

'None at all.' Melanie turned back to stare at the early details on their evidence board. 'That's the problem.'

7

It was two days later when George Waller left a message with Burton to say the post-mortem report was ready whenever Melanie was. The two shared pleasantries while one room away Melanie and Carter were on a call to the victim's ex-wife. Morris had done a fine job of tracking down not only travel information for the woman but also a direct contact number.

'Morris, I could–'

'Kiss me, I know,' Morris concluded her boss' half-compliment with a laugh. 'I'm pulling all the financial records I can find for our victim too, so save some of that praise.'

Melanie and Carter had got through to Penelope Halloway on the second attempt. She'd answered with an airy tone, as though she might have been in the middle of dozing on a beach somewhere. But her voice became more serious after the officers introduced themselves.

'Do you have a few moments to talk with us, Mrs Halloway?' Melanie asked.

'Ms, and yes, of course. What's happened? Norman– Is Norman okay?'

It caused a twist in Melanie's innards that even though the

two were separated, he'd still been the woman's first point of concern. 'Actually, Ms Halloway, it's about your ex-husband, yes. I'm so sorry to be the person to tell you this but he was discovered in his studio three days ago by his housekeeper. He was dead when she found him.' Melanie grimaced in anticipation of the next part. 'He was murdered, Ms Halloway, it seems.'

'Murdered? Jesus Christ, are you sure?'

Carter shot Melanie a wide-eyed look and a shrug.

'Yes, we're sure,' she replied. 'We understand you're out of the country–'

'But I'll be back at the beginning of next week, or I'm due back, I can – fuck it, no, I'll change my flights, I can be home sooner than that.'

'We'll obviously need to talk with you, whenever it is that you do get home. Will you be okay to come into the station to see myself or one of my colleagues?'

'Of course, of course. Give me your number, would you? I can call and let you know when I know my flight details, and when I'll be coming in. What else can I do? Is there anything you need for me to be doing?'

'We'll need you to do a formal identification when you're home. Obviously, given that he was discovered by Ms Ionescu we're as sure as we can be that it's him. It's a formality, though.'

'Christ, Stela. How is she? Do you know?'

'She's working closely with us to identify things that are missing from your husband's studio, so she's still quite involved in proceedings here. She's being very helpful.'

'I'm sorry, did you say missing?'

'We can talk in more detail when you come in, but yes, missing. It wasn't a simple attack, I'm afraid. In fact, it looks as though quite a few things were taken from your husband's studio.'

'His tools? His equipment, you mean?'

'Not equipment, no, his actual projects. It was a number of taxidermy sculptures that were taken. We're not yet sure of just how many but we're working on it.'

There was a long pause before Penelope Halloway spoke again. When she did speak, she sounded genuinely perplexed. 'But who the hell would think those godforsaken things were worth killing someone over?'

Carter smirked and Melanie pretended not to notice.

'I don't know yet, Ms Halloway, but we're going to try our best to work that out.'

Before Melanie and Carter had finished their call with Ms Halloway, the ex-wife had made the generous offer of putting together names that would be worth tracking down in relation to her husband. She seemed convinced they weren't killers, but also seemed optimistic they might offer something of use. After that, Melanie finished the phone call with another chorus of, 'I'm sorry for your loss,' and said goodbye to the woman whose holiday she'd just ruined.

There hardly seemed to be a minute between finishing one call and placing another, though, this one to the medical examiner's office. Melanie called Waller to let him know she'd be there within the hour, and on her travels she stopped to get them both a little something: Waller's tall hot chocolate with too much whipped cream, and Melanie's Americano with an extra shot. She felt as though she could have stuck her head directly beneath the spout of the coffee machine while she queued in line for the drinks, but a socially acceptable takeout cup would have to do.

When she arrived, she held a beaker in either hand and backed her way into Waller's open-plan office-operating suite.

'Shall we?' she said, holding the cups up and nodding outside.

Waller looked pleasantly surprised as he dropped his pen and stepped away from his desk. He followed Melanie back out into the hallway, where it was safe and sanitary to enjoy the drinks, and he took the large cup that he was offered.

'Tall hot chocolate?'

'Yes, George.'

'Extra cream?'

'Yes, George.'

He narrowed his eyes. 'What did you do?'

Melanie matched the gesture in comedic mimicry. 'Nothing, George.'

'I don't believe you.'

'Have the hot chocolate anyway. Worst case scenario, it'll soften the blow.'

The two of them leaned back on opposing walls so they could talk face-to-face as they indulged. But for a minute or two there was a comfortable silence between them.

'You aren't going to ask?' George eventually said.

'Ask what?'

'About the findings.' He tipped his cup back and when he lowered it there was a smudge of cream on the tip of his nose. He went cross-eyed for a second before wiping it away. 'You're usually champing at the bit to know these things.'

'He was stabbed, wasn't he?'

'Well, yes. You saw the state of the crime scene.'

'How many times?'

'Seven by my reckoning. The fourth one should have, likely would have, sealed the deal. The ones after that were, I don't know, rage, momentum. That's for another expert to decide.'

Melanie shook her head in mild disbelief. 'What's the matter with people, George?'

'If you think that's bad then wait until you hear the rest of it.' He drained the contents of the cup and trod down to the corridor to throw it into the nearest bin. 'Come in when you're ready,' he said, pushing his way back into the operating room. Melanie followed soon after.

George was sitting at his desk squinting at something on his computer monitor. He looked up as Melanie walked in but quickly refocused his attention on whatever had held it before. With a cluster of clicks, a string of images unfolded on George's walled monitors. Melanie moved her eyes from one photo to the next until it dawned on her what she was seeing: the victim's clothing. The shirt had been shot from a number of different viewpoints, but each image focused on the same central thing.

'Is that a rip in his shirt?' Melanie said, squinting to see.

'Come on, Watson.' George stood and stepped from the raised platform that kept his desk partly separate from the rest of the room. 'Let's have a look at the poor chap.'

Melanie followed as he trod across the space. 'Why do you get to be Sherlock?'

'Because we both have the same cunning eye for detail.'

There was only one cadaver laid out. Melanie could never be sure whether it would be a busy or a quiet day here, but she was thankful it was the latter. When they were positioned one either side of the trolley, and George had managed to snap a pair of gloves on, he reached up and pulled away the modesty sheet covering the victim. The body had started to discolour, which only made the entry wounds more obvious. Melanie stared at them in turn, hovering over one for a few seconds before moving to the next.

'It's not a pretty one, I'm afraid.'

'The cuts in the shirt,' Melanie said, nodding behind them. 'They're not from these.'

'No, quite right. Step around this side?' he said, his hands already fixed around the victim's arm. When Melanie was standing alongside George, he lifted the weighted arm up to reveal two strategic cuts on either side of the victim's armpit. He gave Melanie enough time to take a good look before resting the limb back in place.

'I don't understand.' Melanie walked back to her own side of the trolley. 'If the killer cut him through his shirt, then why? To make him bleed out?'

George shook his head. 'If I didn't know better, and I don't, so again I might be the wrong kind of expert, but I'd say they're meant to look like small relief cuts.' Melanie looked at him blankly, so he continued, 'In taxidermy, when the artist needs to loosen the skin for whatever reason, they make relief cuts on the body. It gives them, oh, I don't know, wiggle room, I suppose.'

'Do I want to know why you know that?'

'Everyone's allowed a hobby.' He pulled the sheet back up. 'Speaking of which, I wouldn't say your killer is an experienced taxidermist by any stretch. I don't even think these are actual relief cuts so much as cuts that are staged to look like them.'

'But why?'

George snapped his gloves off and balled them up before throwing them into the bin. 'Again, I'm the wrong kind of expert.' He wandered back to his desk with Melanie close behind, and he handed her the hard copy of his report. 'I can recommend a few good head doctors though.' He nodded towards the body on the other side of the room. 'I'd wager that you're going to need one after you find your killer.'

8

Melanie closed the browser and shut her laptop. She'd been reading about relief cuts since she got home, and she was still no closer to working out why someone might leave them on a body. It felt like a sign or a message for something; but there had been a much more explicit message left than these small cuts, so why leave them at all? She'd skimmed through the rest of Waller's post-mortem report and, as he'd said, there didn't look to be anything more remarkable. The stab wounds weren't patterned or methodical; there were no carvings, no other messages left on the body. So, what were they missing?

Melanie sighed, pushed the laptop away from her and ran a hand through her hair. 'Remember a time when you didn't have the stomach for this, Watton?' she asked the empty room, thinking back to before the team's first big case landed.

There were already printouts of the murder scene spread across the opposite end of her dining room table. This seemed to be the primary use for the room now; a second evidence space. Which would be a problem if Melanie actually had company for the evening. There was a clear shot of the message carved into the flooring, sitting on the left-hand side of

Melanie's tabletop display. She'd thought of calling Hilda three times since she'd got home and, as she stared down at the message, she wondered whether it was for the company or the expertise.

She grabbed her phone and pulled up a fresh text – *Dinner tomorrow? x* – and sent it before she could overanalyse the action. Forensics were due to come in tomorrow too, although Melanie had no idea what their initial findings were likely to be in a room that doubled as an open studio. But good company and a bottle of wine were the least she deserved after the last few days, she thought, and it would be something to look forward to. She didn't wait for a reply, but instead went straight to the kitchen to take her frustrations out on the sealed top of a microwave meal. She pierced the lid seven times, all the while thinking of their victim.

When the team filtered into the office the following day, they found Melanie tacking pictures to the evidence board. She'd pieced together four different shots to show the cuts on the body, and she took a deep breath before she explained what they were.

'Do we have a clue?' Carter asked, pulling a seat up.

'I don't know, Shaggy, what do you think?' Burton jibed as she came to a stop behind him. 'Did Waller find something of interest, boss?'

'You could say that. Can we all hover over here for a second?' Melanie waited for Read, Fairer and Morris. 'Halloway died from multiple wounds, seven in total. But then on closer inspection, Waller also found the cuts you can see pinned behind me. It turns out Waller is something of a taxidermy enthusiast and by his reckoning these are relief cuts. Apparently, they're a technique used when the skin of an animal needs to be loosened.'

Read's head pulled back as though he were trying to physically distance himself from the knowledge. He swallowed hard. 'Was someone going to try to skin him?'

'It seems unlikely. However, it does seem like we're dealing with a more complicated case than we perhaps thought.' Melanie paused as the door to the office swung open. Williams, from the forensics team, pushed his way in and hailed a quick hello to the faces that had snapped around to him. 'I'm hoping by this afternoon there'll be something more to share, so keep at what you're doing and we'll reconvene over lunch.'

'It doesn't seem like a lunchtime topic of conversation,' Williams added.

Melanie huffed. 'It is in this job. Shall we?'

The two filtered into Melanie's office and she closed the door behind them. Williams was settled in the visitor's chair by the time Melanie reached her own, and he didn't waste any time in cutting to the conversation.

'I'm going to come clean and admit we're struggling on this one. In a place like that, there's hair and fibre left, right and centre and we're having a whale of a time working out human from animal to begin with.'

Melanie sighed. It had crossed her mind in the early hours of this morning that this might be the case. 'Is there anything we can do?'

'We can keep working. It would help if we had some discernible trace of the killer but the body itself doesn't have any foreign fibres that can't be tracked to another source already in the room. We find a hair and suddenly we find ten fox hairs that match it. The only evidence to suggest a killer was even in that room is the fact that there's a body in it.'

'Are you thinking he was killed somewhere else?'

'No, I'm thinking you have a smart murderer who understands how fibres and hairs are left and traced. We'll keep searching, obviously; this is what we do. But you might have to cut us a little extra slack on this one.'

Melanie ran a hand over her face. 'Of course, Graham, whatever you need.'

'Waller didn't pull anything?'

'Nothing that helps. I'm guessing you saw the victim's clothes?'

'Cuts under the arms? Yeah, I spotted those. They look more like slashes so we're assuming the same knife was used across all parts of the job, but I've got someone double-checking the fabric tears later today.'

'You'll let me know if anything changes?'

'As always.' He stood and Melanie matched the gesture. 'I can make my own way out.'

'It's fine, I need to collar Morris anyway,' she said, beating him to the door. The two said their farewells in the open office and as Williams walked one way Melanie went the other to track down her technology expert. 'Got a second?'

'Have a whole minute,' Morris joked as Melanie pulled up a chair next to her. 'Financial reports?'

Melanie nodded. 'If you've got anything.'

'Well, he certainly didn't owe anyone money. In the last two years Halloway's financial takings went through the roof so he was more than solvent. There aren't any loans that I can find, there's also no mortgage on the house. There's a steady payment going out every month to his ex-wife, alongside bills and all the usual stuff. I've found a lot of entries like this.' She paused and pointed to seemingly random figures listed on a spreadsheet. 'I couldn't make sense of them at first but now I'm thinking they might actually be deposits for orders he'd taken, which makes me think that the last two years weren't a fluke.'

'I looked into him, a lazy internet search is all, but I read something about him starting up these artists' markets, locally. That might explain the influx of work?'

'I can check the timings.'

'That would be gre–'

'Boss?' Carter had come to a halt behind them.

Melanie turned to greet him. 'You've got something?'

'Not exactly, no. You've been asked to attend a robbery in the city centre. Art supply shop has been broken into and most of their till takings have been made away with. It doesn't look as though anything else is missing apart–'

'I'm lost, Carter,' she interrupted him, losing patience. 'What do they need us for?'

Carter cleared his throat. 'Because there's a stuffed parrot in the centre of the shop floor.'

There was a beat of silence in which Melanie looked between Morris and Carter, then to their evidence board. 'Of course there bloody is...'

9

The uniformed officers had cordoned off the Artists' Hideout and they were doing their utmost to keep passers-by a safe distance away. The only exception being one irate individual standing behind the police tape, who Melanie guessed to be the shop's owner. She half-heard their conversation – 'But I need to get in there, I have a right!' – as she ducked under the cordon, shortly followed by Carter, Read and Fairer. She needed all the feet on the ground that she could get for this visit if they wanted to get everything they could from the scene. Before they'd filed out of the office in their separate cars, Melanie had ordered Burton and Morris to keep looking through Halloway's background – namely, look for any connections with their new crime scene.

Melanie took in a quick surveillance of the building from the outside – on the surface it looked like an ordinary art supply shop – and then she stepped indoors. The place looked dishevelled, but the overturned till was Melanie's main point of interest. There was an officer standing nearby already – whether he was waiting for her or guarding the till, she couldn't tell.

'DI Watton.' She extended a hand and the junior matched

the gesture, although he looked initially startled by it. 'Is the till the only point of disruption?'

'As best as we can tell. There's a Mr...' he started but paused to fact-check himself with a glance at his notebook. 'Mr Evans outside who claims to be the owner.'

'Is he the one who called it in?'

'No, it was an anonymous caller to the station.'

'Read?' Melanie called her junior's attention. 'Get a call into the station, see if they can arrange for a copy of that phone call to be emailed over to me, would you?'

'On it,' Read replied, phone already in hand.

'Has he been able to tell you much so far?' Melanie asked, nodding to the man outside who was still raising his voice at an officer.

The young man looked down at his notebook again. 'It's his shop, his building. There aren't huge amounts of cash left on-site but there's a sizeable float, £500 or so, left in the till whether the shop is open or not.'

Melanie took a quick scan around the room. 'We'll need the CCTV footage from those.'

The officer coughed lightly, then said, 'There isn't any, ma'am.'

'Then what are they?' Melanie pointed to the camera perched not ten feet away from her in one corner of the room. She'd already spotted a similar device in the opposite corner too.

'Apparently they're dummy cameras.'

But what would be the point in that? Melanie thought. The young officer didn't offer more information, though, and Melanie didn't press him. There was no point in beating up the messenger.

'Thanks for your help. You're welcome to join your colleagues if you'd like.' She looked outside and the officer took his cue to leave. 'Carter, we've got a right one here,' she said as she walked over to her deputy, who was snapping on a pair of gloves. 'Cameras in the corner? Dummies, apparently, there's no live feed.'

Carter frowned and looked up at the closest camera. 'Then what the fu–'

'I know, pointless.' She cut him off. 'Where are Read and Fairer?'

'I sent them scouting out the back. There's a cordon at the back of the shop, which is where the thief gained entry. That's as much as we've been able to guess at so far. There's no damage to the front door that we can see at a glance.' He pulled at the knees of his trousers to loosen them before squatting. 'It's this little fella that's causing me the problem though.'

Melanie squatted level with Carter, but she refused his offer of gloves; she had no intention of touching the thing. 'How did you get here, eh?' She turned her head to one side and then the other. An onlooker might have thought she were expecting an answer.

The small structure stood nearly two feet tall but a portion of that was the branch on which the parrot was balanced – or rather, fixed. Its head was turned to one side, as though it were looking for something behind it. The eyes had a glint to them but as Melanie looked at the head from different angles she saw that glint wasn't quite there all the time; there was something unnatural about that. But the eyes were the only thing that gave the creature away. Its feathers were a blend of green, blue, and yellow, with intermittent bursts of red as though the artist had realised there was a primary colour missing. They were smooth, fanned neatly to cover one wing that was slightly extended, while the other was tucked against the creature's side. Melanie wondered how deliberate the decision had been to spread its wing like that, a splay of feathers as a sort of centrepiece.

'What am I missing, Carter?'

'What do you mean?'

'I mean, why leave this here? Why go for a specialist artist and dealer, and then go again, for a lesser crime, for a lower level pay off? What are we missing in that?'

Carter exhaled hard. 'Hell if I know. Am I calling forensics?'

'Yeah, tell them they're needed as soon as they can spare bodies. We need a clean sweep of this place, although it'll be more of the same, I suspect.'

'More of the same?'

'If there are too many sets of prints in a studio, I can't see a shop being much better.'

'The door out back was butchered a little,' Read announced as he and Fairer stepped back into the main space. 'But it looks like there's one setting for the back door and another for the front; they've each got a switch on the alarm system out there. So, the thief must have triggered the alarm in the back before they opened the front door to leave.'

'But how would someone hear that?' Carter asked. 'Is it a public space out there?'

'Nope, completely built-up area. The outside space is the wall of the next building.'

'We need to listen to the call that came in reporting this break-in,' Melanie suggested. 'We can cross-match between when the alarms were triggered and when the call was placed. Maybe our witness knew more than they let on. Can you add that to your list?' She directed the question to Read and Fairer, and the latter nodded as he typed the instruction into his phone. 'Carter, forensics? I'm heading for the owner.'

Outside the same man was still talking to officers, although he seemed less irritated by the situation now, which relieved Melanie. She took over from her colleagues, and introduced herself with a smile and a firm handshake. 'My officers tell me you don't have security cameras in this place?' she asked, cutting straight to the point.

Mr Evans rubbed a hand down his face. 'No, no, I don't.'

'The reason for that being?'

He gestured to the open space around them. 'We're in the middle of a popular street. I have alarm systems set up for the front and back doors, I'm careful with the people who work for me. They're mostly art students who'd take equipment and materials sooner than they'd take money. The cleaner is a woman who's worked here for–'

'Does your cleaner have a name?' Melanie interrupted.

'Winnie Hughes.'

Melanie had been hoping for an obvious connection but of course that would have been too easy. She noted down the name just in case and gestured for the man to continue.

'Winnie's the only other person who even keeps a key. All the others drop their keys in the security box by the wall, and I'm always here to open up before they need a key again.'

The box on the wall looked intact but Melanie scribbled a reminder to ask forensics to check it over. *Why have alarm systems and no cameras though*? Something didn't feel right about Evans' protective measures – or lack thereof. 'You didn't open up today?' she clarified.

The man huffed. 'It was meant to be a day off.'

'And how often does Winnie come and sweep the place?'

'Every evening, like clockwork.'

'So, she would have been here last night?'

'Yes.' He snapped the answer, as though bored of the questions now. 'Every night.'

'Thanks for your time, Mr Evans. If you don't mind waiting here for a couple of moments, I'll get an officer to come and take down a few more details and you'll be free to go until we need you for more questioning.' She turned to leave.

'Wait, that's it?'

'For the time being,' Melanie replied, already walking away from the owner. Her three detectives were huddled around each other when Melanie arrived back in the store. 'Did you call forensics?' she asked, focusing on Carter.

'They're on their way already. I explained the situation.' He gestured to the bird.

'They need to sweep the till for fingerprints. Turns out the owner has the shop cleaned every night, including last night, and today the shop has been shut all day.'

'So, the burglar came into a completely clean crime scene?'

'That's my hope. Did you call through about the recording?' Melanie shifted her focus.

'Funny thing,' Fairer started, in a tone that suggested he wasn't going to say anything funny at all. 'Morris intercepted the call that went through to the station to pull a timestamp from it, while we double-checked the alarms out back. The call was placed after the back alarm was triggered, but before the front one even went off.'

Melanie frowned. 'How certain are we that someone wouldn't hear that alarm out back?'

'We could do a trial run of it?' Read suggested. 'Reset the alarms while the owner is here, trip them again while some of us are out front.'

'It's an easy way to see how audible they are,' Fairer added.

Melanie ran a hand through her hair. 'Sure, okay, it can't hurt. He's out front still, waiting for you two, actually. Will you grab him and bring him in?'

The two followed orders and vacated.

'There's so much about this that I don't understand,' Carter said, watching the bird as he spoke. 'If someone called in the robbery before the front alarm was triggered, then how did they know the robbery was happening?'

'I'm not sure, Carter.' Melanie paced to the front of the shop and looked out the window, glancing in one direction and then the other. 'I'm more interested in why a thief would trigger one alarm at the back of a building, where it's safe, but then stroll right out the front door and straight in view of a street camera.' There was a bold black camera fixed to a building across the street, and from this angle it looked as though its view was fixed close to the shop's front door. 'Get Morris and Burton on to the street's camera footage, would you? I want a still of whoever left this shop.'

10

Their trial run of the alarm system had at least confirmed one thing: the noise couldn't be heard from the front of the shop. Morris had also been able to confirm that the call to the station was made between the alarms sounding, based on the timestamps pulled from the shop's system. So whoever reported the crime must have been either in the know about the robbery taking place, or involved in the theft at the time.

'That doesn't make sense,' Carter said.

'Oh, but a stuffed parrot in the centre of a crime scene does?' Read threw back.

'Fair point.'

'Where does that leave us?' Burton asked. She directed the question at Melanie who had her back to the room; she was facing the evidence board still when she spoke. 'It leaves us hoping that forensics pull something we can cross-match.'

'And what's the hope exactly?' Fairer pushed.

Melanie turned to face them all. 'Williams said the murder scene was tricky because it doubled as Halloway's studio, so there were people in and out all the time. Apparently, the place was such a mess the body was the only giveaway that a killer had been there at all–'

'Dead giveaway,' Read interrupted, and flashed a thumbs up gesture at Carter.

Melanie made a concerted effort not to roll her eyes. 'If there's DNA left behind in the shop that Williams can pull then he can cross-match it with evidence taken from the studio.'

'And there should be evidence, because the shop was cleaned the night before the robbery?'

'Bingo.'

'Is no one going to talk about the stuffed parrot, then?' Read asked. Burton threw him a cutting look and he held his hands up in a defensive gesture. 'I'm just saying, it feels like there's something to say there.'

'He's not wrong,' Melanie weighed in. 'It seems like an obvious thing to verify but we'll need to try to match the bird to Halloway's studio somehow.'

'We've got the project log that we can check,' Fairer suggested.

'Or the cleaner,' Morris added.

'How about both. Burton and Morris, can you call the cleaner and get a meeting with her? Maybe she'll recognise the bird from her time in the studio. Read and Fairer, start working through the log and see if you can match the bird with any descriptions.' One by one the team nodded their understanding of the instructions. 'Carter, you're with me.'

'Because I'm in trouble?'

'No, because we're going to have to talk to Archer.'

Stela Ionescu answered the phone within three rings, and she was down at the station within the hour. 'I have so much free time now,' she'd said on the phone to Burton and the officer tried to keep her sympathy in check; she didn't want anything to cloud her judgement of the case. She and Morris escorted the witness into one of the interview rooms and, while she and Burton got settled, Morris excused herself to get the required evidence. Forensics had offered to take the bird, but Melanie had been hesitant to let it go; a good call, as it turned out. The creature had been bagged, tagged and safely stored inside the evidence room. Morris saw herself in with her card and the keycode. She kicked the door open – keeping both hands steady on the base of the bird's structure – on her way back out. She was too nervous to spare a hand getting into the interview room, so she tapped three times against the door with the toe of her boot and waited patiently for Burton to let her in.

'Hands full,' she said, as the door was opened.

Morris wandered in slowly, keeping eyes on the bird, and there soon came an outburst from their visitor.

'Pablo!'

Morris threw a glance back at Burton. 'I'm sorry?'

'Do you recognise the bird, Ms Ionescu?' Burton asked, taking her seat back at the table.

Morris set the bird down with great care. Rather than lowering her arms, she bent at the knees and slid the structure on until it felt steady. Ionescu was already twisting her head to survey the mount from several different angles.

'Ms Ionescu,' Burton started again. 'Do you recognise this?'

'It's Pablo. It's one of Mr Halloway's.'

'And you're sure?' Morris pushed, taking a seat alongside her colleague.

Ionescu looked along one side of the bird and then the other as though making a comparison. 'I'm positive. But someone has cleaned him wrong.' She looked up at the officers then and, as though noting their confused expressions, added, 'They have to be cleaned in a certain way, I said before. Pablo has been cleaned wrong.'

'How so?' Burton asked.

Ionescu pressed the fingertip of her little finger against the protective plastic.

'Ms Ionescu, be mindful because that's evidence now.'

The woman made a clucking sound as though dismissing the claim. 'Here,' she said, still holding the plastic against the bird. 'The feathers have been disturbed.'

'Could that not have happened when the thief took it?' Morris asked, in part to the witness but mostly to her colleague.

Ionescu shrugged. 'It's a basic error for people to make when they don't know how to care for taxidermy. But transit could have done it too, sure.'

'Why is it a basic error?'

'The birds only need to be dusted. I do them every couple of weeks–'

'But you were there every day?' Morris cut the witness off.

'I didn't do all of them every day,' Ionescu replied, her tone matter of fact. 'I did them on rotation, and I did the house every day. But the birds, they need to be dusted in the direction their feathers are placed. Like you're brushing them.' She made a stroking motion with her hand. 'When you brush them in the opposite direction, or when you dust them like a common sculpture, this happens.' She pointed to one patch, then another on the right-hand side of the bird. Morris and Burton both craned their views to follow the explanation.

'So, if this were done during cleaning, you'd guess it was someone who doesn't know much about taxidermy?' Burton asked.

The woman nodded with some enthusiasm. 'No one who knows anything about taking care of animals would do this, no.'

'This has been really helpful, Ms Ionescu, thank you,'

Burton said, signalling the end of this visit. She threw Morris a glance who gave a quick head dip to show her agreement. 'My colleague will see you out now. Unless you have any questions for us?'

Ionescu ran a hand lightly over the parrot. The plastic crackled underneath her. 'What will happen to him? Where will he go, do you think?'

Burton set a hand flat on her chest. 'I'll personally take him back to the evidence room.'

'And then?'

'He'll be taken good care of, whether he's here or in another part of the station.' She used her softest voice, as though delivering bad news, but it seemed enough to pacify the woman. 'Thank you again for your time, Ms Ionescu.'

Burton excused herself, bird in tow, and made her way to the evidence space where the item was stashed again. By the time she was back in the office it was close to what should be home time, but Fairer and Read were still working away on the log, and there were signs of life in Melanie's office too.

'Any luck?' Burton asked as she grabbed her coat from the back of her chair.

'There are quite a few things matching the description of the bird, but we're trying to be strategic in terms of the dates that are listed,' Fairer explained.

'How was the witness?'

'Helpful. Pablo, the bird is called,' Burton said, trying to keep a straight face. Read cocked an eyebrow at her. 'I shit you not. Carter clocked off?'

'Aye, picking up the little one. Speaking of which, Brian, pub?'

Fairer took a glance at his watch. 'One.'

The pair started to pack away as Burton padded across to Melanie's office. The door was ajar but before she could open it she heard the boss' phone ring, so she took a strategic pause.

'Watton.'

Burton could overhear Melanie too clearly and she considered backing away. *But that might make even more noise*, she thought.

'Hil, I'm really sorry. We got a call in... No, it's the taxidermy thing... Forensics have said they might get something back to us this evening... I know it seems like I always do this... Okay, I know I always... How about tomorrow?' There was the rustle of papers, as though Melanie might be hunting for her diary after the fact. 'If you actually know one then that might come in handy... I'm not seeing you because of your contacts... Hil, come on, we see each... Yes, I understand. I appreciate the offer... Can it be of help and of dinner?' Burton winced, anticipating what Hilda's question must have been. 'I'll talk to you soon... Yep, soon. Bye.'

Burton waited a deliberate amount of time before knocking on the door and pushing it open. 'Got a second?' Her boss gestured her in without looking up from her paperwork. 'We talked to Ionescu. She seems pretty convinced the parrot is Halloway's.' Burton shook her head and laughed. 'Christ, what a sentence.'

Melanie dropped her pen and leaned back in her chair. 'How often do you cancel plans with Joe? Like, on a weekly basis?'

Burton shifted uncomfortably. 'Joe and I are married, boss. It's different.'

'You heard, then?'

'A little.'

'Hilda knows a taxidermist. Shocker.' Melanie huffed. 'Who doesn't that woman know.'

'So, we've got an expert witness if we need one?' Burton said, trying to steer the conversation closer to work talk than personal.

'Which I suspect we will.'

'It's nice of her to offer that help.'

Melanie ran her hands through her hair, pushing it away from her face. 'She said I do this all the time. If I do then why is it such a big deal? I've cancelled my fair share, but she's never been bothered before.'

Burton bit back on her ideal response. 'Am I answering as a colleague or a friend?'

Melanie thought for a second. 'Friend.'

'You actually heard what you just said, right?'

But Melanie responded with a furrowed brow.

'Maybe it's because you've done this your fair share of times that she's become bothered.'

Melanie seemed to roll the answer round, tilting her head to one side, then the other. She cracked a half-laugh and said, 'Okay, you can go back to being my colleague.'

11

Melanie sat in her office the following morning with Morris across from her. The young officer was taking quick scans around the room while Melanie looked over her most recent findings – or lack thereof. From what Melanie could see in front of her, it didn't look like there was anything at all to tie the two shops together – which was something she'd been counting on.

'And we interviewed the shop owner?' Melanie asked, still focused on the documents.

'Read and Fairer did, boss, but they couldn't get anything out of him that would tie the two places to each other either. The shop was a regular arts supply set-up. There wasn't anything specialist about it. Both the shop and the studio were doing okay financially. Burton and I can keep looking though. There are a few things we haven't gone over yet.'

Before Melanie could weigh in there came a knock at the office door, and Carter walked in without waiting for approval.

'Sorry, boss, it's worth the interruption,' he said, as though anticipating a reprimand. 'Penelope Halloway has just rocked up in the main reception.'

Melanie pushed back from her desk. 'So much for calling ahead. Morris, keep doing what you're doing but Burton's heading over to forensics today. They always respond better to face-to-face pressure.' She flashed a thin smile to the young woman before turning her attention to Carter. 'Shall we?'

The two walked downstairs in a comfortable silence, broken only when Carter asked, 'So, what kind of woman are we expecting here?'

Melanie let out a half-laugh. 'International jet-setter, she looked quite glamorous from the social media stuff Fairer found.'

'Married to a taxidermist though…' Carter trailed off as he pushed open the door into the reception space. He held the door open for Melanie to follow and then let it fall closed with a clang. There was only one person waiting for them. An older lady who carried herself well, Halloway's ex-wife stood straight-backed wearing high heels, an A-line skirt and perfectly blacked-out sunglasses. 'I'll grab us an interview room,' Carter said out of the side of his mouth as he ducked towards the desk sergeant.

'Ms Halloway?' Melanie said questioningly. When the woman turned Melanie held out a hand in greeting. 'I'm DI Melanie Watton, we spoke on the phone some days ago.'

Halloway reciprocated the gesture. 'Yes, yes, of course we did. I'm sorry, you must think I'm so rude. I said I'd call, I know, but as soon as the wheels touched down this morning I thought I just had to get here and talk to you all, and find out what the hell happened. I mean, what in the hell did happen?'

Melanie couldn't picture Norman Halloway – their dumpy taxidermist – being married to a woman who was as no-nonsense as Penelope Halloway appeared to be. *But then, they did get divorced too*, she thought as she guided the woman towards Carter.

'I have the list,' she started to say as they walked. 'The list of people who might know something, or be able to help.'

With the rush of a second crime scene, Melanie hadn't even thought to chase up on Penelope Halloway's promise of a catalogue of people. She explained to the woman that they'd get to that, though, as part of the formal interview.

'This is my colleague, DS Carter, if you want to go with him...' Melanie petered out as the visiting woman followed the instruction and, after saying her polite hello to Carter, went with him down a corridor leading to an interview room. Melanie walked in close behind them, secured the door and joined them at the table. Halloway was scanning the room when Melanie let out a gentle cough to get her attention. 'There's recording equipment in here,' she clarified, guessing that might be what their interviewee was looking for; it usually was. 'For the purposes of our records could you state your name and your reason for being here.'

'I'm Penelope Halloway and I'm here because – Christ, I'm here because someone killed my husband. My ex-husband.'

'Ms Halloway, we're terribly sorry for your loss and we're appreciative of the arrangements you've made to be here today. Would it be okay if we asked you a few questions about your husband?'

'Of course, of course,' Halloway encouraged, as she ferreted out a folded sheet of paper from her floral handbag. It was an A4 sheet that had been folded a few times over. Once it was flat on the table, she turned her attention to the officers.

'When did you last see him?'

Halloway thought. 'Around four weeks ago. I've been away for three weeks now, and we had dinner the week before I went.'

'Was it just the two of you?'

'Yes.' As though noting something in Melanie's expression,

she added, 'I know a lot of people hate their ex-spouses, but Norman and I weren't like that. We didn't have it in us.'

'It's nice to see that,' Carter added.

'And how were things when you went for dinner?' Melanie asked, ignoring the tangent.

She shrugged. 'Completely fine. Norman had been booked for an artists' market...' She paused to think. 'Somewhere up north, I remember that much, but it was a few months away. He'd had a lot of new commissions come in that he was excited about. I had a lot of travel plans that I was excited about.' She shook her head. 'Christ, it all seems so stupid now. If I'd known that something like this was going to happen...'

'Do you mind me asking why you and Mr Halloway separated?'

'Oh, we got married impossibly young, that was all. Norman was always very happy with married life.' She stopped and smiled as though remembering something and then continued, 'It was actually me that had the midlife crisis.'

'Hence the travel plans?'

Halloway nodded. 'I do a lot of freelance editorial work and content creation. It's nothing that can't be done on the road.'

'And what about Mr Halloway's work?'

The woman rolled her eyes and smiled again; it was nearly a laugh. 'What about it? I hated it, he loved it. But it made him happy.'

'Was taxidermy always his profession?'

'When we first got together, he was an aspiring artist; you know what young men can be like. He painted, taught art, painted some more. It wasn't until around fifteen years back that he got into the taxidermy and he just took to it, like a duck to a mount, he used to joke.'

Melanie side-eyed Carter to make sure he was keeping up

with notes before adding her next question. 'Has he had any problems since he joined this industry?'

'Problems that might get him killed? No.' Halloway tilted her head back and stared at the ceiling. She stayed like this as she continued, 'Norman had friendly competition with other people in the industry, I would say.' She dropped her head and tapped the sheet of paper on the table. 'There are competitions up and down the country, some out of the country, and there were people – God, friends of his, even – who he'd always beat in these things. There were mock hard feelings but nothing that ever lasted longer than the competition day. There have been problems with activists over the years, but less so since we moved to the house, to his house.'

'What kind of activists?'

The woman rolled her eyes again. 'Activists who confuse artwork with butchery. I've put their names on the list too.' She shot the sheet a filthy look, as though she were eyeing the individuals directly. 'There were three altogether, three that I could remember. They seemed to think Norman, and people in the business, generally, would go out killing all manner of animals when people weren't looking. Don't get me wrong, I'm sure there are people like that, but Norman wasn't one of them. Everything he worked with was ethically sourced, which he tried to explain to these people on numerous occasions, but...' she let her speech trail out and waved away the rest of her explanation.

'Do you think these people were dangerous?'

She huffed. 'One of them left roadkill outside of our back door once, and you could only get to the back door by hopping an eight-foot fence at the time. I remember telling Norman it was nothing to do with the roadkill and everything to do with that crazy bitch letting us know she could get onto our property.'

'Was that at Mr Halloway's studio address?'

'We were in the old house when that happened. It's been some years now. Like I said, the names are there. The activists are listed with an asterisk.'

'Ms Halloway, we really appreciate this time. Is there anything else you think we should know about, whether it's Norman, his life. Was he seeing anyone, for example?'

She smiled fondly. 'No, he wasn't. He would have told me that.' She rubbed her forehead. 'I'm sorry, I really can't think of anything else, at least not at the moment.'

'That's completely fine. You've given us a lot to work with already.' Melanie reached across the table for the list. 'I'll take this and we'll get started on contacting the people on the list in the coming days.'

'There are friends on there, as well as colleagues, just in case.'

'Thank you,' Melanie said again. 'DS Carter here will see you out and I promise we'll be in touch as and when we have updates on the case.' Melanie pushed back from the table and stood to leave.

'DI Watton, you'll catch the bastard that did this, won't you?' Halloway asked, but somehow it didn't sound like a question but rather an instruction.

Goddamn right I will, Melanie thought. 'We'll do our best to, Ms Halloway.'

12

It was mid-afternoon by the time Burton strolled back into the office, an evidence folder in tow. The entire team had their heads down, working on one thing or another, with most people chasing up the names that Ms Halloway had given them that morning. Melanie had requested background checks on friends and colleagues, but she'd given Morris the activists as a special treat, explaining, 'I want everything they think we can't get.' Morris had nodded her understanding. Meanwhile Carter, Read and Fairer had started to work through their clusters of names. For an A4 sheet, Halloway had been quite extensive with the details she'd provided them.

Melanie was in her office looking up the details of Ms Halloway herself when Burton came to a stop in the open doorway.

'The wanderer returns,' Melanie said, spotting her.

'And she brings gifts.' Burton held the file up.

'Something for the whole team?'

'I should think so.'

'Well then, round them up.' Melanie stood and followed

Burton into the open space. 'Folks, Burton has brought us something exciting.'

'Thank God because these blokes so far are dull,' Read replied.

'Forensics swept the second crime scene and you'll be glad to know they only found three sets of DNA in the place. Two male and one female. The reason I've been there all day is because Williams was waiting for confirmation that one of the male samples was in fact the owner of the shop, which it turns out it was.'

'And the other male?' Melanie asked.

'What about the female?' Carter added.

'They're operating on the assumption that the female is the cleaning lady, which makes sense given that she was likely the last person in the building. The shop owner has spent so much time there over the years that Williams didn't seem surprised to find residual DNA and fingerprint traces from him around the place. To be sure, or as sure as they can be, they cross-matched all three with the DNA samples pulled from Halloway's scene, and there was a hit.'

'We've got a suspect?' Melanie asked, the excitement clear in her tone.

'We've got a suspect.' Burton handed the folder over to her boss. 'That's a DNA rundown and a name, so we'll need to do a further search ourselves. But it's a young man who's definitely already in the system.'

'Carter,' Melanie started, her colleague already shuffling about behind her.

'On it.' He hit a quick combination of something into his keyboard. 'Hit me.'

'Liam Kinsley.'

Carter typed in the name and leaned back in his chair, awaiting the results. There was a quiet ping as they unfolded onto his monitor. He whistled. 'That's a lot of minor theft and common assault for someone so young.'

Melanie stood behind him to scan the results. 'Flat 87, Walsh Towers. Read, Fairer?'

'Yep.' Fairer stood and Read was close behind him.

'A suspect is good, boss, but this kid?' Carter pointed to the screen. 'Do we think someone would go from minor theft to murder that fast?'

Melanie shrugged. 'People cut their teeth at different paces, Carter. Worst case scenario, we can pin the art shop on him. Best case…'

Kinsley was a gangly young man with shaggy hair and a poor posture; Melanie guessed he would be a good six foot tall if only he could bring himself to stand up straight. Read and Fairer herded him into a room and, as soon as the duty solicitor was available, Melanie and Carter stepped in for the interview. Their suspect was fidgety from the second the officers took their seats, his glance shifting this way then that – anywhere to avoid looking at either of them directly. He even seemed perturbed when the solicitor introduced himself.

'I'm DI Watton and this is DS Carter. Could you please confirm your name for the recording?' The pause after this lasted so long that Melanie was about to repeat the question, but the young man stirred into life.

'Liam Kinsley.'

'Ian Moore.' The solicitor followed, already familiar with this routine.

'Liam, we've brought you here today to talk about a recent robbery.' No sooner were the words out and the fidgeting increased, it looked as though the base of the chair was slowly heating beneath their suspect. 'There's an art supply shop on Fairmount Street, Artists' Hideout. Are you familiar with the property?'

Liam looked to his solicitor, who said nothing. 'I suppose I've walked past it.'

'But you've never been inside?'

'Why would I have been?'

Taking this as his cue, Carter lifted the cover of the evidence folder in front of him and pulled out a sheet explaining the points at which Kinsley's DNA had been found inside the shop. 'The thing is, Liam,' he started, adopting a notably softer tone than Melanie had used, 'we've got forensic evidence that places you inside the shop.'

The solicitor leaned forward to look at the paperwork. 'That sheet could say anything. We're not experts.'

'Neither are we,' Melanie said. 'But our forensics team know a thing or two.'

'They've found a lot of DNA around the shop, especially around the area of the cash till. Can you explain how that might have happened, Liam?' Carter asked.

Again, their suspect threw a sad and expectant look at the solicitor who shrugged in return. If they weren't amid a murder enquiry, then Melanie might be moved to feel sorry for the kid. The fact that he was a repeat offender made it considerably easier to keep her sympathies in check, though.

'Liam?' she pushed.

He shifted, lifting one side of his body and then the other as though trying to give his backside a break from the chair. 'I don't know.'

'Any chance you might have broken in, Liam?' Melanie said. 'That would have done it.'

'DI Watton,' the solicitor cautioned, his tone suddenly firm.

Melanie held her hands up in defence. 'We can place you in the shop, Liam, so there must be some explanation for that.'

'Is there any chance you went in there and forgot?' Carter suggested, using the same meek tone as before. 'Or, you know, Liam, even if you were there for reasons you shouldn't have been, it's okay to tell us that too.'

Melanie held back a frown. She understood good cop, but this was a step too far. She was about to wade in with a counter comment when their suspect opened his mouth, fish-like, slammed it closed, but then tried again.

'If I had been there, what kind of trouble would I be in?'

'It depends on your reason for being there, Liam,' Carter replied.

'If you were responsible for the robbery then action would be taken against you, which I imagine you know from your previous charges.' Melanie left a beat between that blow and the next. 'If you confess to that as well as the murder then it'll go a little easier on us all, in terms of investigations and the trial.'

Kinsley pushed himself back from the table and leapt from his chair before dropping back into it with a heavy thud. He looked as though he'd been physically shocked. 'What fucking murder?' he asked, still a distance from the table. 'I didn't kill the owner, like, I just went in, scrambled about a bit and then took what I could. Jesus.' His tone made the act of robbery sound reasonable.

Well at least that's our first confession, Melanie thought. 'The murder of Norman Halloway, Liam, can you tell us anything about that?'

He looked from one officer to the other, and back again. 'No,' he said plainly. 'Who the fuck is Norman Halloway and why would I kill him? Did he come to the shop? Did he see me?' He moved back closer to the table with each question, shuffling the chair forward bit by bit until he was leaning on the surface that separated him from Melanie and Carter. 'Did he see me?' he asked again.

Melanie narrowed her eyes. She couldn't tell what of this was real and what was faked for their benefit. 'Norman Halloway was the owner of a private studio on the other side of down. He was an artist producing taxidermy–'

'Stuffed animals?'

'Yes,' Melanie replied, flatly. 'He was found dead in his studio some days ago now. He's also responsible for making the structure that was left behind in Artists' Hideout, after you'd broken in. Is this sounding familiar yet?'

Again, the young man looked sincerely startled. 'What fucking structure?'

'Mind your language, please, Mr Kinsley,' Melanie said, deliberately dropping the use of his first name. 'It looks as though this is becoming a bit of a troubling topic so why don't we pause things there?' She looked from Carter to the solicitor, both of whom gestured their agreement; she didn't bother to see how the suggestion sat with Kinsley before continuing. 'DS Carter and I will liaise with our team further. In the meantime, perhaps it would be worthwhile for you to have a discussion with your client about his options?'

'Yes, DI Watton, I'd appreciate that.'

'What options? For what?'

'Interview terminated.' Melanie stood. 'We'll see you both again shortly.' She and Carter left the interview room without another word, waiting until they were a safe distance from the space to begin their deliberations.

'What are you thinking, boss?' Carter asked, climbing the stairs behind her.

'He seemed panicked about the suggestion of murder, didn't he?'

'But not so much about the robbery.'

'Murder is an escalation, though, and even an eejit like Kinsley must understand what that means in terms of sentencing.'

'But why leave the parrot?'

Melanie thought about this for a second longer. 'I suspect we'll get to that later,' she said, but her tone didn't suggest much optimism. She waited outside the office for Carter to catch up. 'We've bought ourselves a couple of hours, either way. Maybe by the time we go back in we'll have something more concrete. Although forensics have already given us good grounding.'

Melanie walked into the office space, followed by Carter, to find the rest of her team crowded around a single desk. Morris was seated in front of her monitor while Burton, Read and Fairer hunched over to garner a look at the screen.

'Anything for the group?' Melanie called out to them as she crossed the room.

The three officers took a step back, giving Morris the space to turn and talk. 'We've got the camera footage from the feeds that are over the road from the shop.'

'Took long enough,' Carter said, coming to join them.

'We've been over it as a group, and I even called through to make sure there wasn't space for a cock up anywhere along the way. But, there's nothing here, boss.'

Melanie felt a twist in her stomach. 'I don't understand.'

Morris turned back to her computer and dragged her cursor along the play-bar of the footage. 'Okay, we know the front alarm and back alarm are on separate circuits. My thinking, our thinking, was that he must have come in the back and rushed out through the front, right?' There was a grumble of agreement from the group. 'But he doesn't.'

She clicked play and leaned back in her seat giving everyone a clear view of the screen. The grainy footage showed the front of the Artists' Hideout and the time stamp in the corner confirmed the date and the time; it was just over one minute before the alarm was tripped. Melanie waited, her eyes on the timer until they were ten seconds away from the alarm going off, at which point she shifted her focus to the door. She kept count in her head – *seven, six, five...* – and waited. Morris had already crushed her hopes of video footage for Kinsley but maybe this would mean another player – *four, three, two...* – someone else they could pull in and tie to Halloway. She took a sharp pull of air as the door opened, it couldn't have been more than an inch or two, and she'd have missed it if she hadn't been looking. It dropped closed again and then nothing – no signs of life, no further movement on the shop front.

'We've watched it right up until people start arriving, boss, and no one comes.' Morris paused the footage and turned back to her superior. 'Someone tripped the alarm on purpose.'

13

Melanie stepped back from the second evidence board – brought in especially for the occasion. Their first one remained blank, showing little to no information about Norman Halloway's death, but plenty about his life at least. The second board was populated with their latest discoveries. Melanie had branched off Liam Kinsley with everything they now knew, little of which made much sense. She'd hoped that seeing everything laid out in one place might spark an idea, and yet...

'What am I missing?' she spoke to the board, but the question was addressed to the team behind her, all of whom responded with stoic silence. She turned. 'It's not just me, then?'

'We need to know whether there was anyone else involved,' Carter suggested.

'With the robbery?' Burton jumped in.

'Exactly. It might be that there was an accomplice, and the accomplice is the person who left the parrot. We just need to crack Kinsley on it.'

'Did the accomplice also kill Halloway?' Morris asked from the back row.

Carter huffed. 'Maybe? Who knows at this point?'

'Okay, we push the accomplice line of questioning. We tell the kid we believe he's nothing to do with the murder, but we also believe his accomplice – hypothetical accomplice – might know something about it. Hence the parrot.' Melanie rubbed her eyes. 'Christ, I've never said parrot so many times in one working day.'

'But outside of work is a different matter,' Carter replied, trying to lighten the tone. 'Come on, we'll lead with the accomplice angle. What else is there? Someone left that bloody bird behind.'

Both officers returned to the same interview room where Ian Moore and Liam Kinsley sat, as though they hadn't moved an inch since the last meeting. Melanie hoped Moore had at least made the effort to speak to his client: someone needed to get answers, especially as she and her team were struggling to.

The four of them walked through the same procedure as before, repeating their names for the recording equipment. But then Melanie let a silence fill the space for nearly a full minute. She reasoned that at some point someone would crack, and she hoped it would be Kinsley. When she saw from the corner of her eye that even Carter was getting fidgety, yet still no one had said anything, she decided to dive in. 'We know the front door alarm was tripped deliberately.' She let the sentence hang there. 'What we can't understand, yet, is why you'd do that knowing that you'd draw attention to yourself in the process. Unless that was the point?'

Kinsley looked from one officer to the other. He shook his head. 'Why would I do that?'

'That's what they're asking you.' Moore leaned forward to rest his forearms on the table. 'My client and I spoke in detail during our little break and he's happy – although happy might be a stretch, to take full responsibility for the robbery itself. But he claims no knowledge of the...' he petered out, searching for the right word. 'No knowledge of the specimen you say was left behind, nor does he know who would have left it.'

'There was no one else involved in the robbery?' Carter pushed.

'No.' Kinsley's tone was flat. 'Christ. I only hit the place because it was meant to be easy.'

Melanie latched on to that. 'Easy according to whom?'

'According to the bloke that told me about it,' he snapped. Kinsley's frustration was obvious, but he didn't seem to register the significance in what he'd said. He watched on as the officers and the solicitor shared the same perplexed expression. 'Fuck sake, what?'

'Who told you about the shop, Liam?' Carter asked.

'And why didn't you mention this during our discussion in the break?' Moore added, but Melanie guessed the question was a rhetorical one. From Kinsley's expression it was clear that the weight of this admission still hadn't fully registered with him.

'I was at my local and got talking to this bloke. Fresh out of the cells, he said, but he didn't seem it. He was nice enough, either way.' He took a breath.

Melanie wondered what the standards were for 'nice enough' among criminals.

'He told me about the shop and said he'd seen some decent money shifted in and out of the place, and he was surprised no one had hit it, with the security there being dead.'

'Security being dead?' Carter repeated, his hand poised over his notebook.

'The cameras were a fix.'

'And a man you'd never met before gave you all of this information?'

'Yep. Fox and Hounds, two pints in.' Kinsley leaned back in his seat and folded his arms. 'Easy as that.'

Except it wasn't, Melanie thought, *because you're here*.

'What did the man want in return for this information?' Carter continued.

'It was idle chit-chat is all. He said it was a shame he couldn't do it, but someone should. He didn't ask for anything in return for it.'

'And you didn't find that at all suspicious?' Moore's frustration cracked, causing a near-squeal at the end of the question.

'Well, I do now.' Kinsley turned to stare at his representation. 'Anyway, he's the only other person who knew about the job.'

'But you didn't tell him anything about when you might do the job?'

'I'm not an idiot.' Kinsley puffed. 'The only way he'd know when I was doing it is if he'd been tailing me.' He half laughed at the suggestion, as though he didn't think it was a true possibility. But Melanie flashed a quick look at Carter and could see he was also taking the idea seriously.

'Mr Kinsley, do you think you're able to describe this man for us?' Melanie stepped in.

'Sure. Quite tall, stocky build. Brownish hair, but he was wearing a cap so–'

'No,' Melanie interrupted him. 'Can you do it in a more formal capacity? If we were to arrange for you to see a sketch artist, for instance.'

Kinsley's eyes stretched wide with what looked to be excitement. 'Yeah, yeah, I could definitely do that. I'll give you a real good description of the guy.' He paused then and tried to level his tone. 'What's in it for me though? You know, what can I expect to gain?' He sounded so sleazy in his asking, Melanie expected him to wink when he'd finished the line.

'Absolutely nothing, Mr Kinsley, other than being in our good graces for a while.'

'What? Nothing at all?'

'Mr Moore, we'll be charging your client with breaking and entering, it goes without saying, and theft, given the substantial sum of money that's missing. Do you have any questions?'

'Only whether my presence is still required here, DI Watton.'

'I don't think any of us need to be here, actually.' She flashed a tight smile at their suspect. 'DS Carter, perhaps you could make sure Mr Kinsley is escorted back to his cell?' She spoke directly to the young man opposite her then. 'You'll remain there for the foreseeable until we can get a sketch artist into the station to work with you.'

'And after that?' he asked.

'After that Mr Moore will arrange for another interview with you, in private from us, where you'll discuss your options ahead of prosecution.' Melanie pushed back from the table before the man could barter for her attention again. 'Mr Moore, I'll see you out; if you're okay here, Carter?' Her DS gestured in the affirmative, so Melanie stepped toward the door, holding it open for the duty solicitor to walk ahead of her.

The pair took a few generous strides down the corridor, bringing them back into the reception space. 'He's quite a character,' Melanie said.

Moore sighed. 'He seems to be, doesn't he?' The man ran a hand over his face. 'I'm sure the next few weeks and months will be good fun.' He tried to force a smile as he held out a hand to Melanie, who reciprocated the gesture. 'Always a pleasure to work with our finest, DI Watton.' He turned toward the door without waiting for a reply from Melanie, but soon back-stepped, remembering one final thing. 'This chap that you think muggins in there can identify, is he the latest murderer you're after?'

The word 'murderer' rang in Melanie's ears as though a gong had sounded.

'It's far too early to say,' she admitted, after some seconds, all the while thinking, *Yes, Mr Moore, yes, I think he might be.*

14

It took Melanie two days to arrange for a sketch artist to visit Kinsley. She left Carter to the official welcome while she caught up with the team, all of whom had been working on their individual tasks. Burton, Read and Fairer had been calling round Norman Halloway's contacts, left behind by his wife during her visit. Meanwhile, Morris had been scouring the corners of the internet to track down the activists that had targeted their victim previously. Melanie didn't know how their investigations were shaping up, but there hadn't been any cries of, 'Eureka!'

She placed the cursory call to Williams in the forensics department to see whether there were any further updates, but they hadn't progressed either.

'There aren't any other DNA matches showing up?' she pushed, knowing the answer.

'Only the ones for Liam Kinsley, DI Watton, I'm sorry.' Williams used his most formal tone, and Melanie could tell she was two pushes away from him ignoring her calls.

'Can I ask a practical question, while I've got you?'

'Fire away.'

'The DNA of Kinsley's that you found at Halloway's scene. Is that something that could have been planted?' The idea occurred to Melanie in the early hours of the morning after they'd first interviewed Kinsley; if he hadn't been to Halloway's, then why could they place him there?

Williams was quiet for a few seconds, as though really giving the question some thought. 'Yes, it could have been planted,' he admitted. 'We didn't find fingerprints of his anywhere in the studio itself, although we did in the art shop. The studio flagged up hair samples though, which could have been placed. If someone had access to his hair, that is.'

Someone must have done. 'Okay, thanks, Williams.'

'You can't place him there for the murder?'

'He's got an alibi,' Melanie admitted. 'Back to the drawing board. Thanks again, for this and for your patience.'

He exhaled a half laugh. 'Any time.'

The two said their goodbyes and Melanie made a note of their exchange on the sheet of paper closest to her; one that was already full of notes and far-fetched theories. She was reaching well outside the box to make their discoveries fit. She checked her emails – a summons from Archer felt imminent – and then closed her laptop. She pushed away from the desk, deciding the lack of any emails might well be a blessing, and walked into the open office.

'Do you have a second?' Morris asked, when Melanie was hardly two feet into the room. By way of reply Melanie headed to Morris' desk and grabbed a seat. 'I've been digging around on these activists: one in prison; one out of the country; one in the wind.'

Melanie held back a groan. 'Okay, talk to me about the ones we've actually found.'

'Fiona O'Grady,' Morris announced as she expanded a browser page to fit her screen. 'She's been in prison for three months, serving a charge for ABH against a man during a protest. She was there in support of animal rights; he was a concerned citizen who didn't want things to get out of hand. The report suggests he somehow tried to move her, or push her away from other citizens, and that's when O'Grady lashed out. Pushed the guy into a wall with such force that he needed stitches to the back of the head.'

'Nice lady. Anything in the file about Halloway?'

'Minor disturbances.' Morris scrolled down the page. 'There are reports of her making a nuisance of herself more than anything else. But here you'll spot the name of our next activist, who's listed as an associated figure.' Morris double-clicked to expand another window. 'Simon Vaar. He also has disturbances listed for the Halloway's previous address but nothing for the new one. The report claims he was loitering outside their property at an anti-social hour, early hours of the morning by the looks of it–'

'There's nothing more serious than the odd bit of loitering?' Melanie interrupted.

Morris's head moved as she scanned the page. 'He was found with a pint of pig's blood in his front pocket on one occasion– oh, wait, no, that was at someone else's house.'

Melanie let out a hard puff of air. 'Brilliant. And he's where?'

'Italy, as best as I can tell from his online presence. For someone who shouldn't want to draw attention to themselves, he seems to be mighty fine with it.' She clicked into another window. There were square images packed alongside each other showing various messages: FISHING HURTS; CLOSE THE LAB; WHEN DID YOU LAST KILL AN ANIMAL?

'How do you know he's in Italy from that?'

'Ah.' Morris clicked a small circle in the top of the screen and a video unfolded. 'He posted this six hours ago, and the video is geotagged so I can track a rough location.'

'Okay. Who's in the wind?'

'Every police officer's favourite question.' Morris closed the windows before opening a fresh one. 'Yvonne Roadick. She's thirty-one, most of her activity has been in and around capital cities although she occasionally focuses her sights on smaller targets, like Halloway. She left roadkill outside of their house on one occasion, according to this.'

'Ah, Penelope Halloway warned us about this one. Did they press charges?'

'Halloway decided not to, but she was cautioned for trespassing. It doesn't look like she had another encounter with them, or at least not one that was reported. But she's got a few addresses listed under the trespassing heading so I'm guessing she varied her targets.'

Melanie let out a noise that was nearly a laugh.

'What?' Morris asked.

'The more I hear of Norman Halloway, the more I think what a nice man he was.'

Morris frowned. 'I guess? I'm sorry, boss, I don't think I fo–'

'I don't know that his murder is anything to do with what's happening here,' Melanie continued. 'A man who no one has a bad word to say about ends up murdered in his in own home. It looks personal, I get it, but how can it be? He didn't even want to press charges against people who were personally gunning for him.' She gestured at the report still on the screen. 'I'm worried we're looking into Halloway because we have to, but we won't find anything. This murder just might not be about him, Morris.'

'Boss?' Burton cut in. 'We're nearly done ringing around the names on Halloway's list. For a bunch of taxidermists, they seem like pretty nice people.' She tried to force a grin. 'A few of them have offered further contacts, people they know Halloway either liaised with or sold work to at one point. Read and Fairer are tying up those details now. But there's nothing new coming in.'

'Let me guess,' Melanie started, 'he was such a nice man?'

'It's never felt like such a bad thing to say that about someone,' Burton replied, looking from her boss to Morris and back again. 'What am I missing?'

'The boss thinks that maybe–'

'And I'm back!' Carter announced as he kicked the door to the office open.

'A girl can't get a word in anywhere in this office,' Morris said quietly, but Melanie caught the grumble and threw her junior an *I'm sorry* expression before she stood.

'How did it go?'

'It's madness that when we first started out these things would take forever.' Carter gestured with a slim cardboard folder as he spoke. 'Now, they turn up with their tablets, they have a chat with the witness and you're away with a sketch before you know it.'

'Carter.' Melanie's tone was firmer. 'How did it go?'

He passed her the folder. 'He'll be submitting a digital copy of it in case we need it in the future for distribution, but he also provided a printout. On the printer that he pulled out of his bag, like it was nothing.'

'You're making yourself sound older than you are,' Melanie said as she opened the file.

The team crowded around her to get a look at the man on the sheet. He looked mid- to late-thirties, with minimal facial hair and a hard stare that came through dark eyes. It looked as though there was light shadowing under his eyes as well, presumably to indicate bags; *which we can all relate to*, Melanie thought. Most of his hair was covered by a peaked cap, but dark wisps escaped from either side.

'So, this is the guy we're looking for?' Read said, looking

from one member of the team to another. 'He doesn't look like anything special.'

'They never do,' Carter replied.

The idle chatter started slowly among the team. Burton seemed to be the only one to notice that Melanie hadn't joined in.

'What's going on?' she asked.

Melanie narrowed her eyes to inspect the image again. 'Burton, I think I know him.'

15

Austerity made crime a hard business to get yourself noticed in. It should be a good thing, really. But for a bunch of low-life thieves and petty criminals who've never been noticed in their lives, it can sometimes just make us want to try that bit harder. If we're dedicated enough to the business, that is. Mam always told me that thieving and poaching and pestering would get me caught one day and something about the idea was exciting when I was kid. The first brush I had with the police in our area felt like a rite of passage: passed your driving test; lost your virginity; got a police caution. The trouble with that is that eventually it makes us ten-a-penny. That's how the police see criminals, don't you think? We're not people, we're statistics; we're not individuals, we're data entries on a spreadsheet. You have to be a kid killing their classmates or a woman on a rampage to get a headline named after you; to get caught.

A mate – more like a mentor, really – told me it was best to fly under the radar when you could. 'Keep your head down. Get in, get the job done, get out. What more is there?' he'd said.

'But what about the thrill?'

'The thrill is getting away with it. Don't get confused about why you're doing this.'

It wasn't to get away with it, though, it never was. It was to take a risk and cause some trouble and get a name. Imagine whole streets knowing who you were because of something you did to someone streets away in the other direction. People try bloody hard to get that sort of reach and reputation. And that's how it started, I suppose. Knocking about at home got hard work as Mam got older and making trouble seemed like a good thing to keep busy with.

'It'll catch up with you one day,' my brother said.

'I hope it does.'

The police used to pound down the front door on any knocking shop or raid going. You'd get real-life action with a detective, up close and personal. They'd introduce themselves and everything, like they thought maybe you'd be acquaintances – or arch nemeses. There was a time when you'd make a game of cops and robbers from it all, have the same police faces chasing you from one hangout to another. But the police like to up their ante too, don't they? In the same way that stealing cars and fencing pills isn't enough; arresting thieves and drug dealers isn't enough. They move up in the world and they reckon they leave us lot behind. How can we ever amount to anything, they might ask; how can we ever become more or worse – or better, depending on the angle you're looking at it from.

Some of us change, though, we really do. Criminals might be ten-a-penny but some'll go the extra mile to get noticed. Some of us like to add flair.

16

Even when she was visiting the office by choice, Melanie felt unnerved at seeing Archer. She'd called the superintendent to ask for an appointment, and Archer had immediately allocated her a time; she was never one to put off meetings. But being left in the office unsupervised while Archer dealt with an emergency elsewhere left Melanie with more freedom in the space than she was used to. She paced around the generously sized room, looking from one commendation to the next, before eventually deciding the visitor's chair was the safest place for her. She settled with the slim cardboard folder on her lap, the one that Carter had given her earlier that day. She drummed her fingers along the cover, still trying to place the man inside.

'Christ alive.' Archer burst into the room with such a force that Melanie couldn't help but jump. 'Sorry, there are small fires everywhere today.' She sat across the desk from Melanie and took a sip from the mug next to her. *It must be cold*, Melanie thought, but it didn't seem to bother her superior. 'Okay, talk taxidermy. You have a suspect?'

'Had,' Melanie corrected her. 'Liam Kinsley seems to have

been a pawn for the art robbery. He isn't– Well, ma'am, frankly he isn't the brightest of bulbs. Someone tipped him off that the shop would be a good hit because security was low-key, which it very much was, and apparently Kinsley didn't think anything more about it.'

'And this someone, they didn't want a cut?' Archer clarified and Melanie shook her head. 'Wow, he really isn't the brightest.'

'The saving grace in dealing with Kinsley is we were able to get a sketch artist involved, to draw up Kinsley's description of the man he spoke to. Apparently they met in Kinsley's local, but he's pretty sure he hadn't seen the man before that day.'

Archer was holding out a hand to take the image before Melanie had finished speaking. She slipped the photo out of the folder and gave it a determined stare. 'He looks like every other criminal we have to find. What else do we know?'

Melanie hesitated. 'I recognise him. But I don't know where from.'

Archer looked as though she were suppressing a smile. 'I don't know how much that helps us at the minute, Watton. Where do you think you recognise him from? Personal or professional matters?'

'Professional, definitely.'

'Maybe you arrested him at some point?' Archer let a laugh slip this time. 'With your record, would you even know?'

It felt like a compliment, but in this context Melanie wasn't sure how to take the remark.

'Could this Kinsley character tell you anything more about the mystery man?'

'That he'd recently been released from prison,' Melanie admitted.

'So, he has previous. Surely that could explain why you know the face?'

Melanie reluctantly agreed.

'I don't mean to be dismissive, Melanie.' Archer's tone was much softer now. 'But if you can't place him then recognition doesn't help us. We'll have to go with good old-fashioned hunting techniques. Do you have a starting point?'

'We know the pub where Kinsley met this man. He said he hadn't seen him there since their first conversation, but I thought it would be a good place to start. We can pay them a visit, circulate the image to see who else recognises him.'

'Good.' Archer looked as though her mind were elsewhere. 'Which pub was it?'

'Fox and Hounds, over on York Road.'

Archer rolled her eyes. 'That's always been a hot spot. It's no wonder that's the root. What other places have made your hit list?' she asked, but before Melanie had the chance to reply she pushed herself away from the desk and crossed to the other side of the room, outside of her junior's line of sight.

Melanie turned to face her. 'Did I miss something, ma'am?'

From alongside a filing cabinet Archer pulled out a large sheet of paper that had been rolled into a tight tube. She gestured with it as she spoke. 'I just thought of something that might be useful.' She carefully unrolled the sheet and spread it across her desk. 'You'll know a lot of these places, I'm sure, but on the off chance.'

Archer weighted down one side of the sheet with her half-empty mug and the other side with a tub of paperclips. It was curling at the corners, but Melanie could get a good enough look to work out what it was: a map of the city. She stood and from a new viewpoint she could soon spot the dots and crosses marked at various points on the layout. Archer stayed quiet for a minute, as though allowing Melanie to take it in.

'The black crosses are crime hot spots that we've noticed around the city. The red dots are public houses, some of which I imagine will be of use,' she explained. 'I know there are online systems for this sort of thing, but nothing beats a good map, does it?' Melanie let out a half laugh and Archer matched her amusement with a smile. 'What did you think I did up here all day, played solitaire?'

'I thought you were more of a sudoku person.'

Archer frowned. 'All those numbers, it's not for me.' She leaned forward on both hands and took another look at the map. 'So, let's match what you've got with what I've got and see if we can get something to work with here.'

Melanie left Archer's office with a list of five public houses – including the Fox and Hounds – that might be worth investigating further. The pair had agreed it was worth circulating the sketch photograph of their suspect in all the hot spots, in case he'd been operating in other areas as well. Melanie pushed her way back into the office with a measure of confidence that the team finally had a direction to move in, and it would be her first announcement to them in the morning, she decided.

Most of her detectives looked to have packed up and gone home for the day, bar one.

'What's got you working overtime, Morris?'

She shot round at the sound of her boss' voice. 'Christ, I didn't even hear you come in. I'm sorry, boss. I'm trying to do some digging around on this Yvonne Roadick woman.' She turned back to face the computer screen. 'People can't just disappear.'

'She's unlikely to be a central figure, Morris. You shouldn't lose sleep over it.'

'I won't, once I've found her.'

Melanie wondered whether this was a professional or ego-led vendetta that her junior was nursing. 'You're a good officer, Morris,' she reassured her. 'If anyone can find her then I'm sure you can. Like you said, people don't just disappear.'

'I've found some cases that might involve her,' she replied, absent-mindedly.

'What cases?' She let a few seconds roll by but when there was no answer she asked again, 'Morris, what cases?'

'Shit, I'm sorry.' She closed the window on her computer and turned away from the screen completely, giving Melanie her full attention. 'Harassment cases, mostly. There are a few reports of roadkill being left on people's properties, which they're obviously reporting, but none of them are sharing any names on who they think it is.'

'If it is her then she's a one-trick pony, surely.'

'Because of what she did to Halloway?'

'Exactly. Are these cases in the area or elsewhere?'

'Mostly elsewhere, and there are huge gaps in between the reports too, like she was moving around a lot when these things happened. There's also only one repeat report so either she just does this once, maybe as a scare tactic for people, or the people stop reporting it after the first time.'

'Either way, she's still not worth losing sleep over.' Melanie flashed a tight smile. 'Someone who's dull enough to leave roadkill over and over isn't anywhere near interesting enough to steal taxidermy structures and then randomly give one back to us.' She tried to laugh but it was more of a tired sound. 'Go home and get some rest,' she said, before she turned and finished the walk to her office.

Melanie packed her essentials and zipped her bag closed. She left the office and locked the door behind her, noting that

Morris had already made a hasty exit. On the way down to the car park, she tried to juggle the more pressing thoughts that were left from the day: *is the Chinese open on a Tuesday? Did I leave any wine in that bottle?*

17

By the time the team arrived the following morning Melanie had already put together a document detailing the public houses they'd be visiting that day – alongside the addresses for each stop. She and Archer had narrowed their early searches down to: Fox and Hounds; Waggon and Horses; Three Horse Shoes; Queen's Arms; and Nag's Head. They'd tried to limit their range in terms of mileage for this first round of enquiries. Depending on what they found, Melanie could decide whether it was worth expanding their search parameters for a second round.

The whiteboard that showed the document caught everyone's attention as they walked in, one by one casting a glance at the locations listed. Read and Fairer were the first to drop their belongings at their desks and join Melanie. Burton and Carter looked caught up in their own conversation, while Morris was busy booting up her computer and her laptop one after the other. *Her priorities are probably right there*, Melanie thought.

'Boss, I won't lie, this looks like a pretty rough pub crawl,'

Read said and Melanie cracked a smile. *Only Read*, she thought. 'You're sending us out to get smashed–'

'Over the head with a pint glass?' Fairer finished his partner's suggestion.

'Carter, Burton, Morris, can you join?' Melanie said, by way of response, and she waited until the other detectives had migrated over before she explained. 'I had a meeting with Superintendent Archer yesterday to discuss the sketch photograph we've got from Liam Kinsley. She agreed the best plan of action is to circulate the image, but her suggestion was that we expand the search zone out from the first sighting, to include other public houses in the city.'

'Why these?' Carter nodded at the board.

'They're hot spots,' Morris suggested.

'Exactly. Archer has details of which areas are more likely to host criminal activities than others, so we thought circulating the man's image there might get us a catch. If he's talked to one person about an easy job, there's no reason to think he wouldn't have spoken to others.'

'So, are we talking to punters or are we talking to landlords?' Read asked.

'Yes,' Melanie replied. 'Bar staff and owners should be the first port of call. It goes without saying the clientele at these pubs probably aren't going to want to talk to the likes of us, though, so you'll need to tread carefully in your plans for speaking to any regulars. Try not to cause any trouble on your travels, is my best advice, but if you need additional support at any point then call it in.'

'Can we shotgun it?' Read said and nodded to the board. 'Which pubs we take.'

Carter sighed. 'You can't shotgun call it.'

'Why?'

'Because you can't call it, you're not a chi–'

'I shotgun Waggon and Horses and Nag's Head,' Burton interrupted her colleagues.

It was the most genuine laugh that Melanie had had for days, and she admired Burton's initiative so much that she said, 'Okay, Burton, deal. Read and Fairer, you'll take the other two.'

'What about the Fox and Hounds?' Carter asked.

'Whoever finishes first can wind up there, as it's the closest to the station. But check in with the other team so they know your whereabouts. Likewise, check in with me so I know you're...' Melanie felt around for the right words. 'Well, frankly, so I know you're alive.' There was a murmur of amusement around the room. 'Morris, what's your plan?'

'I'm still running background checks on Norman Halloway's contacts, the ones that Penelope Halloway left behind. They all seemed normal enough on the phone, but I was wondering whether there were any histories of harassment kicking around with his colleagues.'

'You're looking for an activist link?'

'It can't hurt,' Morris replied, although the statement sounded more like a question.

She was right, Melanie thought, it couldn't hurt. Being thorough with a case like this might save their backsides somewhere down the line. She gestured her agreement. 'Okay, I buy it. Leave Yvonne Roadick out of your search history for the day, though, are we clear?'

Morris gave a reluctant nod.

'Okay, check out opening times for these watering holes and get yourselves sorted. You'll have access to the digital sketch now too, so make sure you've got a copy–' Melanie was interrupted by the squeal of her desk phone from the next room. 'Make sure you've got a copy ready,' she finished, already halfway to her office. She disappeared through the doorway, leaving her team to ready themselves.

~

Melanie arrived at her phone in time for it to stop ringing. She checked the caller ID, but there was nothing listed. *If it's important they'll call back*, she reasoned, and only seconds later they did. She snatched at the handset.

'Watton.'

'Melanie, it's Archer. Was it the Fox and Hounds pub you mentioned, where one perp met the other?'

A stomach turn. 'It was, ma'am.'

'Get yourself down there, would you? It was set alight about thirty minutes ago.'

'Ma'am, I don't understand. Are we talking–'

'We won't know what we're talking until you get down there,' Archer snapped. 'Keep me informed.' It wasn't a question but rather a statement, then she disconnected the call.

Melanie rushed back to the shared office. 'Carter, get your coat.'

'You've pul–' Read started but he was silenced by Melanie's stare.

'What did I miss?' Carter asked, already tugging on his jacket.

'The rest of you are grounded until we get back, at least. The Fox and Hounds has just gone up in smoke. Archer called to let me know.' She saw concerned looks swapped among her team but there was nothing she could do with that now. 'We'll know more as soon as we get to the scene, and we can update you on proceedings from there on.' She didn't wait for a response, just pushed through into the corridor, and pounded down the steps with Carter's heavy footfalls close behind.

The pair tumbled from the station and headed to Melanie's unmarked car. It would be quicker to drive than to walk, and they didn't have time to waste.

When they were close enough to see grey wisps tumbling around buildings, Carter broke the silence. 'We're not thinking this is a coincidence, are we?'

Melanie rounded the street corner and pulled up as close as she could to the building. There were two fire engines, packed with officers who were shifting and angling water to try to kill the flames as they licked the outer edges of the pub. Some of the internal structure already looked exposed and, despite her lack of expert knowledge, Melanie couldn't understand how a thirty-minute fire had managed to take down so much of the building already. Unless someone had gone far out of their way to make it happen.

'I think it's a safe assumption that this isn't a coincidence, no?' She looked the building up and down as she spoke. 'We need to get out there. I'm going to beeline for the officers, to see if we can get an update on this mess. Can you take the crowd? Some of these vultures must have been here for a while now, they might know something useful.'

The cordon around the building was keeping out at least twenty onlookers.

'It'll be my pleasure,' Carter replied, already half out of the car.

Melanie followed him and pulled her ID badge from her pocket, ready to show the cordon control workers who stood between her and the action behind the line. The officer narrowed his eyes at her picture and then back at her before lifting the plastic barrier to let her in. Melanie muttered a 'Thank you,' as she passed from one hectic scene into another.

She looked around for an authority figure among the firefighters at the heart of the action, but under the protective gear the whole team looked equal. She felt a stab of gratitude when someone grabbed her arm and yanked her away from hurried firefighters.

'You can't be in here, it's not safe,' the man shouted through his mask.

'I'm looking for the lead fire officer. Do you know them?' Melanie shouted back.

The man pointed at his own chest. 'I'm a little pushed for time right now.'

Melanie pulled her badge out for the second time to flash the man her picture and rank by way of an explanation. He nodded his understanding but didn't offer anything more.

'I need to know what's happening here,' Melanie pushed.

'I understand that, detective, but we've hardly got this thing under control yet. Keep a distance, would you?' He pointed to a shaded space behind one of the fire engines. 'Can you wait it out there? Believe me, we're trying here. I'll get to you.'

Melanie felt a twinge of frustration; *what other option is there but to wait?* She nodded and paced away, toward the space designated to her. Somehow facing away from the fire increased the sound of it: the crack of the building and the moans of the joints. When she'd been front facing there was a strange comfort in the heat but as it worked through the back of her blazer, she felt a sudden need to get as far into the shaded area as she could. She walked around behind the vehicle in the hope of finding respite from the heat, but there was something else waiting.

Beneath the full heavy tubes that were pumping water onto the blazing fire, there, precariously balanced, was a fox head on a wooden mount – its teeth set in a snarl.

18

Melanie kept a steady stare on the structure, as though expecting it to move, while she fished her phone from her pocket. She thumbed through her emergency contacts and hit dial, sucking her breath in further with each ring.

'Ditch the crowd and meet me behind the fire engines.' She didn't wait for Carter to respond before disconnecting the call. She was already scrolling down to the next name. The addressee answered within two rings, but Melanie beat them to a greeting. 'Williams, are you in the office right now or on a case?'

'In the office, I'm here all day. What do you need?'

'I need for you to get down to the Fox and Hounds pub, do you know it?' She waited for a grunt of agreement before she continued. 'He's been here, the taxidermist killer, I think. There's a fire, but there's a structure.' She realised how jumbled her explanation was, so she paused and forced a deep breath out. 'Someone has set fire to the pub this morning, but I just ducked for shelter behind one of the engines and there's another structure here. A fox.'

Williams snorted. 'Imaginative. Let me grab a kit and I'll be there.'

'Thanks, Williams, I appreciate it.' She disconnected the call in time to catch Carter's eye as he rounded the corner. She didn't say anything, though, she only pointed.

'Jesus H Christ.'

'Can you call the team?'

'All of them?'

'Yep.' Melanie's tone was curt as she eyed the fox again. 'Tell them to bring printouts of Kinsley's mystery man. I want that image all over the place today. Someone must have seen him. Do we have any tape in the car?'

'We must do.' Carter couldn't take his eyes away from the fox either. 'Want me to grab the tape while I call the team?'

'I'll get it. You stay and watch that thing.'

Melanie pushed her way out of the cordoned area and through the hungry crowd. The onlookers paid no attention to the increasing heat, nor the pleas from the fire team asking that they keep their distance. She wondered what they expected to see by getting so close, a flaming victim pulled from the building? *Christ*, she realised, *we haven't even asked who's inside*. She unlocked the car and pulled the boot lid wide. She had to dig around for it, but eventually found two rolls of police tape and she took both for good measure. By the time she was walking back toward the crowd the lead fire officer was on the wrong side of the tape, trying to usher people a safe distance away. Melanie pulled her badge out and came to a stop alongside him.

'Can you please,' she raised her voice over the bustle of the watchers, 'keep a safe distance from the cordon? This is for your protection as well as for the protection of the officers working to get this fire under control.'

There were bursts of questions as she turned away and ducked under the tape again, but Melanie looked as though she hadn't heard. She was on such a determined walk that she didn't even notice the fire officer had followed her, not until he raised his voice to speak over the commotion.

'You couldn't have just asked them to leave?' he shouted.

Melanie bit back on a sharp reply. 'We need them, they're witnesses.' She ripped the end of the tape free and tied it in a hard knot around a small strip of steel at the end of the first fire engine. It rolled out in a neat line and she ripped it again and pinned it to the nearest wall.

'To the fire?' He followed her as she moved, having to duck under this new line of tape.

'No, to this.' She rounded the corner, with the fire officer steps behind, back to where Carter was waiting. She let the newcomer take in the sight of the fox before she explained. 'The reason we're here this morning is we think a murderer planted information in this pub that led to another crime being committed.' She pointed to the fox. 'The murderer killed a taxidermist.'

Without adding further explanation, Melanie crossed to the outer edge of the second fire engine and repeated the same process with the police tape. She'd created a small secure space that the killer must have entered. Although, as she glanced at the grubby concrete, pock-marked with beer stains and cigarette ends, she didn't hold out much hope for a forensic hit. It was Halloway's murder scene all over again.

From behind she heard Carter introduce himself formally – 'DS Carter, I'm second on the case.' – but the fire officer didn't reciprocate.

Melanie didn't understand the man's tension. *He must be territorial*, she thought. But she didn't have the time nor the patience to contend with it. 'Is there anything we can be doing?' she asked, by way of extending an olive branch.

The fire officer lowered his mask. 'Keep a safe distance.'

Then he ducked out of the police's allocated area and disappeared back to his own team.

'Well, he's a delight,' Carter said.

Melanie waved the comment away. 'Did you get through to everyone?'

'Yep, they're all excited and disturbed in equal measure.'

'Aren't we all?' Melanie crouched level with the fox. 'What are we missing, Edd?'

Carter huffed. 'Look, don't think me dramatic, but are we worried this is targeted?'

'Against who?'

He hesitated. 'Against us.'

Melanie rose level with him. 'Walk me through it.'

'I know it's an extreme reading of the text.' He paused and thought. 'Actually, that's not true, I don't know that at all. It *might* be an extreme reading of the text. But we were what, an hour or two away from visiting this place?'

'You think that fire was meant for us?'

'Maybe we weren't meant to be in there, but you've got to admit, one way or another we'd definitely be here to see this. We're a major incident team with a good record, there are strong odds one of us would have been called to this scene. Couple that with the fact it's a pub that ties a recent crime to a previous crime. Couple *that* with the fact there's a goddamn fox here. If it weren't one thing or another or another, we'd be here.'

'Knock, knock.'

Melanie shot round in time to catch Williams dipping under the tape line. He was wearing a full plastic suit complete with booties and she could have kissed him for his efficiency. *But he must be bloody warm under there*, she thought, crossing the space to greet him.

'Before you say anything,' Melanie decided to get in her

reservations before Williams could mention them for her, 'I know it's unlikely you'll get anything. The scene is a mess.'

'Seems to be a theme with this guy, right?' Williams snapped on a pair of gloves. 'You've got your hands full with someone who makes it this hard to scrape a scene for stuff.'

Melanie rolled her eyes. 'Don't we know it. Is there anything you can do?'

'I can bag the structure and–'

'We're going to need someone to consult on that,' Melanie interrupted.

'And you can let me know what you want done with it later,' he finished. 'Plus, I can sweep the area around it for prints, but with the amount of people who must have touched these engines in their lifetimes. Honestly, DI Watton, I don't know that there is much more that I can do.' He looked at the floor. 'Do you want me to try?'

'I'll never sleep again if I say no.'

Williams snorted a laugh. 'I'll scrape and tape anything that looks fresh and we'll cross-match things as well as we can. Don't expect miracles though, okay?' He didn't wait for a response before he knelt to his kit and started to pull out his necessities.

'Boss, the team are here.' Carter gestured with his phone as he spoke. 'Want me to brief them or are you going?'

Melanie watched Williams, who looked to be inspecting the difference between two cigarette ends. 'I think the fox is in safe hands, I'll come with you.' They both ducked out of their private chaos and into that of the fire, which seemed to be more under control now than it was the last time Melanie had braved a look. 'I'll catch up with you. Now things are a little less riotous here, I want to catch the fire officer about the owners to see where we stand with them.'

'Bodies?' Carter asked.

'Nothing that's been mentioned.' Melanie lingered at the

side of the first fire engine looking from one officer to the next, in search of the one she'd spoken to previously. He either wasn't showing his face for her, or he was knee-deep in burnt rubble somewhere; Melanie couldn't be sure which option was most likely. Rather than linger on it for too long, she caught the eye of the first officer that crossed her and she gestured to her badge, which was now hooked over the top pocket of her jacket. The officer nodded, as though in recognition, and lifted his mask. He looked barely old enough to be working the job, and Melanie instantly thought back to the people who'd said similar about her – *to* her – when she'd made detective.

'How can I help, officer?' The young man pushed as though noting Melanie's hesitation.

'I'm looking for information on the landlord, or landlady. Has there been anything said about them yet? I'm not sure where…' she petered out. She wasn't sure whether they were inside or whether they'd made their escape, but it seemed a horrible thing to say aloud.

'We're not too sure on those details just yet, I'm afraid.' Something behind Melanie caught the officer's eye and he paused to wave someone forward. 'This is the man to ask. He's usually in the know about these things.'

Melanie turned and placed a flat hand above her eyeline to block out the growing sun, and there he was, tugging on his protective gear as he walked towards the scene. He made a clumsy show of pushing past the vultures still waiting for their updates, and Melanie noticed that her team wasn't far behind the newcomer.

George Waller ducked under the cordon and came to an abrupt stop in front of Melanie. 'DI Watton, fancy seeing you here.'

19

The day of the fire seemed both to go on forever and last no time at all. It was the following morning when the team were finally sitting down together as a group, eating breakfast sandwiches that Carter had insisted on. He handed a fried egg sandwich to Melanie who shook her head at the offer.

'You have to eat, boss,' Carter insisted, and Melanie snatched the sandwich away.

'How you've got an appetite is beyond me.'

Read crunched down on a piece of gristle. 'This bacon is fried to a bloody crisp.'

There was an awkward silence between the team as one person looked to another, uncertain of whether to let the comment go.

Melanie caught Carter's eye. 'It's too soon to make a joke.'

'Noted.'

She cleared her throat and set the sandwich down on a nearby desk. 'Murder and robbery were just upped to murder, robbery, arson, double murder. Waller called me late last night to let me know that both owners of the pub were pulled from the fire, long-time dead when the officers got to them. He'll be doing post-mortems as soon as he can to verify whether the fire killed them or whether they were killed beforehand, and he'll be in touch when he knows more.'

'Have the fire team been in touch?' Burton asked through a mouthful of crust.

'On the scene there were already talks of an accelerant being used, which seems obvious given the state of the place, but there'll be a formal update when they know more as well.'

Carter nudged the sandwich an inch along the desk towards Melanie. 'So, what now?'

'I'm going to arrange for a taxidermist to come into the station. We've got the fox, and the parrot, and we can make educated guesses with the help of the cleaner on how well they've been looked after–'

'Or not,' Morris interrupted. 'She seemed pretty put out by the parrot's feathers.'

'Was she ruffled?' Carter asked, to the amusement of Read and Fairer.

Melanie shot him a flat expression. 'What did I literally just say?' Carter sank back in his chair like a reprimanded child. 'We'll arrange for a visit from a taxidermist but until then we need to keep that thing as well-preserved as we can. Read and Fairer, you're back on log duty for it. I want you to see whether you can find a description in Halloway's project book that matches the fox; we need that verified as something that came from the shop.'

'We could invite Stela Ionescu back in?' Burton suggested.

Melanie frowned over the suggestion. 'No, it doesn't sit right to keep asking her to come in like that. We need to fend for ourselves, unless we arrive at a point where we really need her. Read and Fairer can trace the fox. Can you log it into evidence when you're done?' The pair nodded in unison. 'Morris and Burton, can you make a start on the pub owners? Getting information about the staff and working out from there might be the best bet.'

'Do you want us to make a list or start making contact?' Burton asked.

'Both.'

'Done.' Morris balled up the foil from her sandwich and dunked it into a nearby bin.

'Where does that leave us?' Carter asked.

'We've got a list of pubs to get through still. The others aren't necessarily targets for an attack, because we haven't got anything that leads us to them. It can't hurt to get this guy's image out there, though, and the more visible he is the more accountable he becomes.' Carter bobbed his head in agreement. 'It'll be worth showing the image to the pub staff when you track them down as well. Just because Kinsley only saw him once doesn't mean other people haven't noticed him around,' Melanie added for Morris and Burton. 'Does anyone have any questions?'

'What's the plan for a taxidermist?' Fairer asked.

'I'll call when we're back from the pubs later. Will the fox keep you busy until then?'

'More than, I should think,' Fairer replied.

'Right then, let's get things moving.'

Melanie and Carter didn't leave any of the pubs having gained new friends or allies – which wasn't a surprise to either of them, but still a disappointment. The owners and managers had at least agreed to keep a printout of the photo-sketch, in case anyone matching the description made an appearance, which was better than nothing. It was late afternoon by the time they were pulling into the station car park.

'Do you need to leave early?' Melanie asked, her head dropped back against the seat.

'My parents are collecting Em, so I'm good.'

'It's not half-term anymore?'

Carter let out a near-laugh. 'No, boss, that was last week.'

Melanie lifted her head and stared off into the car park somewhere. 'How has this guy managed to do so much damage in a week?'

'Maybe he's determined.'

'Or maybe he's been planning this for a while.' As Carter opened his mouth to reply Melanie waved off whatever comment was coming. 'Ignore me, it's been a long day.'

'Maybe the team will have got lucky with something.'

Melanie didn't know whether it was a question or a statement, but she didn't offer a response. She pulled the keys from the car and climbed out, with Carter following close behind. The pair made a hurried return to the office, pounding up the stairs with a determination that bordered on outright aggressive. Melanie sucked in a deep breath before she pushed the door open, as though steadying herself for what was on the other side.

Burton and Morris looked to be buried somewhere under a mound of paperwork, their phones fixed to their ears. It was Read and Fairer that were the first point for concern though. The two of them were in the centre of the room, hovering in front of the evidence board, with the taxidermy fox sitting squat on a nearby table.

'Shouldn't that be in evidence by now?' Melanie asked.

'We found something,' Fairer announced. 'Well, Read found something.' He moved out of the way to reveal the evidence board that had a fresh photograph pinned to the middle of it.

Melanie's eyes stretched involuntarily. 'Where did you find that?'

'Under the fox.'

'The fox was balanced on a fire truck,' Carter said, stepping closer to the board.

'Not under the fox at the crime scene. Actually under the fox, on its base.' Fairer walked to where the fox was balanced, bagged and secure from contamination. The plastic rustled under his touch as he leaned it back to lie on the table. 'We haven't touched it, like properly touched it, but even through the plastic you can feel that it's carved in somehow.'

'Like the message at the first crime scene?' Melanie asked.

'Exactly. But we double-checked the parrot after we found this and there's nothing carved into the base of it. So, this is something new for us.'

'For him, you mean,' Carter said as he walked over to the fox. He crouched down until he was eye level with the underneath of the structure. He seemed to study it for a minute before reaching out to touch it, running his fingers over the indents of each word.

Melanie inspected the printout that was pinned to the board, rather than the real-life message. 'No, Carter, I'd say this is definitely something for us.'

'How did you even find this?' Carter asked, standing upright again.

Fairer and Read shared a guilty look. 'Do you want to tell them?' Fairer asked.

Read rubbed at the back of his neck. 'Not really.'

'Fine.' Fairer looked from Carter to Melanie. 'He dropped the bloody thing.'

20

Melanie handed the photograph over to Archer and stayed quiet while her superior inspected it. The plastic covering of the fox distorted the lettering, but with narrowed eyes the message was clear: REMEMBER WHEN WE MET HERE?

Melanie had spent most of the evening staring at the same image Archer now held. She'd left a copy pinned to the evidence board, as though reminding her team of the new urgency of the situation. But she'd also cautioned them to be extra vigilant on their travels. Archer hadn't been available to talk before they'd all left for the day, which afforded Melanie the unwelcome luxury of taking this development home alone with her. She'd left the image in the centre of her dining room table and stared into it as she ate cold pasta from a Tupperware box. She had tried to leave the image behind when she went to bed, but she hadn't been able to get away from wondering which one of her team was at risk. *Who was that message left for?*

Archer rested the photograph on her desk and rubbed at her eyes. 'So, it's personal.'

'It looks that way, ma'am.'

'What lines of enquiry do you currently have open for this?'

'We're waiting for forensics on the scene where the fox was found. Waller has the fire victims in for post-mortems, and the fire inspector hasn't delivered a report for the fire itself yet. Burton and Morris have compiled lists of employees from the Fox and Hounds too. They've contacted some but not all of them.' When she spread it all out like that, Melanie felt like there was some hope for them.

'This message,' Archer said, tapping the photograph. 'There's no doubt about who wrote it. It seems consistent with the first message?'

'I'm not qualified to comment on that.' Melanie locked eyes with her superior and she felt the weight of what was unsaid between them. 'I can arrange for it to be looked at.'

'I think that would be wise. It's best to be sure, or as sure as we can be at this point. Is there anyone due to come into the station today?'

'Not that I'm aware of.'

'Keep it that way. Have interviews arranged with as many staff members as you can, for tomorrow and the day after. Today, you're digging out old cases.' Melanie must have looked taken aback so Archer continued. 'The whole lot of you, Mel, not just you. If it's personal, then there'll be a connection between one of you and this godforsaken pub.'

'You said yourself it's a hotspot. Do you know how many cases we'll trace back there?'

'Then you'll make yourself a long list of suspects.' She picked up the photograph and dropped it onto Melanie's side of the desk. 'You need to take this seriously, Melanie. This isn't just a threat to your team.'

Melanie frowned. 'I don't understand.'

'This could just as easily be about you.'

~

Before Melanie had been dismissed by Archer, the senior officer had made promises to chase up all the outstanding reports regarding the case. 'I'm not saying they'll be with you by lunchtime, but it might pull them in a little sooner.' She'd already been looking through the contacts list on her phone as she spoke. Archer also suggested distribution of the photo-sketch on a wider scale – 'It might be time for a press conference on all this,' she'd said – but she promised Melanie further details on that soon.

'What did the head honcho have to say?' Carter asked as soon as Melanie stepped into the office. The team was distributed around the room, perched at their own desks, but it was clear from their positions and expressions that little work had been happening. *They're waiting for some much-needed guidance*, she thought.

Melanie couldn't remember seeing her superior quite so unnerved, but she decided not to share that with the team. 'We need to chase down all cases that involve any of us and that pub.'

'*All*?' Read dropped his feet off his desk and sat upright. 'Does she know how many cases that'll be?'

'Yes, Read, I suspect she does.' Melanie rubbed her forehead. 'She thinks it will give us a list of likely suspects, though, and she's keen for us to have more angles to tackle this from.'

'Did she say anything else?' Burton asked, as though trying to change tactic.

'She's going to push people to get their reports to us sooner, and she wants the handwriting verified from the first message to the second message, assuming that can be done from something carved.'

'Will Dr Addair do that?' Burton asked, using a formal tone

that Melanie suspected was deliberate, given the last time the two of them had shared a mention of Hilda.

'I'm going to call her office now to see if she's available for that. I'll get details from her regarding a taxidermist too while I'm on. That's something we can chase up when we've waded through our work history. Is everyone okay to get started?' There was a disgruntled sound that moved around the room, one desk at a time, and Melanie took that as agreement. 'I'm next door if anyone needs me,' she said, already halfway to her office.

She closed the door behind her, desperate for the privacy. She knew Hilda's work telephone and mobile by memory already, but she dialled and re-dialled the office line three times before she let it ring out fully.

Hilda answered on the fifth bell, and Melanie wondered whether she'd recognised the station number and waited deliberately.

'Dr Addair.'

'It's Melanie.'

There followed a too-long pause. 'Is everything okay?'

'It's kind of a formal matter that I'm calling about.'

Hilda let out a huff. Melanie could practically hear the, *Of course it's a formal matter*, that Hilda hadn't said. 'How can I be of use to you?'

'There was a message left at the first crime scene, carved into the floor. There's a third crime scene now and there was another message left. Archer has asked whether there's a way to match the handwriting between the two.'

There was hardly a beat between Melanie finishing and Hilda speaking. 'Were they both carved into wood?'

'Yes.'

'I don't suppose there's any way of knowing whether the same knife was used?'

Melanie recognised this professionalism from overheard

conversations. She felt uncomfortable that Hilda was using the same tone with her now.

'The knife was recovered from the first crime scene, so it won't be the same one exactly. I suppose it could be the same type, but there's no way of knowing for certain.'

'You have photographs of both?'

'I do. The second one is a little distorted because there's plastic over th–'

'If it's clear enough to read the message then I'm sure it will be fine,' Hilda talked over her. There was the sound of pen scratching against paper in the background. 'I can take a look this evening, if that suits, and email my thoughts tomorrow.'

'Thank you, Hilda.'

'You're welcome. Is that everything?'

Melanie took a deep breath. 'You mentioned a taxidermist when we last spoke.'

'I see. I can...' Hilda trailed off as though distracted. Melanie waited quietly until the sound of rustling paper stopped and Hilda spoke again. 'Teddy Yardley is the best bet for consultancy work. He's a quiet chap too, trustworthy. I can email over his details when we're finished here, or tomorrow, whichever suits you.'

'It's you doing me the favour, so, whenever is good.'

There was another long pause between them before Hilda spoke again. 'You should have his details in your inbox now. I don't know what his availability is like.'

Melanie quickly keyed in her password and clicked the icon for her emails. The message from Hilda unfolded in front of her, containing the taxidermist's details – name, phone number and email – and nothing else. She hadn't even included her signature, which stung beyond Melanie's understanding.

'Are you okay?' Hilda asked, and Melanie realised she'd been quiet for too long.

There might be a murderer after a member of my team, or me, but... 'Of course. Are you?'

'It sounds like work is difficult.'

It occurred to Melanie that Hilda meant okay-professionally, not personally. 'Things are ramping up around here but we're managing okay. Look, Hilda, how we–' Melanie felt ready to take the plunge, but Hilda interrupted her again.

'You really don't need to finish that sentence.'

'But then you won't know how it ends.'

Hilda exhaled hard. 'What a loaded comment.' She let out a small and insincere laugh. 'Take good care of what's happening at your end, would you? I'll be in touch.'

Hilda disconnected the call without waiting for a reply, but Melanie held the handset against her ear for a second longer. She finished her unsaid sentence privately to herself, and then set the desk phone down in its cradle.

21

It was later that day when Melanie wheeled the blank whiteboard out of the lift and into the hallway. She had to back her way into the office space, pulling the contraption along with her. She was halfway through the room before Carter jumped to her aid, at which point she urged him away with a narrow-eyed expression. Melanie pulled the fresh board in front of their existing evidence, shielding the crowded images of bodies – human and animal alike – and burnt-out interiors. The blank white space was a welcome sight but there was a turn in Melanie's stomach as she grabbed the nearest board-marker and began to write. Drawing a line across the top of the board, she then drew additional lines from top to bottom, marking out six clear columns.

'We're going with Archer's idea then?' Burton asked, coming to a stop behind her boss.

Melanie didn't answer, but instead continued marking up the board until the team's names were written across the top, one in each column. By the time she was finished, all of her colleagues – bar Morris, who remained glued to her computer – had crowded around to see the spectacle.

'I'm guessing this isn't going to be a fun bonding activity?' Carter asked.

'How do you even imagine that going?' Burton replied.

'Easy, we'd start with a round of Never Have I Ever and th–'

'No, Carter, you're right,' Melanie cut across him. 'It isn't anything at all to do with bonding, unless you've got some shared cases that fit into two columns.' She flashed a tight smile and set the board-marker back on the desk next to her. 'The message we found at the fire is obviously meant for one of us. To try to keep us safe and keep the investigation moving, we're going to need to narrow that down to the most likely members of the team.'

'Wouldn't that be you and Carter?' Morris shouted.

'Because we're old?' Carter retorted.

Morris turned to face the team. 'No, because you're the longest serving officers out of us all. Statistically, given that the pub was a hot spot for crime, it seems likely you'll have more connections to the place than the rest of us.'

Melanie nudged Carter with her elbow. 'And I am not old.' She addressed the whole team again. 'Morris may well have a point, but just because Carter and I are longest serving doesn't mean we're the only ones with grudges out there. We need to look back through case files to see what connections we've all got with the property. Whether we raided it, whether we cuffed someone there; Christ, even if you've got a uniform call-out that went bad ways, we need to know about it. From there we can start narrowing it down by who's got an axe to grind, who's in prison, who's...' Melanie rubbed at her forehead. The variables felt endless. 'It'll give us a starting point at least.'

'We can match the lists with people who are still inside, versus people who have been recently released. That might be another good plan of attack for it,' Morris said, as she crossed the room. She handed Melanie a sheet of paper with seven names written on it.

'Good thinking, that would help.' She took the sheet and glanced it over. 'What are you giving me?'

'My names.'

Carter glanced at his colleagues with a cocked eyebrow. 'And how did you do that?'

Morris smirked. 'Because I guessed what she was doing.'

Melanie pulled up the details from Hilda's email and tried to focus only on the phone number she needed. She needed to stop her vision being swamped by the blank space around the contact information, but Hilda's curtness still stung even as Melanie punched in the digits to call. The line rang out six times before a voicemail cut in – 'The person you are calling is not available at the moment...' – and Melanie slammed her phone down, only to immediately pick up the handset and hit the redial button. This time someone answered after two rings.

'Hello?' A male voice, but Melanie couldn't guess whether it was old or young.

'Hi there, I'm looking for Teddy Yardley. Are you–'

'Did you call a minute ago?' He sounded out of breath.

'Yes, I did. I'm DI Melanie Watton calling fro–'

'Oh, God, is it Mum? Has something happened?'

Melanie had barely made her introductions with the man, but she'd already decided she wasn't keen on his conversational etiquette – or lack thereof. 'No, Mr Yardley, I'm calling about a case I'm working on at the moment. We're investiga–'

'Norman Halloway's death? Hilda said someone might call.'

The interruptions were frustrating but at least they were

getting somewhere. 'I'm glad Hilda forewarned you. It's a bit of a strange case we're working here, but we'd like someone on hand to help us with examining certain taxidermy structures. Hilda said this might be something you'd be available to help us with. Is that the case?'

'What sort of examinations?' His tone was loaded with suspicion. 'I don't feel comfortable dismantling things, or cutting any of Norman's work open, if that's what you need.'

'Did you know Mr Halloway?' Melanie asked, picking up on Yardley's use of the first name rather than surname.

'Not as well as I would have liked. I've admired his work for years. We met once or twice at various shows, exchanged pleasantries. He was a good man.'

'We don't want his work dismantled. We do need to know how it's been cared for though; whether it's been done well or whether there's anything amateur about the treatment.' A long pause followed so Melanie tried further reassurance. 'We obviously want the work to remain as we found it. We're strictly interested in the outward appearance of things.'

On the other end of the phone there were pages being turned. 'This week?'

'If you're available.'

'I can do Thursday afternoon. Let me find a...'

Melanie hesitated. 'Thursday afternoon will be fine if that suits you?'

'I can't find a pen,' Yardley announced. 'Oh, wait, I found a...' he trailed off again. 'Yes, Thursday afternoon. It's in my diary. Should I bring anything? Is that a stupid question?'

'Only yourself, Mr Yardley.'

There was a pause, as though he were making a note of this somewhere. 'I can do that.'

The two said their goodbyes and ended the call. Melanie

scribbled *Thursday PM* along the top of a scrap piece of paper before dropping her head gently against the desk.

'Christ alive.'

'That bad?' came the reply from her doorway.

Melanie looked up to see Burton. 'I think Hilda might have lumbered me with the strangest taxidermist she knows.'

'Are there any average Joe ones, really?' Burton lowered herself into the visitor's chair opposite her superior. 'You'll be glad to know the chaps have managed to turn this into a fun group bonding exercise anyway, by competing for names on the board.'

Melanie huffed. 'The more names they have the more research they do. More fool them.'

'If it gets them working.' Burton shrugged. 'Morris has put her names on the board. She's found three who are still in prison, one who looks clean, the final three she's still looking over.'

'She doesn't waste any time, does she?'

'Never. Speaking of which, I've got a growing list of fifteen. I'll be looking over them this afternoon. But I've also managed to contact bar staff from the pub, and we've got three interviews scheduled throughout the week.' Melanie opened her mouth to reply but Burton beat her to it. 'I know we're working through old cases, but we may as well strike while the iron's hot with the current witnesses too.'

Melanie winced. 'I'd watch your phrasing.' The two shared a laugh. 'Old cases can be something people keep working on over the coming days, but we need something, Burton. We're rapidly running out of angles to come at this from.' Melanie picked up a discarded copy of the sketch-photo that was lying on her desk and looked it over again. *There's something...*

'Do you need a hand going through your old cases? Morris has already offered.'

'I might take her up on that. Yardley, the new taxidermist, he's coming in on Thursday, so I have a few days to make a dent. We'll see how things go...' she petered out, staring hard into the image of the man's face again. 'Pin that to the board outside, would you? I don't want anyone losing sight of that face until we've got a lead.'

22

The following day, a visitor by the name of Jason Quelch sat across the desk from Melanie. While he flicked through his paperwork, she idly thought about his distinct surname. From his sour expression, she guessed there had never been a name that was so apt for a person before. He'd arrived from the fire services a day later than he promised to, and it took a phone call from Archer just to get this meeting arranged – or rather, rearranged, Melanie thought, still waiting for the man to start.

He coughed and set the paperwork down in his lap. 'My team have done an extensive search of the premises and they were marginally assisted by your forensics department who poked about the place throughout...'

Melanie nodded along as he spoke, scribbling notes on his unprofessionalism on the pad next to her. *Marginally*, she wrote, alongside the words, *poked about*. She wondered how Quelch kept himself upright, with the obvious chips on each shoulder. A handful of seconds passed before Melanie realised that the note-making had quickly shifted into not paying attention at all.

'I'm sorry,' she said. 'Can you repeat that last detail?'

Quelch sighed. 'Are you familiar with fire reports?'

'I've seen one or two in my time,' Melanie replied.

'Then perhaps we can talk through this now, and you can make notes at a later point?' He looked towards the pen in Melanie's hand, which she immediately dropped.

'Of course.'

'As I was saying, we found traces of petrol thrown heavily about the outside of the property. Most of it looks to have been left at the back entrance, which was actually the front door of the landlord and his wife.'

He wasn't chancing them getting out alive, Melanie thought, but refrained from making a note.

'There was some found on the doorway to the basement but, thankfully, the team arrived in time to start their extinguish of it all before it reached that point. There were gas tanks in the basement of the pub, plus copious amounts of liquor, so had the fire worked its way through then God only knows what we'd be dealing with.'

'Could you back-tread a second? There was petrol thrown nearby an inside door?'

'There was petrol thrown about the whole place inside.' He lifted his report. 'I'm getting to that. Aside from the amounts left around the basement, it looks to have been liberally scattered around the bar area, but not behind the bar, which is interesting. Seats and cushions doused, et cetera and so on.'

Melanie wanted to stop him – to remind him what that et cetera and so on had led to.

'There weren't any signs that petrol had been distributed in the upstairs of the property, but the staircase and steps were also doused so it likely wouldn't have been long until they burnt through. In a building with that much wood and soft furnishings, the fire would have spread fairly fast to the ceiling of downstairs, therefore the floor of upstairs.' He collected his papers together and leaned forward to drop them on Melanie's desk. 'They're the prominent details within the report but that's your copy, for the investigation and for your own perusal. There's nothing too obscure about it though.'

Melanie realised that he'd heard little, if anything, about the larger investigation this fire was attached to. She decided that was a good thing, for someone with Quelch's laid-back attitude. She had enough to contend with, with Read and Carter's wise cracking.

'Thanks a lot for coming in to hand this over, and to cover the major details.'

There was a brief pause. 'Am I dismissed?' he asked, with the same superior tone he'd adopted earlier.

Melanie let out a light laugh. 'Yes.' Quelch's face dropped at the brevity of Melanie's reply. 'Following the route we came up will get you out again, but I'm sure one of my DCs will help if you need it. It's been a pleasure.' Melanie's tone was deliberately flat, and she didn't stand to shake hands as the man collected himself together to leave the room. She let out a quiet, 'Bye then,' as he walked out, though she was looking at her computer screen as she spoke – despite there being nothing on the blacked-out display.

Melanie skimmed through the report at a slower pace when she was alone. She digested the details and tried to resist the thoughts of the poor people who must have been trapped inside. *But I wonder how long it took them to realise.* She shook the thought away, but ones similar to it stayed with her right until the final page of the read, which confirmed the fire was arson. Her stomach turned over as she set the paperwork on the growing pile of reports balanced on her desk. *Theft to murder to theft to...* the charges were getting uncomfortable for Melanie to tally. But it made her even more driven to catch the man at the helm.

~

Melanie was talking Carter through the fire report when Burton and Morris stepped back into the office. They'd been tackling interview number two of the bar staff team, and Melanie had to hope they'd brought back a lead. Interview number one was a man who, according to Morris, just looked relieved when he was finally unleashed from the place; his concern was less about identifying the man and more about avoiding charges, as though he'd be hauled in for some unknown offence. But Melanie didn't have the time or want to pursue nervous witnesses at the moment.

'Did we get lucky?' Read asked before Melanie had the chance to.

'Don't ever use that phrase at work again,' Morris snapped back, and then smirked. 'But yes, we did.'

'Tell us what you know,' Melanie commanded.

'Interview number two was with an Alison Kemp–'

'Or Ali,' Morris cut in. 'Like Cher, or Beyoncé.'

'And that's actually how she introduced herself on the audio, so you can all have a listen to that special moment. She works five nights a week at the pub so she's familiar with the regulars there. The photo-sketch she recognises and she's sure she's served him on several occasions, but she can't give us a name. It's a drawback, but she's worked at the pub for eight years and she seems certain that if she can't give us a name then he must be a newcomer.'

'So, she can't think of a reason why he would have been inside the pub when the place was closed?' Melanie asked.

Burton shook her head. 'She said if she doesn't know him, the owners wouldn't have either. They're a tight-knit group at that particular watering hole by all accounts.'

'Oh, criminals drinking together, imagine that,' Fairer added in a light tone.

'Wait, he was in the pub when it was closed?' Morris backtracked to Melanie's question.

'Bingo. Jason Quelch turned up with the fire report today–'

'I'm sorry,' Read interrupted. 'Quelch. We're all just going to let that go?'

Melanie picked up her explanation before Carter had the chance to reply. 'The fire report shows that there was as much petrol inside the building as there was outside, so, yes, he was definitely inside the property prior to the fire starting. He doused the downstairs thoroughly but didn't touch the spirits, which is as interesting as it is disturbing. He also went in the back door, not the pub door, and he doused the stairs while he was at it.' Melanie tried to get the details out in one rush, before someone could interrupt her with a question – or worse still, a joke.

'Fuck.'

She wasn't sure who it came from, but she echoed the sentiment. 'So, what now?' she asked the room.

'Morris and I have got another interview pencilled in for tomorrow. Third member of the bar staff that we've managed to get hold of.'

Fairer picked up without missing a beat, as though Burton had triggered a chain reaction around the room. 'Read and I are tracking down as much of Halloway's work as we can. We thought, not only through the logbook we found, but we might get lucky looking over emails and orders that he placed, as well as orders that were placed through him.'

'Good thinking,' Melanie confirmed. 'I've got Teddy Yardley coming in tomorrow to take a look at the taxidermy we've already got to hand. I'm hoping he can give us some tips on how to handle the bloody things to actually pull some forensics from them. And that just leaves you, Carter?'

He flashed his palms in a gesture of surrender. 'Where do you want me, boss?'

'I'm glad you asked.' Melanie flashed a wry smile. She set her hand down heavy on her junior's shoulder. 'That leaves you chasing down Waller's office for the autopsies.'

Carter let out a huff. 'I thought Archer was chasing down reports.'

'Well, two bloodhounds are better than one.'

23

Melanie had expected someone of Norman Halloway's size, stature, and age to walk into the station the following afternoon. Instead, she was greeted by a man who couldn't have been much younger than herself. He wore thin-framed glasses that sat on the end of his nose, as though he didn't really need them, but they complemented the outfit; one befitting a trendy high street barber. He was wearing a fitted waistcoat and appropriately creased trousers; each leg scored where an iron had been run down the front and back. Nothing about the mid-thirties man felt reminiscent of the older Halloway. Yardley, Melanie thought, could be confused for a stiff teacher at worst; at best, he belonged to a flock of hipsters.

He took two steps into the station and took a quick look either side of him. He spotted Melanie on this scan of the room and, as if they were familiar acquaintances already, he came to greet her with a hand extended. 'You must be DI Watton.'

Melanie reciprocated the handshake. 'You must be good at guessing.'

He laughed lightly. 'Hilda told me what to look for.'

Melanie was desperate to push the issue and ask for further

details. *How would Hilda even describe me to someone else?* But in the interest of maintaining professionalism she bit back on the desire to ask.

'I've got the evidence sealed off in a room for us, if you're okay to get started?' Melanie gestured towards a corridor leading out from the far side of the room. 'I don't know how much Hilda will have told you about the case,' she said over her shoulder. 'But we're dealing with a parrot and fox.'

'A whole fox?'

Melanie couldn't decide whether the question was a strange one to ask. She came to a stop outside the door. 'It's just the head,' she replied, as she scanned her card through the lock.

'Mounted. Interesting.' Yardley used a tone that suggested he really did find this detail an interesting one, and again Melanie felt questions bubble up inside her.

She allowed herself the luxury of asking just the one. 'Does it make a difference?'

'Oh, to the process of taxidermy, absolutely. Halloway has done some good foxes.'

Melanie flashed a tight smile as she pushed the door open. 'Well, let's see how this one fares against the others.' She stepped in and held the door open for her visitor, before clicking the lock closed. When she turned around, Yardley was already staring intently at the creatures on the table. 'As you can see, they're intact and safe with us.'

With an unexpected abruptness, Yardley pulled out one of the chairs and positioned it a good metre away from the edge of the table before sitting down. He held his stare on the specimens with such a fierce concentration that Melanie was almost nervous to speak again, for fear of interrupting whatever was happening.

'Is there anything you need?' she asked, when another few seconds had passed.

'More details.' He held his stare for a beat longer before finally looking at Melanie. 'What is it you need from me, I mean?' He flashed Melanie a warm smile, as though the stone-cold stare from seconds ago were nothing more than part of his process.

'We'd like someone to inspect the structures, because we haven't been able to–'

'There's been a firm no to forensics, yes?'

Melanie nearly tripped up over his phrasing. 'Yes.' She hesitated. 'Yes, it was a no to forensics. So, these are exactly as we found them. An employee of Mr Halloway's – actually, the woman who used to clean the structures for him – she came in to take a look and she seemed quite upset by some disturbance to the parrot's feathers, on one side.'

Yardley stood and craned his view around the parrot as Melanie spoke.

'But, beyond that, we don't know much about them other than they were taken from the murder scene, and given back to us at other scenes. We bagged both straight away.'

'Okay, that's brilliant news.' He took his glasses off and felt around in his bag for a second, before pulling out another pair. From the size of the lenses, Melanie guessed they were magnifying spectacles of some kind. 'So, I'll need gloves. I have my own, but maybe it's best if I use yours? I'll need a dust sheet, too. You know, something plastic to put underneath them. It might be worth getting evidence bags as well.'

'You think you'll be able to get something from them?'

'Well, if they went from crime scene to bag, then anything useful – or, useful to you, I suspect – will still be on them. If we can catch as much of that as we can, your forensics will have– well, something. And something is better than nothing?'

'At this point.' Melanie pulled her phone out of her pocket and called up a blank text screen. 'I'll get one of my colleagues to bring in everything you need and then we can get started.' She typed the list, thumbed down to Carter's number, and hit send. 'He shouldn't be long.'

Yardley leaned back in his seat as though getting comfortable. 'So, how do you know Hilda?'

Burton and Morris had been talking to Zaki Underhill, another interviewee from the pub staff, for nearly twenty minutes. He'd managed to tell them about his employers, how long he'd worked at the pub, how they treated him like family; the barman had nothing but good things to say, it seemed. Burton noticed tears in his eyes on more than one occasion, and she couldn't help but feel for him in his grief – then an interview on top of it all.

'Mr Underhill, if you wouldn't mind, we'd like you to look at a picture for us,' she said, shifting the conversation to their real reason for being there.

Morris pulled out the image from a thin cardboard folder and slid it across the table. 'We think this man might have started to visit the pub recently. Does he look at all familiar?'

Underhill took his time to study the photo. 'I threw this guy out.'

Burton leaned forward. 'Recently?'

'A few weeks ago, I think. He's been in since, though.'

'So, he wasn't barred?'

Underhill laughed. 'In an area like that? You'd have to do something pretty bad to get barred from anywhere. No, he wasn't. But he was trading details for shops and shit, the best places to hit around town.'

'Meaning, shops to break into?'

'We've had it before where guys set up like, I dunno, trading circles almost.' He laughed. 'Like kids with their trading cards. They'd swap details on places they'd hit before, or places they'd heard were easy. We tried to break that shit up whenever we could.'

'But this guy.' Burton tapped the image. 'This guy was doing it recently?'

'Yeah, I overhead him talking some of the younger guys through places around town like there was a damn roster for it. He was giving out so much I thought he might have been one of you, you know, like a plant or a honey thing. But yeah, I didn't want that on my shift, so I asked the guy to leave.'

'Was he amicable about leaving?'

'He was, actually. He asked whether he could come back, I said any time, as long as he didn't bring his nonsense. Next time I saw the guy he ordered his pint, kept himself to himself. That was the end of it.'

'Would you recognise him if you saw him again?' Morris jumped in.

'No bother.' He looked at the picture. 'This is a pretty good likeness you've got, though.'

'Mr Underhill, would you mind if we kept you on record? We might get to a point in our investigations where we need an in-person identification and it would really help if–'

'Say no more.' The man held up a hand. 'I'd rather be on your good side.'

The three shared a laugh before Burton formally closed the interview. Morris offered to see Underhill out, leaving Burton to head back to the upstairs office with at least the beginnings of good news. Another eyewitness who could place their missing murderer in the pub, and a criminal connection trying to keep good with the police. *It couldn't hurt*, she thought, *to have an inside man for once.*

24

Carter took a deep breath before he pushed the double doors open. The air in the next room would be laced with chemicals and cadavers, and he wanted to take the outside freshness with him as best as he could. He soon spotted Waller hunched over an open chest, with bloodied gloves half-buried in whatever was left of the person on the table. Seconds later, Waller's hands emerged holding what Carter knew was an organ, but he couldn't take looking at it long enough to guess which. He let out a small retch that caught Waller's attention, and with a faint sigh he set the item down in a large dish next to him. He used fingertips to ease down his face mask, leaving two dark red blotches on the fabric still covering his chin.

'Monkey,' he said with some delight. 'I was expecting the organ grinder.'

'After what you just...' Carter paused and took another deep breath. 'After what you just pulled out of there, I'd think about your phrasing more.'

Waller laughed. 'No, I said what I said.' He pulled the mask back in place and continued his work. 'What can I do for you?'

His voice was muffled through the fabric and Carter took a step closer to hear him.

'Can you stop what you're doing for a second?' he asked.

Waller looked up over the top of his glasses. 'You wander in here unannounced...'

'Okay, fine.' Carter closed the gap between them. 'I just can't hear you very well through the, you know, the face thing.'

'Mask.'

'Exactly.'

Waller stood upright and pulled the shield down again. 'I think I would have preferred the grinder. You're here about the fire reports?'

'She's asked me to chase the autopsies.'

'Of course she bloody has.' Waller dropped the implement he was holding, causing a metal clang to bounce about the room, before crossing to the closest waste bin. He put his foot down on the peddle as he snapped his gloves off, and used unbloodied hands to disrobe himself of his plastic coverings. He rinsed his hands clean and asked, 'There? All better. Let's get this over with.'

'The reports are done?' Carter asked, following Waller to his desk.

'They're done but not written. You can have my notes and that's all you're getting. The reports will be with her when I've written them.' He turned to face Carter with a raised finger. 'And before you ask that, the answer is: at some point.'

Carter closed his mouth and nodded.

Waller dropped himself heavily in his desk chair and ferreted through the papers in front of him. Faced with his own scribble, he squinted to decipher the handwriting before shaking his head and reaching for his glasses. Carter hovered near the doorway, already braced for his exit, but Waller wasn't in a rush. In his waiting moments Carter found himself distracted by the various photographs and charts that were pinned up on the wall next to him. A corkboard collage of death, it looked as though Waller had a cluster for all his active cases – and there were a lot of active cases. Carter felt a pang of guilt for bothering the bloke.

He scanned through row upon row of images, both repulsed and enamoured. It wasn't long before he arrived at a cluster of images showing something blackened – *no, two blackened, lumps?* Carter thought, studying the picture with narrowed eyes.

'Ah, you've spotted our victims,' Waller said, grabbing Carter's attention. 'Those burnt offerings are the bodies in question, I'm afraid. Male and female, that much we know.' Waller let out a little laugh, but Carter couldn't reciprocate. 'I think it's fairly obvious what they died from. I suspect Watton's worry is that they were murdered ahead of the fire, is it?'

Carter's stare was fixed on the images again.

'Monkey,' he pushed. 'Is that what she's worried about?'

Carter turned to face Waller and gently shook his head, as though trying to loosen the memory of the images. 'Sorry, no. I don't know. She didn't say what her suspicions are, but she's looking to tie up loose ends with the fire thing as a whole, I think.'

'She's heard from forensics then?'

Carter flashed a tight-lipped expression. 'Petrol, it seems.'

'No one has any imagination these days.' Waller turned back to the papers he'd pulled together on his desk. 'Look, there's nothing especially surprising here. The fire spread throughout most of the building so, as you'd expect, it was smoke inhalation that got the victims. The male – I have his name somewhere.' He paused to look over his sheet, and then sighed. 'The male showed stress to the heart, I'd say he was dangerously close to cardiac arrest, which again isn't uncommon with victims of severe smoke inhalation. Both have singe marks inside the bodies, nose hairs for example, and–'

'They didn't burn?'

Waller let out a curt laugh. 'No, Carter, people who die in fires seldom do.'

'But the pictures?' He gestured next to him.

'Post-mortem.'

Carter breathed a heavy sigh of relief which was met with another laugh from Waller.

'You thought they'd fried?' he asked, his tone too casual for such a question.

'Well, look at them.'

Waller dropped his glasses back on the desk. 'DS Carter, there's so much for you to learn.'

Carter held a hand palm up. 'Hard pass. Nothing else for me to report back?'

'As I said, there was really nothing unusual.' Waller rubbed at his eyes. 'Look, how's Watton doing with all of this?'

'She's fine, why?'

'Because it's an ongoing case with mounting bodies and it must be killing her.' He huffed. 'No pun intended.' He stepped down from the raised desk space and came level with Carter. 'It must be difficult for someone like Mel to be taunted, that's all I meant.'

'She isn't being taunted,' Carter said, sounding defensive.

'Well, this chap is taunting one of you, Monkey.' He trod back in the direction of the cadaver he'd left behind. 'Is there anything else or can I get back to my actual job for today?'

'No, thanks, Waller. That's everything.' Carter took another look at the collage next to him. He didn't know much about the ins and outs of this examination room – he'd actively tried to avoid knowing – but one thing he knew was that the bodies he could see now were stockpiled somewhere, waiting for Waller's attention. And the thought chilled him.

He tried to brush away the images before he could make too detailed a memory of them, and headed towards the door.

'Oh, Carter?' Waller pulled his attention back into the room. 'Send the organ grinder next time, would you? She has a much stronger stomach for these things.'

25

Melanie waited for the team to take their seats around the table. She watched Read unfold sandwiches from a cooler box, and it struck her how young members of the group really were. As though adding another reminder, Morris grabbed the seat next to him; her attention was set on piercing a hole in the top of her Capri-Sun juice.

'What are you, twelve?' Read asked.

'Says the boy eating his home-made sandwiches from a superhero lunchbox,' Fairer replied before Morris could.

'Hey,' Read started, with a chunk of sandwich already balanced in his mouth. 'Danger Mouse is a national treasure and if you were in a crisis–'

'I like to think if Fairer were in a crisis he'd call one of us,' Melanie interrupted.

'Obviously, I'd be first choice. But Danger Mouse should always be your second.'

'What...' Carter came to a stop at the edge of the table, and looked from one colleague to another, as though waiting for an answer to something. 'What did I miss?' He directed the question to Melanie as he pulled out a seat next to her.

'Office politics,' she replied. She pulled three sheets of paper from the folder in front of her. 'Everyone ready?'

'Isn't Morris done?' Read said, with a half-laugh as he nodded towards the board. 'Her minor contributions are already listed.'

'What, am I wearing a kick-me sign today or something?' she replied. 'Yes, I'm ready, because I'm here as moral support for everyone – apart from Read.'

'Excellent. Fairer?' Melanie tried to steer the conversation.

'I've got twenty-three names that I thought would help–' Read interrupted him with a whistle. Fairer rolled his eyes. 'But taking into account things they've been arrested for since, and those who are still inside for previous arrests, I'm looking at around nine.'

'Want to write them up?' Melanie said and she awaited a nod from Fairer, who stood and rounded the table to get to the board. 'Read?'

'Boss, don't think me rude, but what are we likely to gain from this?' Carter asked.

Melanie sighed. They'd been over this so many times already; it was tiresome to keep having to fight him when all she was doing was following orders herself. 'Carter, you know why. It's been two weeks now since the fire and we have literally nothing, apart from a few people who sort of recognise the picture.'

'What about the tip-line?' Burton asked.

Archer had come good on her promise of distributing the photo-sketch they had of the man who had encouraged Liam Kinsley to burgle the art shop. There had been a small press conference the week after the fire which Melanie, by request, hadn't been included on. The thought of facing off with the likes of journalist Heather Shawly – who wouldn't miss a press conference if her life depended on it – had been too much.

Melanie felt bad enough about their lack of evidence, without the press chiming in. Archer had established a tip-line after the press conference, though, asking for anyone who recognised the man to contact the police immediately.

The few people who'd been in touch could give shaky versions, at best, of their knowledge of the man pictured. There were a handful of specifics – phone calls immediately after a sighting, on two occasions – but by the time the uniforms had arrived their mystery man had disappeared, again.

'Nothing of use,' Melanie said, her tone defeated. 'I know it's tedious but consider it the chance for a humble brag; at least you can boast about everyone you've put away,' she joked with Carter before turning to address the team. 'We need suspects and we're not getting anywhere with what we've already got, so we're just going to have to work backwards for a while. Anyone got any names they want to add to the board?'

Read leapt from his seat. 'I actually have nineteen names for the board.' He took a bow on his way to writing them up and Carter gave a too-enthusiastic cheer for his colleague. Melanie would let them have it this time; if turning this into a game helped them to get their work done then so be it. 'When I was in uniform the Fox and Hounds was on our usual walkabout route so I had my share of run-ins. Some are more major than others; there's a lot of minor drugs crimes here, but there's a dealer or two as well.'

'I'll give bonus points for violent crimes,' Carter added, scanning his own list now.

In what Melanie assumed was meant to be a flirtatious way, Read winked and said, 'There might be one or two hidden here.'

'Burton?' Melanie asked, regaining focus.

She responded shyly. 'I've got twenty-six to add.'

'How?' Read span around.

'Because I also worked uniform, dummy.' She crossed

behind the table. 'Only I worked the city centre pubs.' There was a murmur of understanding from the group. 'I also helped to crack dog-fighting rings, of all things, but that's bumped my number up on the violent crimes front. There are one or two who were heavily involved with crimes against animals.' She turned away from the board to talk to Melanie. 'I know it's probably a long shot but with the whole taxidermy thing–'

'I'll take long, wide or otherwise for shots right now.' She looked back to her own list then and wondered how many names might have slipped around the outskirts of her parameters. 'How are we doing for violent crimes across the board?' she asked the room.

'I've got to be honest, boss, most of my worst ones are still inside,' Carter replied. 'I didn't get that many busts when I was starting out. There are a few that are focused around the pubs, or crime circles that have been known to drink at certain watering holes. But my best are grievous bodily harm and actual; and they're still serving time.'

'What about their associates? Anyone with a grudge against you there?'

Read snorted. 'I suspect there are plenty with a grudge against him.'

'Any big enough grudges for someone to want to kill you?' Melanie rephrased the question and spotted Read opening his mouth again. She held a finger up to pause him.

'Honestly, no.' Carter sounded disappointed with the admission.

'What about you?' Burton asked Melanie. 'Anyone with a grudge worth killing you over?'

Melanie looked down at her papers again. 'I think I need to go back over this before I add my names. You're on to something with the animal crimes. Morris, can we sweep for that? Across the board, I mean, for recent arrests in the area?'

'Sure, we can try. I'll need specifics for what you're after though. Time-frame?'

'Last ten years?'

'Geography?'

Melanie opened her mouth to answer but the phone's shrill ring from her office interrupted her. 'Hold your thought.' She wasn't expecting a phone call, and with this case on the cards every call she got seemed to bring more bad news.

'Carter, write your list up,' Burton instructed her senior as though their roles had been reversed. 'There's no point eavesdropping, she'll tell us what we need to know.'

'While she's not here, can I throw something to the group?' Morris asked, grabbing the attention of the others. Their stares alone were encouragement enough to go on. 'Look, my list is obviously sparse, so, I looked at the boss's old cases.'

Carter let out a theatrical gasp. 'How did you find the time?'

'I know my way around a computer system, what can I say? There's no way we're going to shave her list down to a realistic number though.'

'Have you got her number?' Read asked.

'I stopped at thirty-five, and that's when we were only looking at cases that involved the pubs. There's a touch of violent crime in there, but nothing involving crimes against animals, violence against animals, serious violent crime stats – yet.'

'The list goes on.' Carter ran a hand down his face. 'So, what's your worry, Morris?'

She lowered her voice. 'I'm worried it's her. I'm worried there's someone after her.'

'Break it up, folks.' Melanie interrupted the confessional. 'We've got a call-out.' She nudged Carter. 'Something dead has been left outside The Boar's Head. Uniform got the call and thought of us. Isn't that sweet?'

'Do we know what the something is?' Carter asked, crossing his desk to grab his wallet and badge. 'I'm not keen on the surprises this guy leaves behind.'

'Well, get keen.' Melanie waited for him to join her at the door. 'Because this time he left behind a witness.'

26

Melanie and Carter pulled up outside The Boar's Head two minutes before the forensics van did. Under Melanie's instruction, Carter had called them during the drive over; while Melanie had been busy flouting speed limits to get them across town in record time. The pair sat in silence while Williams gathered his kit together in the back of the van. But, as Melanie moved to open her door, Carter asked, 'What are we expecting to find, exactly?'

'How should I know?' She opened the door without another word, and left her junior sitting in the passenger seat for another handful of seconds before he exited the vehicle too. Melanie wished she had an answer for him, but this whole case looked to be structured around questions she couldn't riddle out; the last thing she needed was Carter piling on. *Between that and the mammoth task of their previous cases coming up*, she thought, but tried to shake away the annoyance rising as she closed in on Williams.

'It's going to be something pig-related, isn't it?' he asked, snapping on a latex glove.

Melanie cracked a smile. 'Don't you think he's more original than that?'

Williams considered the question as he unfolded evidence wrappers from a larger roll, and stuffed two inside an outer pocket of his bag, readying them for immediate use. 'Do you know, I don't know that he is.'

'Can you taxidermy a boar?' Carter asked, coming to a stop next to them.

'Boars are massive, though, Carter.' Melanie turned to Williams. 'Aren't they?'

'It depends on where they are in the life cycle.' Williams rubbed his eyes. 'Conversations that you have at the workplace. Shall we?' He nodded towards the pub.

From the information that had been telephoned through, Melanie knew they were looking for the back entrance to the building rather than the front. Although the marked car they passed on their walk to the rear of the pub tipped her off that they were in the right place. Melanie could see someone moving about in the back of the vehicle; she ducked to get a look, but the person looked to be in a state of distress, throwing themselves from one side of the seat to the other.

'Did they say the witness was agitated?' Carter asked, as though sharing Melanie's observations. 'Or drunk? Drunk might make sense, given the scene.'

'They only said there was a witness. But I feel a bit short-changed already.'

The three of them rounded the corner to the rear of the bar, one after the other, and came to a stop in front of two uniformed officers. Melanie didn't recognise either of them, but she'd never lost the worry that she'd met and forgotten fellow officers somewhere along on the job; it had happened once or twice already.

The younger of the two men stepped forward with an

extended hand to make an introduction. 'I'm PC Bates, this is PC Janaway. We're the first and only officers on the scene,' he said, formally, as though pre-empting a question.

'I'm DI Watton,' Melanie reciprocated. 'This is DS Carter.'

Williams waved a gloved hand. 'I'm looking to not be contaminated.' He laughed. 'But Graham will be fine. What do we have?'

Melanie admired Williams' efficiency. She was also eager to get the reveal over with.

PC Bates fidgeted on his feet, as though searching for a proper reply. 'Honestly, we're not entirely sure. There's something...' he trailed off, as though not knowing how to finish.

'In a jar,' his colleague spoke from behind him.

'I beg your pardon?' Carter asked, his tone cracked with surprise.

'There's something in a jar,' PC Janaway repeated.

'Yes, what my partner said is exactly right. There's something – in a jar.'

Melanie glanced at Williams who said, 'Formaldehyde, most likely.'

'But would a taxidermist have that?'

Williams shrugged. 'That's not a question for me.' He turned to the PCs in front of him. 'May I? I assume it's...' he pointed in the general direction behind them and waited for nervous noises of confirmation before he walked in that direction.

While Williams busied himself in the background, Melanie set about finding out more. 'The man in the back of the car? I assume he's the witness that was mentioned in the call earlier.'

'He is, but I've got to warn you that I don't know how much use he'll be,' PC Bates admitted. 'He's an older chap, seems very disgruntled. We didn't get much information out of him about where he'd come from, or even why he was here.'

'No signs of inebriation either,' PC Janaway added. 'That was our first thought, but he blew into a breathalyser just fine and he's clean as a whistle.'

'I don't understand,' Melanie replied. 'Did he call this discovery in himself, or was it the owners of the pub?'

'Neither. There's a sign in the front window to say the pub is shut for two weeks. The owners are on holiday by all accounts. It's a note to say there's no cash left on the premises, which seems mighty sensible of them in this day and…' he petered out on seeing Melanie's stern expression. 'The station got a call from a concerned citizen who said they'd seen a man loitering at the back of The Boar's Head pub and that it might be a worth a look.'

'That citizen leave a name?' Carter asked.

'No.' Melanie and PC Bates replied in unison. The uniformed officer was wide-eyed at their synchronicity. 'Of course they didn't leave a bloody name.' She ran a hand through her hair.

'DI Watton?' Williams called out. 'I think you'll want to see this.'

Like a perverse trophy, Williams held a small jar up to the sunlight as though trying to gain a better look at the creature inside it. Whatever it was curled into itself, its four feet collected, as though knotted together. With another turn of the jar, Melanie saw what she thought was a squat snout, attached to a sleeping face. The jar was full of not-quite-clear liquid, which she thought might be the formaldehyde Williams had guessed at earlier, a substance that would have been used to preserve the animal.

'If I had to guess, I'd say a small boar.' Williams squinted into the jar as he spoke. 'It could be a piglet, I suppose. There are likely tests we can run to determine that. Although asking Dr Waller wouldn't be a bad move either.'

'Why would he know?' Carter asked, looking to the left of where Williams was crouched, as though trying to avoid any direct eye contact with this latest discovery.

'It's not uncommon for medical students to have these around, so it's something Waller might have come across as a student. I know a couple of fully trained doctors who keep hold of these things too, though, so that's another reason.'

'We can get him to check it over. Can you bag it, Williams?' Melanie turned without waiting for an answer.

'DI Watton, I'm not quite finished,' Williams replied. When Melanie turned, he was already wrestling the container into a bag that looked far too small for it. 'There's something that I assume is for you. I can take photographs but I'm afraid we'll have to contact the owners if you want the stone lifted entirely.'

Melanie's gut clenched as she walked closer. She leaned to look behind him on the doorstep of the pub and there, written in bright white chalk, was their next message:

A SMALL ONE. AS YOU'RE STRUGGLING.

27

Police work isn't what it used to be – or maybe I mean, police officers aren't what they used to be. It's all CCTV and technology tracking nowadays. But what if someone's off the grid – or only very recently back on the grid? Does that make them invisible somehow? Like a smoke and mirrors trick where the police can only see you from certain angles. It must be frustrating for them, and that's a good thought. Frustrating that they've only got so many cards they can play and if someone trumps them, someone trumps them. What more is there for a poor police officer and their team to do? I'd find it too much, I think, having people beat me time and again. I'd find it too much never breaking the law, either, although there are police that do it. They're the real experts at not getting caught, aren't they, the ones who make off-duty trips to criminals in back alleys without anyone ever knowing what's happened. That's a skill set.

'You're not a mastermind,' Mam said. 'It'll all come right in the end.'

'What will?'

'Justice.' She said it with spite, which was how she said most things by the time I was running round the streets with animals in tow. She didn't mind taking the money from it all, though, didn't mind where her housekeeping came from, even though I was the only one of the lot of us to be earning anything – making a living.

'It's not a living you're making,' she said.

'Keeps a roof over my head, though, Mam, and yours.'

She'd tut and tend to my dogs, then, as though she hadn't heard.

But it did make a living and it stopped her from losing the house more than once, so she could hardly moan – she did, but she shouldn't have done. The foul life I was leading saved my brothers' hides more than once too. So there's something to be said for it all.

It changes, too, in the same way that policing does. For every trick they've learnt there's a counter-trick that someone, somewhere has thought up as a means for dodging detection. If the criminals weren't better than the police then there'd hardly be any crime left at all, and what sort of a world would that be? It'd put more than just the filth out of business. You only need look at local prisons to see what a thriving enterprise crime is. Although I can't help but find fault with a system that locks criminals up together for prolonged periods of time with nothing to do but swap war stories – or tips, to think of them another way. And I'm not so proud that I'd pass up the chance to learn from the experiences of people around me. It's a cast-out-kids club, where you find out what works and what doesn't. Then you can improve your act.

From teenager to mid-twenties I came to think of being a criminal as like being a good magician. That must make the police a bunch of wide-eyed kids sitting in the audience. The thing with audiences, though, is they're always busy looking for a wire. So they often end up missing the sleight of hand...

28

Melanie slammed the car door closed with a force that made Carter jump in his seat.

'The smug bastard.' She rested her forehead against the steering wheel and took in two gulps of air before sitting upright. 'Start making phone calls, would you? Morris needs to get us a list of all the care homes in the local area that the old fella could have walked in from. Hopefully when they get him into the visitor's room at the station he'll be comfortable enough to talk, or at least look at a bloody picture.' She pressed the ignition button and the car kicked into life. 'Read and Fairer need to get background checks done on the owner... owners, how ever many there are involved with the pub. They might be able to pull staff too. We need to find out what sort of criminal connections they have, especially if their names ring a bell with any of us. Have you had any dealings with the pub before, in an official capacity?' She glanced quickly at Carter as she asked.

Her junior looked genuinely unnerved; whether it was her driving or the speed of her thoughts, though, Melanie couldn't tell.

'I'm sorry, Edd.' She tried to soften her voice.

'For what?' He was scrolling through his phone already.

'Being – I don't know. Rattled.'

'It's allowed, boss. Just give me time to catch up with the calls?' He put his phone to his ear. 'We'll have them all on this by the time we're back, don't worry.'

'It's not like I've been keen on the arsehole from the off, but this just takes the biscuit,' Read announced. He was hunched over to look at Morris' computer monitor when Melanie and Carter walked in.

'Did something else happen?' There was concern in Melanie's voice as she crossed the room. Fairer lingered by Morris' desk too, although his outrage seemed more contained than that of his partner.

'This arsehole.' Read pointed at Morris' screen without further explanation.

When Melanie craned over to look at the offending article, she saw a photograph of the message that had been left behind for them at the crime scene. Williams must have emailed it over already – and emailed it to the whole team.

'Morris, did you get the list of care homes?' Melanie asked, trying to take control of the situation, despite her shared aggravation at the message.

'I did. Burton's on it.' She turned and nodded to her colleague. Melanie looked behind her to Burton's desk and the officer flashed her a downward thumb to indicate a lack of luck in her phone calls so far. 'I am – or I was, before that email came in, looking through databases of vulnerable people living in the area that we know of, and that we can access. They're not exactly readily available, but if he has a listed condition then it might be that he's on a register somewhere. I thought it was worth a shot?'

'Everything is worth a shot at this point. Have you lads had any luck?' Melanie asked.

Fairer was the first to reply. 'We're waiting on the search engine to run the names listed at the pub. There's a landlord and an owner. The names didn't ring bells with any of us for previous crimes, and there weren't any priors flagged, but they're written on a Post-it for you on your desk just in case.'

'Thanks, Fairer.'

'I was helping,' Read added, defensively. 'But then this happened.'

'Close that. The last thing we need is a distraction,' Melanie issued the instruction and Morris duly followed, clicking back to the databases she'd been working on. 'Carter, can you call ahead to Waller's office and see if he's around this afternoon? We need to know whether we can take that pig in.'

'I'm sorry?' Morris turned.

'It might be a boar, we're not sure yet.'

Morris faced her computer again. 'Sure, that would make more sense.'

'I'm heading downstairs to see whether we can get a name for the witness. They should have checked him in by now. Anything happens, call me?' She waited for a noise of confirmation from each team member before she flashed Carter a tight-lipped smile and mouthed, 'Thank you,' before she passed him.

She couldn't remember a time in their working together when she'd been so irked, and Carter had been the calm one, but she didn't like the dynamic. When she'd escaped the confines of the shared office, she took a second to gather her thoughts. Melanie leaned against the wall of the first quiet corridor that she came to and folded over, resting her hands on her knees. She forced herself to take deep breaths in and out until she felt steady. She didn't know much about the man downstairs yet, but she guessed he wouldn't take well to confrontation. It would take a softer approach.

Melanie made it down to the station desk without another wave of panic hitting her, which felt like an accomplishment. The desk sergeant was busying himself with a phone call but held up a single finger to signal Melanie to wait.

'Yes, yes he was picked up by The Boar's Head pub, I believe, earlier today.'

Melanie's ears pricked up at the half-conversation.

'He's perfectly fine, miss, although our officers would like to speak to him. It's possible he might have been the witness to a crime earlier today... No, there was nothing violent, as I said he's... Yes, he's in one of our visitor's rooms now... No, it's different to an interview room.' The man rolled his eyes at Melanie. 'I have the officer here, yes, she's waiting to... I can certainly ask, miss, yes.' He covered the phone. 'Might you speak to her?'

'Of course.' She took the phone. 'DI Watton speaking.'

'I'm his granddaughter.' That was the only introduction given; Melanie didn't have time to ask for more before the woman jumped in with further questions. 'Can I come down to get him, please? He isn't happy outside of his house usually and God knows how long he's been out now, and he might have even missed his meds.'

'Is your granddad prone to trips out like this?' Melanie wondered whether the witness was an accidental one, or whether this was yet another dead-end planted by their killer. *Could he be that calculated?*

'It happens sometimes, but not often. The Boar's Head is special to him. He met our nan there. If he goes anywhere, he'll go to places where he went with Nan.'

'I hope you don't mind me asking, but what is it that your granddad suffers from?'

'Alzheimer's,' the woman said in a flat tone, as though it should be perfectly obvious.

Melanie held back a sigh. 'Of course, you're welcome to come down to get him any time you're ready to, and we'll do our best to keep him comfortable until then. We haven't been able to get a name...'

'Laurence. Or Larry, sometimes.'

'Thank you, and one more thing...' Melanie tried to keep her tone level, hiding the growing disappointment coursing through her. 'I'd appreciate the chance to show him a picture of the man we believe he might have seen at The Boar's Head, if you think that wouldn't be too stressful for him.'

The woman was quiet for a moment as though fully considering the request. 'It'll really depend on how he is when I get there.'

It was clear from her tone she wasn't open to negotiations. In a similar position, Melanie thought she probably wouldn't be either. They agreed for the woman to come down to the station as soon as she was able to.

'Did she call us?' Melanie asked when the phone was safely back in its cradle.

'After the hospitals, she called here. Poor woman,' the desk sergeant replied.

'Laurence, or Larry, she said his name is. Has he asked for anything?'

'Only a cup of tea with three sugars.' He laughed lightly. 'Simple things and all that.'

Melanie only wished things could be so simple. She could at least report back to Archer that they'd got themselves a witness; it was just a shame that he was unreliable at best...

29

The granddaughter – Ona Newent – was both younger and more attractive than Carter had imagined she might be, but he tried not to let the thought show. He'd extended a polite enough greeting after the desk sergeant had called to alert him to the visitor's arrival. Melanie had already stepped out of the office – pig in tow – to see what she could find out from Waller. After dealing with Melanie earlier, though, the woman looked surprised to see a male officer greet her.

'I'm afraid DI Watton has had to step out on associated business,' he explained, and her obvious confusion eased. 'I'll be taking you in to see your grandfather. He's been waiting in th–'

'Is he okay?' she cut across him.

'He is. He's even managed a chat with one of our officers who took a cup of tea into him.' Carter smiled to seal the reassurance and it looked to work. He thought of this situation in different terms – if he were tracking down a missing daughter who'd taken herself for a walk, for instance – and it conjured his best sympathy voice. 'Shall we go through?'

The woman smiled in agreement and Carter led the way to one of the more hospitable rooms the station boasted. Laurence was sitting and staring into space with what must, by now, be a lukewarm cup of tea cradled between his hands. Carter felt a twinge of sympathy, sadness even, but he tried to keep his face neutral as Ona approached her grandfather.

'Hello, you,' she said, sitting down next to him. She used a much softer tone than the one she'd afforded Carter, and he wondered whether she saved this voice for moments like this one. 'You've given us the run-around today, old man, haven't you?' She nudged him lightly with her elbow then and he turned to look at her, as though only just noticing she were talking. His face lit up with recognition and Ona smiled. 'There you are.'

'Josie.'

Her smile drooped. 'No, Granddad, that's Mum you're thinking of there.' She turned to Carter. 'Mum passed away about two years ago. That's why he and I are...' she trailed off. 'Closer.'

Her grandfather tapped at her arm, pulling her attention back. 'Can we go home now, love?'

Ona's expression lifted. 'I should think so. You've had enough adventure for one day.'

'Actually, if you wouldn't mind,' Carter said, and both visitors turned to face him. 'We'd love for your grandfather to look at a picture for us, if you both think that would be okay?' He looked from one to the other; it felt strange not to include the older chap in the conversation – or not to at least try. 'He mentioned something to our colleagues about having seen a man outside the pub. We were hoping he might look at a photo-sketch for us?'

Ona looked back at her grandfather who flashed her a wide smile. 'Fancy being an eyewitness in a top-secret police investigation to catch a mob boss?'

The man clambered to his feet and rolled up the sleeves of his cardigan. 'Do I ever!'

Melanie and Waller were sat on opposite sides of an empty examination table with the jarred remains between them. Waller quietly studied the specimen while Melanie studied him; his eyes narrowing now and then, his head shifting to a different angle and then shifting back seconds later. He'd leapt with joy when he saw what Melanie had brought – 'God, it's been a while since I handled one of those.' – and immediately reached for two sets of gloves, so they could remove the item from its bagging. But since they'd settled down, there had been this stoic quiet.

'What are your thoughts, George?' Melanie finally asked.

He sat up straight, his back cracking from the sudden movement. 'What is it you think I do here?' Melanie opened her mouth to answer but he held up his index finger. 'Don't answer. I dread to think what accusations you might throw. But I don't do animals, that's for certain. You need a vet.' He laughed. 'Actually, it's probably too late for one of those too.'

'Come on, George, I need you to be serious on this. You said you'd seen one before?'

'Medical school. Two heads. Poor thing. It turned out to be a prank by one of our lecturers. She brought the real deal in the week after though. It wasn't especially relevant, of course. We all had a basic understanding of anatomy by that point. I suppose we were all, I don't know, morbidly curious?' He stood from his seat and let out another laugh. 'I suppose some of us never grew out of that.'

'So, where would someone get one of these?'

'It isn't from the taxidermist's?'

'There's nothing in the photographs of the scene to suggest Halloway collected these, nor is there anything in his own written log of the specimens he'd handled. I checked before I came here. It might have been something personal, I suppose, but there was no sign of the murderer having entered the home, only the studio.' She rubbed at her forehead; a tension headache had been building there for hours. 'I called the wife but there was no answer. If she returns my voicemail I'll be able to check whether she recognises it. But – shit, George, I literally don't know what else to do with this. The taxidermy was bad enough.'

He bent at the knees to lower himself into Melanie's eyeline. 'Do you like ginger tea?'

'I'm sorry?'

'Ginger tea. Have you ever tried it?'

Melanie faltered. 'I can't – I can't say I have, no. What does that ha–'

'Come on, my treat.' He walked away from the table, snapping off his gloves as he went, and then stepped up into his office space. He shrugged off his white overall, then ferreted around in the pocket of his coat to find his wallet. On standing upright, he nodded to the door. 'Café out front is usually dead at this time of day.'

'What about the pig?'

'Don't worry, he'll still be here.'

Melanie couldn't remember having a social drink with Waller before; *if that's what this is meant to be*, she thought as he carried a tray over to her. There were two personal teapots, along with two cups and saucers.

'They've got ginger cake,' he explained. 'But we'll see how the tea helps.'

'With what?'

'The headache.' He smiled as he sat opposite her. 'You rub at your forehead when you're getting a headache, but that won't help with the pressure.'

'And the tea will?'

He shrugged. 'At least you're taking a break.' Melanie went to pour her pot and he set a hand on hers. 'It needs to brew.' She leaned back heavily in her chair, as though deflated by the announcement. 'Do you want to talk about it?'

'The case?'

'If that's what's causing the headache.'

She sighed and leaned forward on the table's edge. 'It's driving me crazy, George.' *And it feels like a relief to admit it.* 'This guy is out there, invisible, it seems, but it's like I'm waiting for him to pick off a member of the team. All these little bloody notes, and none of us can work out why he's leaving these things behind, or what the Halloway connection is. I mean, why Halloway? Is it the taxidermy? But we've ruled out activists, and taxidermy is humane anyway.'

Waller checked his watch and then leaned across the table to pour Melanie's tea. 'Keep going. You're not done.'

'We've distributed his picture everywhere we can. We've gone through our old cases. I haven't gone through *all* of mine, obviously, but my cases to a point. But without forensics or witnesses or cameras even, we're at a bloody loose end all the time. And the smarmy git is right, we did need another clue, and after that pig stunt we need another clue still.'

'Try your tea.'

She sipped at the hot brew and the ginger burnt on the edge of her lip. It wasn't unpleasant, and neither was this opportunity to talk so openly about the case.

'Have you even considered that you're at danger too?' Melanie waved away the suggestion, so Waller pushed, 'Mel, I'm being serious. It's all very well looking after your team but you have to make sure that protection measures are in place for yourself.'

'What can I be doing?'

'Did you talk to her highness?' There was animosity between Waller and Archer that stretched back longer than Melanie knew. Neither of them had ever offered an explanation, and it never felt right to ask. 'She's your superior officer, you should be talking to her if you feel there are problems with the case.'

'There aren't problems with the case, it's just–' Melanie's ringtone cut across her explanation. She pulled the phone from her pocket and flashed the screen at Waller: it was Archer calling.

'Christ, I must have said her name too many times.' He rolled his eyes and concentrated on pouring his tea.

'Superintendent Archer... Yes, I'm just at Dr Waller's office now... He's examining the specimen for me... No, I know that, I just thought... He's a medical professional... Yes, he's seen this sort of thing before...' Melanie looked at the screen of her phone to check the time before setting it back by her ear. 'Of course... That's no problem... I'll be there... I'll take care, don't worry... Bye.'

'Are you in trouble?' Waller asked from behind his teacup.

'She wants me back at the station for a meeting in about an hour.'

'Team meeting?'

'One to one.'

Waller let out a low whistle as he set his cup down. 'Let me get that cake after all.'

30

Melanie had left the blinds of her office open just enough. Burton had been watching her for nearly half an hour, and the senior officer was yet to move. They'd had an influx of new cases in recent weeks – burglaries, one case of arson, rumours of a new drugs ring – but nothing had grabbed Melanie's attention quite like that evidence board did. The first time Burton noticed, she'd come into the office earlier than her colleagues to double-check paperwork that had kept her awake half the night. But when she pushed through into the shared space, she'd noticed lights were on in Melanie's room. Through a crack Burton watched as her boss looked from one side of the evidence board to the other, re-familiarising herself with burnt-out buildings and taxidermy structures. Burton didn't think that Melanie had noticed her to start with, but in the two weeks since, Melanie had become less secretive about her fixation on the case.

'She's still watching it?' Carter came to a stop beside his partner. Burton wasn't the only one who'd noticed at least, and the shared responsibility made her less uncomfortable somehow.

'It's been twenty-five, maybe thirty minutes. I've seen her shake her head a few times.'

'She's worried about us,' Carter said, as though answering a question.

'I'm worried about her.'

'Carter,' Read raised his voice. 'We've got a call in about a break-in at another art gallery in town. Have we got someone to cover it?'

Carter looked from Read to Melanie and back again. 'Take down the details and tell them to keep the scene secure. We'll be there within the hour.'

'What are you doing?' Burton asked, her voice a hushed whisper now.

Carter cleared his throat. 'I'm laying bait.'

Melanie stared out of the passenger window. The art gallery was a good twenty-minute drive away and neither she nor Carter had felt moved to make conversation in the first thirteen minutes of it. It was her job to be here, she knew – but she also knew Carter's plan.

'I could be back at the station,' she eventually said, her tone sharper than intended.

'Staring at the evidence board?'

Carter's tone was equally cutting, but Melanie suspected she deserved it. 'Yes,' she admitted, and their silence resumed. Nearly a full minute had passed when she added, 'I'm worried about you all, Carter, that's what it comes down to. Just because he's been quiet for a few weeks now, it doesn't mean he's gone.'

'But without another case, how will we find him again?'

'This isn't his work.' Her tone was sharp-edged again; she

made a concerted effort to control it. 'This is someone trying to break into a portrait gallery and make a fast buck.'

'So, it's not worth investigating?'

Melanie sighed. 'That isn't what I said, or meant.'

'Without taking new cases, we're not going to find him again. Without finding him, we won't get any new leads.' Carter's tone was somehow soft and firm all at once. Melanie wondered whether this was how he spoke to Emily. 'Plus, Archer specifically instructed us to take new cases.'

Archer had specifically instructed *Melanie* to take new cases, he meant, and he wasn't wrong. In their last catch-up meeting, before the taxidermy case was officially shelved, Archer had stressed the importance of not letting other investigations fall by the wayside in favour of a big break. 'I'm not accusing you of glory-hunting,' she'd said, and Melanie had replayed the non-accusation several times since. It hadn't even crossed her mind that that's what Archer had meant, until she'd brought it up. But wasn't what Melanie was doing. She was protecting her team, and after weeks of people trying to coax her back into the field, she felt a rising frustration that others didn't share her worries.

'I'm here, I don't know what more you want, Carter,' she said, with the hope that it might draw a line under their discussion. When he opened his mouth to respond Melanie shut him down. 'Before you add anything else to this, you'd be wise to remember who's actually the senior officer here.'

From Carter's expression it looked as though he gave her warning some real consideration, before swallowing whatever he'd been about to say. They went the last five minutes of the journey in perfect silence after that, until Carter took the turning into the gallery's private car park.

'Do you want me to call Burton?' he asked.

Melanie unbuckled her safety belt and flashed him a confused look. 'Why?'

'Because you don't really want to be here?'

'Carter.' She was already reaching for the handle. 'Don't be an arse.' She flashed him a smile to reassure him and without another word the pair exited the vehicle.

The car park was near empty. It had been easy enough for them to drive straight in and, as Melanie looked from one corner to another, she noticed there didn't seem to be any cameras on this back part of the property. *Clumsy*, she thought as she looked around the side of the building, spotting an alleyway that must lead to the front door.

'Why wouldn't they have cameras back here?' she asked Carter from two steps ahead.

'Maybe paintings aren't the only thing they're dealing?'

'Would they have called us in at all if that were the case?'

The two stopped out front and assessed the building. The gallery was clearly marked up for its purpose, with vertical banners either side of the front door boasting the name Imperial Arts. Melanie scouted the buildings opposite and spotted there were street cameras and front-of-shop cameras on the street lamps and buildings respectively, so at least they had eyes out here. *That doesn't help us much with that back entrance though*, she thought, with suspicion bubbling.

'We heading in?' Carter asked, his foot already on the first step.

'After you.'

They were greeted by anxious smiles from two women loitering in the foyer. Melanie could have met both women in a completely different setting, and she still would have guessed they were something to do with the arts industry. Their clothes were a mixture of denim and suede – with expensive fringes – and their haircuts angular, as though sculpted rather than cut. Melanie and Carter were hardly three steps into the building when both women rushed to them, falling over themselves to make their introductions.

'You must be the detectives, yes?' one asked, her voice cracking as she spoke. She extended a hand, 'I'm Ursula, Ursula Vale. I'm one of the gallery owners, with–'

'Honor,' the other woman interrupted. 'Without the U,' she added when she saw Carter pull out his notebook.

'Surname?' he asked.

'I don't have one.'

Bloody artists, Melanie thought as she shook hands with both women in turn. She introduced herself before launching into the formalities. 'Can you walk us through what's happened here exactly?'

'We have an alarm system that's quite sensitive,' Ursula explained. 'It has to be, with the items we tend to keep in stock. While we were getting ready this morning, I guess it was around six, six thirty? We can check the exact time.' She looked at Honor who gave a single head dip in confirmation. 'It was around then that our phones went off, to say something had triggered the alarm. We raced down here, which in hindsight I suppose wasn't the best thing to have done. But we did. There was no one here by the time we arrived though.'

'You're sure it wasn't a false alarm?' Carter asked.

'The back door has been jimmied open. That's why there was a delay between us getting here and calling you. We did a sweep of the gallery, upstairs and down. We wanted to check whether anything had been taken,' Honor explained, her tone more level than her partner's.

'And has it?'

'No, nothing at all.'

'Have you ever had anything like this happen before?' Melanie asked, her attention caught now by the artwork around her. 'You have some really interesting pieces here. It must be quite a target for anyone looking for high-end work.'

Honor smiled, as though taking this as a compliment, but it was Ursula who replied. 'We've never had any problems, no. I don't even understand this.' Her tone began to rise in pitch. 'Why would someone break in and not take anything? Surely that's too much of a risk?'

'It might be that the alarm spooked them,' Carter explained.

Melanie thought for a moment then asked, 'Nothing was left behind, was it?'

'I'm sorry?' Honor asked, her eyebrow raised in what looked like scepticism.

'We've had some strange incidents over the last few months where break-ins have taken place, but rather than something being taken, something was left. Was anything left?' The owners exchanged a quizzical look. 'Never mind,' Melanie said, snatching back the idea. 'You have the interior and exterior alarms, but I didn't see any cameras?'

'They're hidden, out front and out back. Ursula and I have both seen galleries thrown over, all because people could dodge the cameras. It's easily done if you believe anyone in the industry. So, we had ours stashed. I can show you?'

'Please,' Melanie replied. 'Can you do a walk round with Ms Vale?' she half-asked, half-instructed Carter, before taking Honor's lead out to the front of the building. 'It's quite a smart move on your part, to stash the cameras where even police officers can't spot them.'

'Ursula took some persuading.' Honor spoke over her shoulder as she pushed through the double doors leading on to the street. 'She seemed to think the cameras would be a deterrent, that if people could see them they'd be less likely to try something like this. We've been here for nearly five years now, though, and this is the first time anything...'

Melanie froze on the steps of the gallery. Honor was still speaking, but the noise had trailed into something undiscernible. Cars interrupted Melanie's stare, but she kept her eyes locked across the street. Everything about the man looked the same, right down to the shading around the eyes. In person she still recognised him, but she couldn't place where from. She hurriedly tried to convince herself it was nothing, merely an uncanny likeness. Which she might have believed, if the man from the photo-sketch hadn't been staring back.

31

Melanie launched herself from the steps of the gallery. She ran into oncoming traffic, not caring about the dangers as the man across the street bounded away. There was a cacophony of car horns and shouts but she stayed determined, dodging bumpers and pedestrians alike as she made her way from road to pavement, and then down the busy street ahead of her. She pulled her phone from her pocket and eyed it long enough to dial Carter's number. He answered before the first ring had fully sounded, and he'd obviously been waiting for the call.

'Boss, what the he–'

'He's here, Edd,' Melanie explained, the speed of her run making her breath fall heavy into the receiver. 'He was waiting outside the gallery for us, for one of us, I don't know. I'm following him along the opposite street, he's pushing through crowds and – oh, shit, Edd, hang on.' The man ahead ducked unexpectedly into a side street; Melanie had to slow her pace to make the same turn, before pounding against the uneven concrete again to try to shorten the distance between them. 'Deermount Street, he's veered into there. I'm still following him.

Call patrol cars, and the team, get them out and on the look-out as soon as possible. There are only a few ways he can turn from he–'

'I've got it, I've got it,' Carter reassured her.

She disconnected the phone and slipped it back into her pocket, giving her full attention to the task at hand. While the man in front powered through the crowds, crashing into anyone not quick enough to move, Melanie slowed her speed by pausing to throw apologies in her wake. She sidestepped people as best as she could, feeling muscles yank this way then that as she shifted her body but tried to maintain her speed. She felt the beginnings of a burning sensation inside her chest and tried to breathe through it. But the sharp turn into Georgian Street caught her by surprise. There were more shoppers there, more people to try to avoid and as her steady breaths became ragged pants Melanie knew the distance between her and her quarry was lengthening.

For the first time the man looked back over his shoulder and, as though noticing Melanie's lag, he stood entirely still. Melanie was so stunned by the change of pace that she stopped running herself. She wondered what had spooked him; *had he been hoping for Carter?* Her chest heaved as she took in air. One step at a time she tried to close the distance between them, but she soon realised that for every step forward she took, her target took one back. He didn't seem concerned with anyone who might be behind him, only concerned with Melanie, and how she might calmly navigate these crowds.

'Police, please, can everyone move out of the way!' Melanie raised her voice and held her badge high above her. Her tone was frayed around the edges with irritation as people persisted in blocking her path. She pushed between a group of young girls who were busying themselves with freshly bought make-up, and when she looked up the man had stopped entirely again – but this time he wasn't standing alone.

'It's not much of a cat and mouse this, is it, DI Watton?' he shouted above the crowd. He'd made a human shield of a terrified woman. Melanie guessed she must be late twenties, early thirties at a push. Less concerned with the woman's age, though, Melanie soon spotted the curve of a baby bump. Her hands were reaching to hold her stomach, but were stuck a distance away due to the man's firm grip on her shoulders. Melanie wanted to run to her. *But how might that make him react?*

'We'll try again another time,' he announced, before launching the woman. He moved her as though she weighed nothing, aiming her towards a crowd of young men in suits as they walked, talked and laughed their way past the spectacle.

Melanie saw the woman tumble into the crowd like a thrown bowling ball, her body off balance with the force of the push. She closed the distance to the victim just in time to see her pregnant belly land hard against the concrete. Melanie looked from victim to perpetrator; he was walking backwards still, one hand raising as though to wave.

'Fuck,' she snapped, pulling out her phone as she scrambled to her knees alongside the woman. 'I'm a police officer,' she explained. 'I'm going to call for help, okay?' The woman nodded along with Melanie's words as she spoke into the phone, alerting the emergency services to what had happened and what her location was. 'Please hurry?' she asked, knowing the redundancy of the plea; they would get here as soon as they could, she knew. She disconnected the one call and replaced it with another. 'Carter, I lost him. He's heading north on Georgian Street and he's got maybe a two-minute head start.' She looked down at the woman, discomfort and worry clear from her expression. 'I can't leave my post.'

~

Melanie had managed to contact the victim's husband during the ride to the hospital. She had been desperate to resume the chase, to find out what headway the team had made without her. But as the expectant mother had been bundled into the back of the ambulance she'd begged – 'Stay with me, please, would you?' – through heavy pants for Melanie to come too. Despite her need to catch the guy, Melanie hadn't had the heart to say no to someone in such obvious distress – and the worried looks swapped between paramedics had only helped with her decision.

She'd been pacing the corridor, half-waiting for the father to arrive and half-waiting for Carter to call, when the latter finally came through.

'Anything?' Melanie asked, her voice cracking with exhaustion.

'We didn't get him, boss.'

'Bollocks.' The word came out louder than intended, and she noticed an older couple give her a side glance from their seats. She mouthed, 'Sorry,' then moved closer to the doors. She shoved her way past incoming traffic, not stopping to apologise for the shoulder bumps along the way. One man grunted as he pushed past, but she had bigger worries than politeness. 'Have there been any reports made? Damages, people hurt? He was tearing through town like a lunatic, someone must have seen something.'

'The good news is there's no way he wasn't caught on camera. There haven't been reports of disruptive behaviour, but we've got switchboard at the ready for it. They know to direct all of that straight to us. Morris is pulling security footage that we can readily access from the ground you covered. Burton, Read and Fairer are all contacting shop owners too, for any CCTV angled towards the street or even the doors of shops.'

Melanie ran a hand through her tangled hair. The team were doing everything they could be, she knew, but this feeling of helplessness was too much.

Carter lowered his voice as he spoke again, 'We're going to get the fucker, Mel.'

She smiled at his efforts to soothe her. 'We'd better.'

'We've got eyes on him now; there's no way we can't identify him from this. Plus, Morris is unnervingly excited about using the facial recognition software.'

Melanie had to laugh at that. 'Thanks for rallying them, Carter. I'm waiting on the husband still but as soon as he's here I'll head over to the station. Keep me posted?'

'Always. Hey, how's the mother doing?'

Melanie thought back to the journey here: the gas and air; the cries for help; the call ahead to warn accident and emergency. 'I don't know,' she admitted. 'I'll keep you posted too.'

The two said their goodbyes and disconnected the call. Melanie hovered by the doorway for a while longer, checking her phone every few seconds as though she might have missed a call in that time. The husband had been on the other side of town when Melanie got through to him, but she'd hoped he'd make it through the traffic sooner than this.

'I'm sorry, officer?' someone asked from behind her.

Melanie turned to see a woman her own age, suited in blue scrubs. 'DI Watton.'

'The young mother you came in with is asking if you can call her husband again.' She spoke softly, as though Melanie were also a patient. 'You might want to stress that it's a matter of urgency.'

'I'll try again,' Melanie said, already thumbing down to the number. 'He knows everything in terms of the incident, but I'll tell him she's asking for him. Maybe I can get a car to get him or something, if he's struggling to–' Melanie was aware of the rising panic in her voice, despite her efforts to keep her tone steady. She was almost grateful for the doctor having set a hand down on her forearm, bringing her fumbling explanation to an early stop.

'It might be worth stressing the circumstances have changed since his wife was brought in, and she could really do with her husband right now.' Melanie locked eyes with the doctor; she was desperate for there to be a better conclusion than the one she'd jumped to, but the doctor only added, 'I think you understand what I mean? Of course, I can't give out specific details about a patient's case, and her husband...'

The explanation continued but Melanie didn't catch what came next. She'd been given enough ammunition for one day.

32

Archer had called ahead before visiting the office. The entire team was still in place, trying to track down as much information as they could about their suspect. Read, Fairer and Burton were watching through CCTV footage in forward motion to try to speed up the process. Meanwhile, Morris had already pulled footage from street cameras; she'd got three blurred images of the man's face that she'd attempted to match against facial recognition. Nothing was of a high enough quality yet, but at least they would have a string of images to release to the public in a press conference – which Melanie assumed was what Archer wanted to discuss with them all. Although why she wanted the whole team in place for that, Melanie was less certain.

The officers stood to attention when Archer entered the room, and Melanie thought she saw a smirk of enjoyment on her boss's face. *This must mean she's in a manageable mood*, Melanie thought, taking a step ahead to put her at the forefront of her crew. 'Ma'am, I can only apologise for–'

Archer held a hand up to stop her. 'Don't. I'm not here to dish out reprimands for the day's work. He caught you entirely off guard and there's only so much that any one of us could do in that situation. The reason I'm here is to discuss what happens next.'

'We're currently looking over the CCTV–' Melanie started but Archer cut her off again.

'Apologies, DI Watton, but it's late in the day and it might be timelier if I explain what's going to happen next and we can save questions for the end.' She paused and waited for a nod of agreement from Melanie before continuing. 'This individual is now in the public eye. There have been news reports about his behaviour today and there have already been suggestions that he's the man we've been hunting over the last several weeks. I don't want anyone to confirm or deny the latter to people outside of this office. What I would like is for most of you to spend time working through surveillance footage as late as you can stand to this evening. I've got a meeting with select media outlets pencilled in for the morning, people we're on good terms with. I'd like to save the full press conference for when DI Watton and DS Carter are back in the office in a couple of days.' Archer paused to catch her breath but didn't wait anywhere near long enough for Melanie to jump in. 'When the press conference does roll around, though, I'd like DI Watton and DS Carter to be as prepared as possible, and something close to a name or at the very least a clear picture of the suspect would be beneficial. We'll open a fresh tip-line, which DI Watton and DS Carter will manage for the foreseeable.' Again, Melanie opened her mouth to interrupt so Archer rushed the rest of her explanation, as though pre-empting any objections. 'Because they'll both be on desk duty with immediate effect when they return from their days off.'

'Ma'am, I can't speak for DS Carter, but I don't personally feel that I need time–'

'You're taking the time off, DI Watton, it's not open for discussion.'

'With all due respect, ma'am, I don't see how time off, or desk duty, is an effective use of DS Carter or myself as resources for the team. We're the senior officers.'

'And you'll remain as such, but you won't be on the streets, DI Watton, and you'll save us both time and energy if you accept that now. You've spent a lot of hours trying to determine who it is from your team this man is targeting and now we know it's you, or Carter.'

'We can't know that for certain,' Carter intervened.

Archer looked surprised at his comment. 'Of course we can. Any one of you could have taken that call out to the gallery today. If you hadn't been who he was looking for, wouldn't he have simply left the scene?'

Carter opened his mouth to respond again but thought better of it. But his eyes soon widened at another realisation. 'Ma'am, my daughter. When I'm here she's either–'

'I'll take your home address, your parents' and your ex-wife's before I leave,' Archer said, answering Carter's unspoken concern. Melanie knew the mother – the mother's loss – from earlier in the day had shaken him. 'DI Watton, is there anyone that we should discuss protection for, or do you feel comfortable pressing ahead with the new arrangements?'

Melanie thought briefly of Hilda; of the last time they'd spoken, and the forced professionalism that made a veil for everything they weren't saying. 'No, ma'am, thank you. I don't have anyone,' she admitted, adding another blow to a brutal day.

~

After putting together her official statement for the incidents that had taken place, Melanie stuck her head out into the open office. The team were still busy, following Archer's commands and working through CCTV. Much to Melanie's dismay, Archer was still present and accounted for too. She was hunched over Morris' desk while the pair talked in hushed tones, and Melanie felt a twist in her stomach at being so far removed from operations. She'd never felt more determined to catch this man but in all the hoops he'd had them jump so far, she'd never felt more disadvantaged than now. Without anything more concrete or constructive to offer, she did the only thing she could think of that might still make a difference.

'Pizza, or do we fancy something else?'

'Pizza,' Read answered without missing a beat.

'Don't we always have pizza?' his partner replied.

'But can you ever have too much pizza?' Carter added, looking up from whatever paperwork was keeping him busy.

Archer stood upright but stayed alongside Morris; Melanie guessed they must have business still to finish.

'The rest of you should eat, so order in. It's on me. DI Watton and DS Carter should be heading home by now.' She made a show of looking at her watch. 'It's well past your clocking out time for a desk day.'

Melanie tried to take the comment on the chin and flashed her superior a tight smile. 'Of course, ma'am. Do we need to be escorted home?' It was a bluff on Melanie's part; she wouldn't accept an offer like that even if Archer extended one, but she wanted her superior to know she was taking the changes seriously.

'Only if you'd feel more comfortable with one?'

Melanie looked to Carter, deflecting the offer.

'I'm fine without,' he said, and Melanie agreed.

Both of them collected their belongings and powered down

their workstations. The remaining members of the team shouted their goodbyes without looking up from their tasks. Melanie wasn't sure whether they were trying to minimise the impact of the change, or maximise their work time; knowing the team, it could well have been both. It didn't sit right with her to be leaving Archer behind as the senior officer, though, despite her enthusiasm – 'It's been a good few years since I got the chance for a late night working a case' – at being more hands on with the team. If anything, the enthusiasm had added to Melanie's discomfort; it should be her spurring them on; it should be her buying the food.

She took the stairs two in front of Carter and they were a floor clear of their team when he said, 'Now, on a scale of one to ten–'

'Fuming.'

'Thought so.'

Melanie stopped on a small landing and leaned back against the wall. She was exhausted, and from the pitying look Carter flashed her she guessed she must look how she felt. 'She's making exactly the same call that I'd make in her situation,' she admitted, her tone hard-edged. 'But it doesn't mean we have to be happy about it.'

'Do you think he's after you?'

Over the hours since the chase Melanie had played back what the suspect had said several times over. He knew her surname and rank, but that could mean anything. The cat and mouse reference didn't hold any significance for her either.

'I don't know, Edd, is the honest answer.' Her colleague looked deflated and she wondered what answer he'd been expecting.

'Got time for a drink? Emily is staying with my parents tonight so I may as well make the most of the time.'

'How can I pass up an offer like that,' Melanie said, turning to trek down the final steps ahead of them. She reached the main exit and felt in her outer pocket for her ID card. 'That's weird.' She checked the other side, and the inner pockets too, in case in the rush she'd stashed it somewhere else. 'It looks like I didn't grab it at all.'

Carter held up his own card. 'DS Carter to the rescue.'

'I should check...'

'Come on. It'll be there.'

Melanie sighed. It had already been a day and a half, and she knew Carter would be right. She moved aside to let her colleague scan them out of the building. They spent the journey to the car park discussing where might be a worthy watering hole for a midweek drink. After the names of four different pubs had been mentioned, Melanie started to feel like they'd circled back around to the start of the case.

'Carter, as long as it's cold and boozy, right now I really don't care.'

'Okay.' He thought for a moment. 'Yep, cold and boozy I can do.'

33

Melanie stared at the ceiling, counting out the seconds until a full minute had passed. She couldn't remember the last time she'd had a day off in the middle of a week, which also meant she couldn't remember what to do with a midweek day off either. She thought of the housework she could get done, which would keep her busy for at least an hour. There must be a friend who she could ring too, she thought, reaching for her phone from the bedside table. She thumbed through her recent contacts – Carter, Carter, Burton, Burton, Burton – and exhaled hard at the limited options. The team should only have been in the office for half an hour by now, although Archer's determination from the previous evening left Melanie wondering whether their late night might have been followed by an early morning too. Regardless of their start time, though, it was far too early to be pestering them, she knew that much. *Could I call Carter, then?* She wondered how her junior was managing the early hours of his day off; was it this hard for Carter, or did he have more to fill his time?

She felt herself slipping into a dangerous avenue of thinking. Eager to nip lonely thoughts in the bud, she set her phone back on the bedside table before swinging her legs out of bed. She would shower, clean, and go into town. She didn't need anything but being out felt like a better idea than being in, and by that time of day it might be a sociable enough hour to call Carter, she reasoned.

Melanie had only taken two steps towards her bathroom when her phone began to hum, vibrating across the surface of the table. She launched herself across the bed, landing hard on her front, but managed to catch the call before her voicemail cut in.

'DI Watton.'

'Is everything okay?'

She'd never been more grateful to hear Hilda's voice.

'Hilda, hi.' Melanie righted herself on the bed. 'Of course, is everything okay with you?'

'I called the office and they said you're on leave.'

Melanie held back a sigh. 'Only for a day, maybe two. Probably one.'

'Because of what happened yesterday? I saw you were caught up in it.'

'Superintendent Archer thought DS Carter and I could do with a break after it all.'

'I see, and what are your thoughts on that?'

Melanie felt a torrent of feeling rise in her throat. Could she share that much with Hilda, especially after everything? She'd called, after all, and she'd asked. And yet...

'I think she has fair reasons. You know me, I'd always prefer to be on the job.' No sooner had the words escaped Melanie's mouth than she hit her palm flat against her forehead.

Hilda let out a hard huff. 'Yep, I know you. I'm in the office myself, so I should get a shift on. You take good care, won't you?'

'Did you call the office for something to do with the case?'

'I'm sorry?'

'You said you called the office, and they said I was on leave.'

'Oh, oh, no.' Hilda faltered. 'I called to see you were okay. I saw some news reports and...'

The pair fell into an awkward silence, and Melanie felt torn between finishing their phone call and clinging on to the contact for dear life. But Hilda made the decision for her. 'Take care, Mel, okay? I'm here if there's anything.'

'Of course, me too, if you... Have a good day.'

Melanie disconnected and caught the call time on the screen of her phone: they'd talked for five minutes and thirty-two seconds. What would she do with the rest of the day?

Melanie couldn't decide whether she was doing everything in extra quick time, or whether the day around her was moving slowly. She sat down at 3pm having decided it was likely a mixture of the two. The house was cleaner than it had been in months, and she was finally up to date with her washing, and her household paperwork. She'd visited town and decided that unless you needed new clothes or new electrical equipment, there wasn't much the city centre could offer. She'd toyed with the idea of getting a coffee somewhere – a fancy one, the type she always saw shared by a non-friend on her social media feeds – but she'd opted for making her own at home, where she could sit and overthink in peace.

She was halfway through her drink when she pulled her phone from her pocket, with every intention of calling Carter. But instead she thumbed down to Burton's number. If her colleague hadn't answered by the third ring, she decided, then she'd disconnect the call.

'DC Burton speaking,' she answered on the second. But she must have seen the number calling before she answered.

Melanie wondered whose company her junior must be in to be still using her official phone voice.

'Can you talk?'

'For a second or two, I can.'

'Any developments?'

'I'm not sure we can say at the moment.'

Melanie swallowed a sigh. 'Burton, don't hold out on me.'

There was a rustling noise on the other end of the phone. When Burton next spoke, Melanie realised she'd covered the receiver to excuse herself from whoever she was with. 'I'll just be a moment... No, it won't take long.' Melanie thought she heard Read in the background. She felt her leg begin to tap rhythmically, the denim of her jeans scraping against the edge of the coffee table with each jerk. From the noise down the phoneline it was clear Burton was carrying her to privacy. 'I really can only talk for a minute, boss,' she said after another few seconds had passed. 'Things are busy and it's hard to get away.'

'Busy, like leads?'

'Archer has kept us busy while she's been liaising between us and the media team.'

Melanie couldn't help but feel her colleague was being deliberately evasive. 'She's told you to keep quiet, even with me?'

Burton moaned, and Melanie could sense her conflict. 'She hasn't said with you specifically, no, she's just told us to watch ourselves during phone conversations and email exchanges. Christ, basically anything that sees us swap information digitally.'

'She thinks our digital comms are vulnerable?'

'She doesn't know. After last year...' Their last major case had given the team a crash course in hacking and dark web dealings; Melanie could understand why her superior wouldn't want a repeat of that. 'She's got the technology team checking things over, so we'll have extra security in the next couple of hours.'

'Why isn't Morris doing it?'

'Morris is busy with other work.'

'That's as much as I'm getting?' Melanie knew her tone was sharp, but she struggled to keep her frustrations in check.

Burton let out another quiet noise of discomfort. 'Yes, boss, that's all you're getting. I'm sorry, but I really have to get back.'

'She's running a tight ship?'

'Archer has had to step out on other business.'

Leaving you in charge, Melanie thought, but she'd pressed her colleague enough already.

'Boss, make the most of the next day or so. Why don't you put your feet up, watch the news?' Burton suggested. Melanie could hear movement down the phone, as though Burton were backstepping into the office – signalling the close of their call. 'I'll see you soon.'

'Take care of yourself, Burton.'

Melanie dropped her phone hard against the coffee table and thumped back against the sofa. *Watch the news?* She replayed Burton's advice, wondering whether it was a random choice of viewing or whether there was some significance to it. Either way, Melanie needed the noise of something happening. She stood to grab the television remote and flicked straight to the local news briefing two channels away, and there it was, plastered across the bottom of the screen: Superintendent Beverley Archer.

'We're not accepting questions at this present time, no. The major incident team is working hard to determine the identity of the individual involved in the recent disruptions through the city centre, though, and we would be grateful to hear from anyone who recognises the man pictured.' The screen cut away from Archer to show a handful of grainy images. Archer's voice continued over the top: 'We'll be providing news outlets with these images which means they'll be shown regularly. If you do recognise this man, you're encouraged to call our tip-line as a matter of urgency, the number for which is displayed below.' The screen switched back to Archer then, her expression stone-set despite the flashing bulbs and bustle of journalists. 'We've also been able to isolate a partial number plate for a vehicle that we believe the perpetrator escaped in. The team are currently working to locate this vehicle also. Our sympathies, of course, go out to those who were affected by yesterday's disruption, and we'd like to reassure the public that we're making every effort to locate this man, and we'll report updates as we feel able to...'

34

It was two days later when Melanie and Carter were allowed back into the office. Archer had called them both the night before to let them know they were needed back on the ground. The following morning they entered together as though conjoined by their exile, and despite arriving early, the team were already at work ahead of them – a running theme, Melanie thought, as the office door clanged shut behind them. No one looked up from their workstations, but Archer did appear from Melanie's office. She felt a twist of anxiety at seeing her superior so settled in her domain. *But her office is much nicer*, Melanie soothed herself, *this isn't a permanent set-up*. Archer crossed the office to meet them and exchanged pleasantries with a fake smile that didn't suit her; it only made Melanie all the more nervous at what might be coming.

'Let's get the good news out of the way, shall we?' she asked, and Melanie noted the implication of bad news. 'DCs Read and Fairer are working on the partial number plate that DC Morris managed to pull from the CCTV footage, taken on the day of the chase. It looks to belong to a Vauxhall Vivaro. The brand of car was visible from the badge showing, but the angle and quality of the footage made it hard to see much else.'

'How did you determine the model?' Melanie asked. She didn't mean to sound like she was poking holes, and yet...

'You can thank DC Burton for that. She was working with Morris when the van was spotted, and she spent a good portion of time scouring the internet for lookalikes. I believe she also spoke to a local dealership who helped her in the matter, but you'll have to verify that fully for yourself.' Archer smirked and cocked an eyebrow, flashing an expression that asked, *satisfied?* Melanie managed to reciprocate with a smile before her superior continued. 'The chaps are trying to track down vans of the right model and colour that correspond with the partial number plate, and ones that are tied to the area. There'll be updates over the day, I'm sure.' The firmness of her expectation told Melanie everything she needed to know about what had happened while she was away; Archer had ridden the team hard to get these results. But as much as Melanie wanted to protect them, she had a nagging feeling about the good work being done in her absence.

'Well, that is good news,' Carter said, filling the pause. 'Can I ask where we are today, ma'am? Press conference, is it?' He sounded almost hopeful.

'That'll be tomorrow, I'm afraid. Morris has managed to pull some more accurate images of the suspect from the reams of footage that we pulled initially. There's no hiding him, thanks to that rundown you gave him.' She flashed Melanie an encouraging glance. 'We're hoping that another day working on the facial recognition will crack the mystery of who he is. She's doing some – I don't know – tweaks to software. I haven't asked.'

Melanie half-laughed. 'In my experience it's best you don't.'

'Where's Burton loitering?' Carter scanned the room.

'Ah, she's readying DI Watton's workload for the day. I've set up in an interview room for you downstairs with everything you'll need to be getting on with. DS Carter, you'll find a sizeable stack of paperwork waiting on your desk.' A tight smile followed, as though she were braced for confrontation, but nothing came.

'Well, if there's anything you need...' Carter trailed off before excusing himself. He stopped along the way for a hello with Read and Fairer but soon settled in at his own desk.

'Shall I get downstairs to meet Burton?' Melanie asked, trying to keep her tone neutral, trying also to show willing. She had a horrible feeling that whatever was waiting for her would be grim in comparison to Carter's paperwork – and that was saying something. Still, she was eager to oversee her team, and she knew that lines would have to be toed now to make sure that happened.

'Let's walk? I can explain on the way.' Archer held the door open for Melanie, who stepped out ahead of her. 'Now, the bad news is that you're still on paperwork.'

'I guessed that much, ma'am.'

'In your absence, I asked DC Morris to pull your previous cases relating to the Fox and Hounds pub.' Archer let the sentence hang, as though giving Melanie time to digest the information. 'Because I'd wager that given the time you set aside for yourself to go through those old cases, you probably didn't go through them fully.'

'Ma'am, when you asked–'

'You don't need to humour me, Melanie. I'm not asking whether you went through them, nor am I reprimanding you for the fact you didn't. You head up a busy team and you've had a long career, I do understand.'

Melanie was grateful for the soft accusation, because she couldn't deny its truth. While the team had been busy going through every past case relating to the crime scene, Melanie had skimmed the top of her cases. At the time it didn't seem to matter, but now...

The two pushed through into reception, where Burton was waiting for them.

'DC Morris was kind enough to pull the mugshots from your previous cases, complete with the name of the individual pictured and a summary of their arrest.' *Which must have amounted to a fair bit of overtime*, Melanie thought. 'They've been printed and placed in ring-binders for your perusal over the next day or so; how ever long it takes, in truth. I recalled you saying you recognised the photo-sketch but couldn't place him. Now's your chance.'

Melanie glanced at Burton who flashed her a tight smile.

'I think that's a good idea, ma'am,' Melanie announced, forcing enthusiasm.

'I'm glad to hear it. Burton will take it from here. I imagine all the heavy lifting has been done by now?'

'Yes, ma'am. All of the folders are waiting.'

Archer reached forward to squeeze Melanie's forearm. 'Enjoy.'

Melanie was going into her third hour of looking through photographs. They'd all been lifted and shifted by Burton, stacked into cardboard boxes and left here in no particular order. Melanie wasn't sure how many were left, but she thought that by now she'd looked through close on a hundred arrests. She also had a growing urge to buy Morris an apology present; a bottle of wine, or at the very least get her an extra day of holiday.

There were a handful of images left to look over for the current folder. Melanie promised herself a break after; to see the light of day, perhaps even to check on the team. Archer surely couldn't begrudge her the luxury of a human face that didn't belong in a binder for five minutes. Although she'd looked over some of the best cases of her career in these hours, and she had to admit it buoyed her spirits to see how well she'd done in the days of being a fresh detective. She'd revisited a drugs bust from fifteen years ago; a case involving forged licences and immigration papers from three years ago; animal abuse, theft, dogfights from...

Melanie looked up from the arrest listings and into the eyes of the man photographed. He looked younger. The bags under his eyes weren't quite so pronounced and his hair, shaved close to his head, didn't show signs of grey. But it had been seventeen years since this photograph was taken. The longer she looked, the more similarities she could see between the criminal pictured and her quarry from the other day. She read down the charges listed, many of them small-time arrests – pet theft, animal fights, publishing inappropriate materials online – leading to one final blow – grievous bodily harm – that resulted in the longest sentence of them all. It was only when she came to this final arrest that she saw the criminal's release date too: seven months ago.

She pushed through the door of the interview room, taking care to close it until it locked behind her. But she made the rest of the journey without such care, pushing past fellow officers and pounding up the stairs, pausing only once to catch her breath. She held the photograph of the man in question in one hand, her curled fingers creasing the printout. In the weeks of working the case she'd never felt as close to tracking him down as she did now. An image and a name would close the net around the man who could be responsible for this whole mess. If nothing else, it gave them a fresh place to start, which they desperately needed. But for the first time in weeks Melanie at least had a good feeling about a lead – about this man, being the exact man who'd got her running.

With another large pull of air she closed the last of the distance, falling through the office door with a clatter that caught the attention of most of her team. Archer, again, was present in the room but Melanie was glad of her audience this time. She crossed over to her superior, holding the image out in front of her like an offering, and Archer took a step forward to take it. While Melanie panted air back into her chest, Archer assessed the photograph.

Seconds later, and in perfect synchronicity, the pair shared their announcement: 'We've got a name.'

35

Pencils were already scratching against papers when the three officers entered the room. The space had been set up for a relatively large-scale press conference, and the local rag writers were out in force to fill the seats. Melanie thought she recognised one or two national writers in the audience too, but she tried not to let her eye linger for long. She hovered around the seat in the centre of the table, making room for Archer to pass through to the chair on the far side of her. Under normal circumstances, an attending superintendent would have headed up a press conference. But Archer and Melanie, with support from Carter, had planned this down to the last detail. It had been Melanie's suggestion – 'If he's trying to get to me, shouldn't I be front and centre?' – and the other two had readily agreed. With Melanie and Archer seated, this left the final spot waiting for the recently reinstated Carter. Archer hadn't wasted any time in getting him back on active duty and, while he'd tried to hide his relief and excitement, Melanie could only imagine how pleased her junior must feel.

Melanie poured herself a glass of water and, as though this were a signal that proceedings were about to begin, the room shuffled to near quiet. She'd always loved these before moments, when the position of power fell entirely to her; even with Archer lending support, Melanie still felt a tingle at what she was about to reveal. She cleared her throat, commanding silence from the final few chattering journalists, and then launched into their major announcement. The three of them had agreed there shouldn't be a slow burn for releasing details, not now they had a person of interest, and the best way to get their suspect was to make sure there were as many pairs of eyes looking for him as possible.

'The major incident team has been working to determine the identity of a suspect who, many of you will likely know, caused a string of disruptions through the city centre recently. Not only did he cause distress to many citizens, but he also caused serious harm to an expectant mother...' Melanie had to concentrate especially hard to make sure her tone didn't waver during that part of the announcement. She needed to keep her composure throughout; that was something else the three of them had decided. He'd be watching, they guessed, and weakness would be a poor show.

'You can't let the bastard know he's got to you, Watton, do you understand?' Archer had asked, her tone determined and fierce. Melanie had found it infectious and had nodded along enthusiastically with her superior's guidance. But it was another thing holding that ferocity for the length of a whole press conference.

'We believe he may also be connected to a number of thefts that have taken place in the local area over the last few weeks,' she announced, much to the murmured delight of the writers in front of her. 'As I said, MIT has been working hard to determine the identity of the individual and we believe that our person of interest is one Roderick Stone, who's local to the area. He's had encounters with members of our team before,' Melanie paused and took a deliberate swallow to steady herself. 'We also believe him to be well-known for dealings with several criminal organisations in the area. The images you'll see on the screen behind us,' she said, prompting Carter to click the monitors into life, 'show the stills pulled from CCTV footage, taken from various city centre establishments. This following image is an older mugshot of Stone, taken from when he was previously incarcerated. This was for a series of violent crimes, most notably acts of bodily harm.'

They were also crimes Melanie would rather leave long behind her. Her pursuit of Stone the first time round had been long-winded and laborious, made up of charges that couldn't stick and crimes that escalated. She wasn't exactly eager to tread back over old ground. Although she knew it was only a matter of time before her team got the full scoop on this new character. She'd given them the bare minimum so far, with the press conference taking up most of her time and energies. But they needed to know who they were facing off against.

'We'll be monitoring a tip-line and asking that members of the public stay vigilant for sightings. Should anyone at all see Stone, they're advised to call this tip-line immediately and under no circumstances approach him. The number itself is in your press packs, and we'll be distributing it to media outlets for televised distribution as well.' Melanie took a deep inhale and a sip of water, quietly congratulating herself on getting through the exact speech they had planned, and without her anger cracking through. But now came the part they couldn't plan for. 'We'd like to open up the room for questions, should anyone have any.'

Journalists threw their hands into the air like year ones desperate to answer a basic maths question. Melanie tried to be strategic with her choices, sharing answers that she was comfortable voicing – 'No, the public isn't in any immediate danger... Yes, we have leads to follow in terms of isolating his location...' – but not every question could be answered so easily.

'I take your point that the public isn't in any immediate danger, but what about the expectant mother he targeted?' The question came from a young man sitting on the front row. Melanie didn't recognise him from a local publication, but she took an instant dislike to him for his question alone. 'Are we meant to believe he won't harm others?'

'To clarify a point there, the young mother from the city centre incident was not the target of any particular attack. We believe that Stone, during pursuit, made a snap judgement and it had a poor impact on a member of the public–'

'I'd call a miscarriage more than "a poor impact".'

The interruption came from the back of the room. Melanie knew the voice without seeking clarification on its owner. She couldn't remember Heather Shawly having missed a single one of the press conferences. *Why would she grant us the good grace of starting now?* Melanie thought, while trying to suppress an eye roll. She looked up to direct her response to Shawly.

'Forgive the euphemism,' Melanie started, 'but I didn't think it appropriate to discuss the health concerns, or misfortune, of an innocent member of the public during a press conference.' At that she turned to stare down the rest of the room. 'Are there any further questions?'

'I have one, actually,' Shawly replied. 'By your own admission, DI Watton, Stone likely only targeted that poor mother because he was being pursued.' Melanie felt her gut tense; she knew what was coming. 'Is it fair to say, then, that the loss of her baby rests on the officers – sorry, officer, who was pursuing Stone to begin with?'

Melanie opened her mouth, but Archer beat her to the punch. 'Miss Shawly, I will tolerate you being here as a member of the free press, but you will not fling accusations at hard-working officers while you're in attendance. Is that much clear?' Archer waited for a response but when one didn't arrive she added, 'Let's not forget that you and I have come to blows at these meetings before. It seldom ends well.'

For you, Melanie thought, but Archer was too professional to say it herself.

Melanie was almost disappointed at the ease with which Shawly clambered off her soapbox following one reprimand. The journalist noted something down and flashed Melanie a cocked eyebrow, before the questioning was picked up by another journalist who leapt on the silence. Whether it was Archer's display, or whether there really were no difficult questions to be asked, the rest of the event came together with relative ease. But Melanie still heaved a sigh of relief when she and her colleagues were out of the room.

'Well handled,' Carter said, flashing Melanie a quick look.

'Yes, you took all of that well, DI Watton. I imagine it'll irk Stone when he sees it.' Archer seemed pleased by the idea.

'Apologies, ma'am, but are we sure that's a good thing?' Carter asked, his hand rubbing nervously at the back of his neck.

It was Melanie's turn to beat Archer to the punch. 'He doesn't want me to be handling things; he wants me to be unsettled. If I'm not unsettled, he'll up his game. If he ups his game, he'll get clumsy.' She looked to Archer for approval and the two shared a quick smile.

'Okay, sure, that makes sense.' Although Carter didn't sound convinced. 'But, why does he hate you so much? Could we swing back around to that?'

'DS Carter, you're letting yourself in for an afternoon of story time with a request like that,' Archer said, side-stepping to move around the other two officers. 'I think I'll leave you to catch your team up, DI Watton. Godspeed.'

36

It was nearly the end of the workday. The press conference had been a relative success and, since she and Carter had escaped from the ordeal, Melanie had spent the rest of the day putting together packs on Roderick Stone for her team to study. It wasn't until she'd compiled the various cases connected to him that it dawned on her just how much history they had – just how many reasons he might have for coming after her now. Melanie had asked the team to seat themselves in the briefing area, in front of the evidence board – she was keen to keep the current case at the forefronts of their minds – so she could address them all together. Looking out across them, she relished the feeling of control this gave her; it had only been a short while since she'd worked the case with them, but it felt good to be heading it up again. Despite the niggling concern at how long this would last.

Melanie handed out the slim packs of information to her team as she started talking. 'I've put together some basics about Roderick Stone, largely relating to my past dealings with him. You'll see a list detailing all of the charges and accusations I questioned him over–'

'*All* of these?' Burton was already skimming the pages.

'All of them.' Melanie leaned on the edge of a nearby desk. 'The full reports for all of the cases are available on the system, and I've collected them into a single folder for ease of access. Obviously, with the amount of them, it didn't seem right to put the station or the environment through that amount of printing.' She tried to sound light-hearted but there wasn't enough gentle humour to hide the meaning behind her words; she and Stone had history, and lots of it. 'I'll discuss those cases in a little more detail as we go along but I think it's important that you know some of Stone's background, too, to get a better idea of the sort of man you're hunting.'

'One who hates animals and humans alike, by the looks of it.' Morris' eyes widened as she spotted another entry. 'Wow, really hates them, okay.'

'Stone grew up on the Brookmyre Estate. He was one of four sons born to Tanya Stone, father unknown to the lot of them. We could never quite work out whether the four brothers had the same dad, or whether they were half-siblings. We never found reason to pursue the father, or fathers, though. The best we could tell is that he or they cut and run, and Tanya was left to raise the boys. But on an estate like Brookmyre, it wasn't long before one son or another fell into trouble. Roderick was the likely suspect for most things. His early efforts were before my time, but you can find details of most things in his folder as it reads on the system. He and I didn't cross paths until his first round of animal fighting when he was in his early twenties. We had reason to believe he was convening several dogfights in the local area. I was part of the team to bust up the fights themselves, and see the animals into proper care, but no one was ever willing to turn on Stone for it.'

'Were they scared of him?' Read asked.

'Wait until you get to the end of the file,' Fairer said by way of explanation.

'Were the fights a front for anything else?' Burton added. 'Drug smuggling, money laundering?'

'There was never evidence to suggest that. Stone could clear a tidy profit and there never looked to be a greater motivation for it. He was involved with all sorts of things over the years and frankly his motivation for half of them is questionable.' The beginnings of her walk down memory lane brought everything back for her; the state of the animals when they'd been seized, the escalations of Stone's crimes in the period around the fighting too. She'd known he was trouble from the first time she'd laid eyes on him; getting something to stick had always been another matter. 'There were countless reports of domestic animals going missing around Stone's time on the estates as well, and some of them ended up as part of the fights. Some of them were never found.'

'Why animals? I don't get it,' Fairer asked.

'Was he cutting his teeth for something?'

Melanie raised her eyebrow at Burton's suggestion. 'That was always my theory. I hauled him in at every chance I could, and I don't mind admitting that. He was a time bomb, and I made several cases that he was a killer waiting to happen.'

'But?'

'But, Burton, you can't arrest someone for their intention to hurt others, as I was so frequently reminded by my team at the time. So, I kept pulling him in on minor charges until he eventually attracted the attention of other members of the force.'

'For what?' Morris asked, skimming the folder as though looking for her own answer.

'Drugs ring?' Read looked up.

Melanie clicked her fingers. 'Bingo. The Fox and Hounds was a hot den for it, and I got word from a source of mine that

Stone was making waves there. He was thought to be on good terms with the landlord at the time, who was shifting drugs for extra pocket money at the weekend; meanwhile Stone was using the back of the premises for fighting.'

'What a cracking venue,' Carter said, his tone flat. 'So, the pub holds some significance for the two of you?'

Melanie shrugged. 'Apparently? No more or less than any other pub where I'd pulled him up over the years, but it looks as though it meant something to him.' But she knew exactly why Stone had chosen that place above others; it was the first time she'd let him see exactly how much he'd crawled under her skin. She hadn't even been on duty when she'd approached him there. But there was no mention of that on record anywhere, and Melanie hadn't carried the incident quietly for this long only to blurt it out these years later.

'Touching.' Carter threw his folder down on the empty seat next to him. 'Fast forward?'

'When he wasn't arranging for animal fights, he was training animals – dogs, mostly, although there were rumours that he was dealing with larger predators, illegal imports. The truth of it was that he was either killing an animal, or training an animal to kill another animal, and that last part is where he slipped up. There was one dog in particular – a pit bull, not that that takes much imagination – who he kept with him often. Christ knows what he did to that dog to turn it into what we found.'

Despite her pleas, the animal had eventually been destroyed. Melanie had offered to try and find a centre for it, a specialist who could put in the hours, but her DI at the time had said there was no turning back for it. Melanie had been in her boss' good graces for bagging Stone; but even that hadn't won her this favour. 'Later in his career, Stone took to taking that dog, and others, out to the farms between here and the next town across.'

'Worrying livestock is what did it?' Fairer asked, his head

buried between pages as though he were following the print version of Melanie's narrative while she spoke.

'Worrying livestock is what started it. I fought tooth and nail with the team across the way to get those cases and every time someone gave the bastard an alibi for the time of the attacks all the same. There were cattle being torn apart every other week and we couldn't do anything for it. He was tormenting those farm owners as best as he could. So...'

'One of the farmers took things in hand,' Morris completed the explanation.

The man's face was entirely caved in by the time Stone was finished. The farmer's wife had called the police as soon as the confrontation had started, and Melanie had leapt on the report when she'd got wind of it – but the fight was well underway. Stone and two friends had taken four dogs over to the Loughdown Farm, a good twenty-minute drive out. The howls from the fields and the barking had raised the farmer, Thomas Mullins, Melanie remembered. He'd inherited the property – and the cattle – some years before this, and he couldn't stand to see it leave the family. She had visited him and his wife in the months after the attack. His face had taken longer than expected to heal, and it was still showing signs of the beating by the time Mullins' wife had taken Melanie to one side and asked her not to come around anymore. *An unwelcome reminder*, the other woman had phrased it, which had seemed fair at the time – and still did.

'But I cuffed Stone, there and then. His mates were brought in, animals taken, several more tracked down besides that. People didn't mind turning on him when he was in custody.' She half-laughed. 'There are dribs and drabs besides, you'll find it all in there.' She nodded to the folder Burton was still clutching. 'But that's the meat of what happened between us.'

'How long did he get?' Carter asked.

'Nine years, which it looked as though he served in full.'

'So, the animals, the violence, everything. It's all just escalated while he's been inside,' Read announced and then took a glance around the room, as though he'd asked a question. 'Is Halloway collateral? For the sake of getting animals?'

'Some things can't be brought back to life,' Morris repeated. 'Because of everything he did, I guess? Is that it?' She looked from one colleague to another.

'In the coming days I'm going to be going back over everything Stone and I shared during my time gunning for him. I have personal notebooks still, more like diaries really. They're boxed up at home. I'll bring them in, check them against the official reports, anything I can be doing to help you. From the safety of my desk, that is,' Melanie added, trying to raise a laugh. 'I know there are a lot of unanswered questions. But we'll have our time when we get him back into the interview room...'

37

I think they call it face-saving. When one person has one version of events that they share with folk; something that makes them look better than what actually happened. People paint her like the second coming when she's on the news: DI Melanie Watton catches criminal; saves a baby from a burning building; rescues a cat from a fucking tree. She might look like a good police officer on the surface of things but she wasn't always that way. There were times when she was looking for me, when she went right off the beaten track just to get her way. Maybe that's how she wound up heading a team; she probably cornered someone behind their local boozer one evening and rough-talked her way into the job.

'I'll get you, you know.' She was close enough for me to feel the heat of her. It was something special, it truly was. I'd never been that close to a copper without having my rights read to me. 'You might think you're getting away with this shit, but you won't, I'll see to it.'

'Is that a threat, DC Watton?' I asked, laughed and stepped back. I can still remember the force of her fingertip pressing into my chest. She pushed hard and then gave a little shove, as though she might knock me down completely. Cocksure, she was. 'Are you allowed to go around touching chaps without their permission? Here I am,' I spread my arms out, 'minding my own business, and you're–'

'You're scum, is what you are.' She swayed backwards and it crossed my mind that she might have hit a boozer herself before coming my way. But she steadied. 'Something will stick.'

'You'll see to it, will you?'

She closed the gap between us again. 'You can bet on it.'

'In that case...' I closed what distance was left between us; my belly pressed against the flat of her stomach and I thought she'd move away but she stayed stock still, and then I knew I was in trouble with it all. It takes a strong woman not to back down from a bloke twice her size in the pitch black of a pub car park. There'd never been an officer to make me feel quite so wanted. 'I look forward to seeing more of you.'

She didn't say anything else. She backed away, though, at long last, and kept a stare on me. I wouldn't break eye contact; I've never been the first to back down. Even when her back was to me, I kept a look on her. *She might come back*, I remember thinking. Two mates, ones who'd watched the beginnings of it unfold from the doorway, came out to check me over.

'You've been out a while?'

'Smoking.' I squashed out my third cigarette. 'I just wanted some air.'

'She's got a thing for you, lad.'

I laughed. 'She won't get anything to stick.'

'Don't think that's what he meant,' the other chimed in. He held out an open packet of smokes for me and I took one. Watton had left me chaining. 'How many coppers do you know who pay house calls out of hours?' He sparked up. 'Not something I've seen before.'

'Well,' I lit up with him, 'maybe you just haven't found the right woman.'

When her promises caught up with me, there was almost something friendly about sitting opposite her again. The lot of us – me and my handler; Watton and hers – sat in quiet while my appointed brief flicked through papers and made a mess of working out which charges to defend first. Then the formal introductions were made.

'Can you state your name for the tape, please?' DC Watton asked.

'Don't you know it?'

'It's a formality.'

I edged further down in my seat and leaned back to get a good look at her. 'It's nice to see you again, you know. After that night at the pub, I've thought about this a lot.'

She narrowed her eyes. There was a flicker of something that I'd wager was nerves. 'Your name, please.'

That's when I knew she hadn't told anyone. And I felt like a right little secret.

38

Melanie had spent three days office-bound, and she was already toying with the idea of scratching a tally into the underside of her desk. Archer had implemented new rules that meant Melanie could no longer walk to her car without supervision either – although Archer had called it 'protection' – which meant that leaving the station at the end of a work day had become a group activity. There had been talk of upping her protection further, but she'd made a case against it, arguing that Stone had been vying for her attention, not her life, so the physical risk was minimal. Archer had reluctantly agreed – 'We'll be reviewing this on a rolling basis,' she'd said, getting the last word – but the talk of security at all had set the team on edge. Melanie felt as though the whole operation were being run behind closed doors from her. Although in many ways she thought that was the proper protocol for it. Still, being so far removed from the team meant that her contributions were a fraction of what she would normally bring to a case of this importance – and she didn't like the feeling.

'Lunch?' Burton's voice was a welcome intrusion.

Melanie hadn't realised how much time had passed with her

just sitting. 'Can you come in, and close the door?' She motioned her colleague into the room and Burton followed the instructions. She sat opposite her boss, straight-backed and alert as though expecting an interrogation. *She knows what I'm going to ask*, Melanie thought, one hand gripped into her hair to keep it from her face. 'How much can you tell me?'

Burton sighed and relaxed her posture. 'Nothing.'

'Because there's nothing to tell?'

'Because...' She hesitated. 'Because Archer doesn't want us to tell you what's happening.'

'Will Carter tell me?' Melanie asked, trying a different tactic.

'Not if he knows what's good for him.' Burton softened. 'Only because – well, not only, but not just because either. I'm sorry...' she petered out and took a deep breath, as though steadying herself. 'We're trying to keep you safe.'

Melanie picked up her mobile. 'I'm going to phone through to Archer, see if I can have a chat with her. It isn't fair that you're having to pussyfoot around me, and no one on this team knows Stone better than I do so there must be something I can be doing here.' She sounded optimistic, but the reality was that even when Melanie knew she could be being targeted, Stone still hadn't been a flicker on her radar for it. She knew that was a point against her. But she believed she could redeem herself from it. 'We just need to talk division of labour.'

Burton flashed her boss a pitying look and Melanie tried to pretend she hadn't seen it.

'So, that's a no to lunch?' she asked, standing from the visitor's chair.

Melanie smiled. 'Bring me something back.'

Twenty minutes later she sat across the desk from Archer, waiting for her to finish a call. Melanie had spent so much time in this room over the years, she felt she knew it almost as well as her own office. So the recent addition of a photo frame on the desk – angled at such a way that the photograph inside was visible – stood out almost immediately. She tried to be subtle in case her boss should turn and catch her in the act, but Melanie couldn't resist taking a stare at the subject of the picture: a wild-haired, muddied puppy. Archer had never given away the slightest hint of her life outside of this office, but something about this scamp must have won her over. Melanie tried to guess at the dog's age – he could only have been a few months – but she was startled out of the assessment by the phone slamming back into its cradle.

'Apologies, as always.' Archer sounded how Melanie felt: exasperated. 'He's a handsome thing, isn't he?' She nodded towards the photograph.

So she had seen me, Melanie thought, as she nodded her agreement.

'A live wire, but a handsome one.'

'You've recently got him?'

Archer frowned. 'It's kind of a dog-share situation. My neighbour, he's elderly, lonely, able. We talk across the fence from time to time and he'd mentioned wanting a dog, but feeling too old for one, and – why on earth am I telling you this?' She half-laughed.

It was nice to see a softer side, Melanie thought, but she didn't know how to put that into words without causing offence. 'It's nice to hear about something other than work,' she tried, and from her expression Archer seemed to agree.

'Long story short, we both wanted a dog. He felt too old and I felt too busy.' She turned the photograph towards herself. 'But it was overdue in many ways. Now, why are you here?'

Melanie laughed at her superior's abruptness. 'I need some guidance with the case.'

Archer frowned. 'What case?'

'Stone's.'

'You're not working that case.'

'But I could be.'

'No, DI Watton, you couldn't be. It's a conflict of interest in more ways–'

'Hear me out,' Melanie cut across her, but Archer snapped back.

'No, Melanie, there's nothing to hear out; not from your side at least, but I'll reiterate mine. The only reason you haven't been pulled from duty entirely is because you're a credit to the station, and to your team. I understand they need you and that you can guide them on a consultancy basis, but that doesn't involve hands-on work, and it can't involve hands-on work. Do you understand me? When this thing is wrapped up and boxes have to be ticked, I don't want any doubt in anyone's mind that we did this in any other way than by the book.'

Melanie felt reprimanded, but she still sat quietly, waiting for the second wave that she sensed was coming.

'To add to that...'

There it is, she thought.

'Your safety is on the line. Stone knows we're looking for him, and that we're positive of his ID now. Carter and Burton have been talking to known associates left, right and centre since that press conference, and while we might not know enough yet, what we do know is that he's gunning for you.'

Melanie had noticed her colleagues were out of the office for longer periods than usual, but she hadn't felt ready to push the issue with them. 'Who have they been speaking to?'

'The names on the extensive lists that you provided for them.' Archer leaned hard on 'extensive' and Melanie felt a sting from it. 'We're looking in all of the right places for this guy yet we still can't find him, and if your role was being played by any single member of your team you'd have very different thoughts on the matter.'

'You're right–'

'And another thing– I'm sorry, what? You're not pushing back?'

'I have and it hasn't worked.' She felt too tired for the argument. 'You're right, if this were any member of the team then I'd be signing them off and putting patrols on their property until the situation was resolved.'

Archer spent too long considering the admission, and Melanie worried she'd put ideas in her superior's head. 'I don't want to sign you off duty, Mel,' Archer said at last.

Melanie felt herself grow tense; it sounded like a 'but' was coming.

Archer opened her mouth to speak but the trill of her phone ringing interrupted her. She leaned over to check the caller ID before answering. 'I'm sorry, I need to take this. Archer... Where did you find it? ... I see, where is that in relation to... I see... What sort of condition...'

Archer shot hooded glances at Melanie throughout the conversation. *This is to do with him*, Melanie soon decided. She made a show of looking around the room as though uninterested in the phone call; in truth Melanie was straining her ears to see whether she could decipher which member of the team was on the phone. If it were Read or Fairer; they'd found a vehicle. Burton or Carter; then it must be a person.

'And have you called forensics in?' Archer asked. She checked her watch. 'Did they give you an ETA?... No, she's with me...'

Melanie couldn't ignore the call now. She locked eyes with her superior, but Archer didn't give anything away.

'I'll let her know this latest news... I'm sure, yes... Make sure you report to DS Carter, though. I don't know when I'm next likely to speak to him as he's... Yes, there... Okay, good work, DC Read...'

The van, Melanie thought. She inched forward in her seat, eager for an update as soon as Archer had finished the call.

'They've found something?' she pushed, as the phone collided with its holder.

'The van, yes.'

'From the day of the chase?'

'It seems your DCs have gone around the houses to track down the relevant vans registered to the area, with a number plate ending in the right figures. They soon found one registered as stolen. I dare say it won't be much of a surprise to you that Stone looks to be the thief behind the crime. From there they've tracked it through cameras, and now here we are.'

Melanie felt a flicker of excitement in the base of her stomach. 'This is good news, though, right? If we're homing in on things like this, then they must be getting closer to him.'

Archer looked less enthused. 'The van is in perfect condition, so Read has ordered in forensics to do a full sweep. It looks to have done some mileage since being taken, but Stone, caught on camera too, thanks to your Morris...' Melanie felt a flicker of pride in her team. '...abandoned it in the field over the back of Loughdown Farm.'

The name hung in the air; the farm where Melanie had finally cuffed Stone.

'I see.' Melanie didn't understand it all yet. The fresh leads and new information felt like a break, but one that she didn't know what to do with. 'Well, it's good that we found it,' she finally said, desperate to fill the silence.

'Of course we did,' Archer agreed as she pushed her chair back from her desk. 'He made it quite impossible for us not to.'

39

Carter stood well clear of the vehicle, letting forensics do their sweep in peace. He'd seen Williams work enough times now to know he didn't need his hand held. Carter and Burton had been liaising with a pub-owner in the next town across when the call had come in about the van discovery, and they'd raced over to meet their colleagues. If he was honest, he was amazed Melanie hadn't turned up as well – instructions from Archer be damned – but in her absence he knew the role of senior officer fell to him. He ignored Read's attempts at jokes and remained steady, stern – and nervous beneath the surface.

'Why has he left it like this?' Burton asked, coming to stand next to her partner.

'What do you mean?'

'In such good condition. It's like a shitty, brilliant present.'

Carter's composure broke allowing for a snort of laughter. 'Yep, that's exactly what this is. I can't tell you why yet though. I'm no DI Watton.' The two shared a comforting smile. 'Talk to Read and Fairer, find out the steps they took to get here, would you? Read mentioned something about catching Stone on camera? Let's see if we can't work out where he'd been or where he was going before this.'

'What about you?'

He nodded towards the van. 'I've lost count of how many samples of something or other Williams has pulled from the back of that now. I'm going to play boss.'

Carter came to a stop a metre back from Williams, who was crouched on his knees inside the van. The technician was wearing a visor that worked as a magnifying glass, blowing up the fibres and textures of the vehicle's interior. He looked so focused on the task ahead of him that Carter didn't have it in him to interrupt the work, so he quietly waited until Williams took a break. He looked up and took two deliberate and long blinks, as though clearing his eyes of something, before he moved the glass shield out of his line of vision.

'Ah, DS Carter. I couldn't work out what I was looking at there.' He waddled to the edge of the van and set his legs over the ledge, perching on the bumper. 'You're much less aggressive than DI Watton is about these things,' he commented, but the remark sounded more playful than critical, so Carter let it slide. 'How is she?'

Carter wasn't sure how honest he should be. He tried for something middle of the road between completely calm and totally erratic. 'She's handling it as well as any of us could.' Williams made a face of understanding, as though he might know the hidden message of the remark. *Everyone knows what she's like*, Carter thought, with a pang of feeling for his boss. 'She's eager for results whether she's here or not though,' he said, trying to steer the conversation.

Williams pointed to a kit box some distance away from them both. 'You see all of the sample lines across the top there?' Carter turned and grunted his confirmation. 'They're fibre and hair samples from the back of the van, and I'd wager that all of them are animal.'

Carter frowned at the news, but his forehead smoothed with a quick realisation. 'This is the van he used to move the taxidermy from the first crime scene?'

'I mean, I don't do the detective stuff, but I'd wager on that as well.'

Carter kicked into life with a burst of enthusiasm. 'How close are you to being done?'

'Another half an hour will finish the preliminary stuff but in truth–'

'Can you get the whole thing back to the forensics lab today?' Carter interrupted.

Williams flashed a look of annoyance. 'In truth,' he continued where he'd left off, 'we could do with getting the whole thing back to base, to sweep the back of the van entirely. I've taken hair samples from the front too, and they do look human, so I'll be able to run samples to confirm the driver, the same applies for fingerprints. Still, I'd like to know that we've pulled as much from this as we can.'

Hair samples, fingerprints. What's this guy thinking? Carter tried not to be grounded by these small mercies, but he couldn't shake the feeling they were somehow being played by their suspect. 'Okay, make whatever arrangements you need and let us know what we can be doing. But when you get the van back, in between sweeping for hair and prints, would you see whether you can get any traces of blood?'

'You're expecting some?' Williams replied, lowering his visor back in place.

'I am if this was Stone's first getaway vehicle...'

~

They were technically ten minutes away from going home, but none of the team were rushing. Instead, they were seated in front of the interactive whiteboard, while Morris orchestrated a screen share. Carter and Burton needed to see blow by blow how they'd managed to track the vehicle to the field – including a stop along the way.

'Even criminals need to get petrol,' Morris explained, clicking through a series of staggered images that clearly showed their suspect pulling into a petrol station and climbing out of the van from the driver's side. She hit another two buttons and clicked in for a closer view. 'This is definitely one and the same man who DI Watton chased through the city centre, so we can confirm that much, and it doesn't look as though there's anyone travelling alongside him for this drop off at least.' She pointed to the shadow of the passenger seat with her cursor.

'That's great, Morris. We need to get in touch with the petrol station to see how he–'

'Cash,' she said with a smile.

'The cashier said he was a very polite man,' Read added, in a tone that suggested the very idea was ludicrous. 'In terms of screen time we lose him about five minutes after this.' There were accompanying clicks throughout Read's explanation, as Morris played out the last of their footage. 'We plotted out the journey he'd taken up to that point and took a wild guess.'

'Which paid off,' Burton said, giving her colleague a congratulatory punch on the arm.

'It paid off big time, so well done, everyone.' Carter tried to sound cheerful; he didn't know how Melanie managed it. He took another glance towards her office. *Where the hell is she?* They hadn't seen sight or sound of her since they returned to the station earlier in the day, and that alone seemed suspicious. But Carter couldn't let the team get side-tracked. 'Forensics have taken the whole vehicle in for inspection now but it's going to be a few days before we get any results back from that. I've hurried them as best as I can.'

'Can we set the DI on them? That usually gets people shifting,' Fairer asked, and the team shared a gentle laugh. Carter realised they must all have the same worries about Melanie's lack of presence. He'd call Archer before the day was out, he decided.

'Morris, you mentioned something earlier you wanted to share?'

She cleared her throat. 'While you were all out chasing the van, I started poking around in Stone's more recent history. He's obviously a control freak, and he evaded capture for so long that it's hardly a surprise his nose was put out of joint when he was finally apprehended. But doesn't this seem like an awful lot of trouble for revenge?'

'People have snapped over less,' Read replied.

'People as methodical as Stone though? He knew exactly what he was doing when the first team were trying to pursue him, and even now, he knows what he's doing with us. There are brains there, so I wondered about the logic.' She closed the CCTV screens and pulled up what looked to be a scanned document. 'This is the death certificate for Owen Stone, Roderick's youngest brother.' She kept quiet while the team scanned the details.

'He died while Roderick was in prison?' Burton clarified.

'Yep, and did you spot how he died?' Morris motioned with the cursor again.

'Blunt force trauma,' Fairer said, mostly to himself. 'He was murdered?'

'Murdered by someone Roderick Stone owed money to.' Morris sounded smug and Carter could understand why; this was some motivation. 'I tracked down the team that worked the case at the time–'

'Wait,' Carter interrupted, 'why didn't that come to us? Watton would have been around then.'

'Because the murderer was already being investigated in three other cities. When the murder took place, it briefly came across our desks but never made it as far as MIT because so many other areas had a vested interest in it.'

'How much money did Roderick owe?' Burton asked.

'Now that, I couldn't find out.' Morris closed the window and leaned back in her chair. 'But I'm waiting on a call back from the detectives left over from the original cases, although they look to be dotted around different cities now. I'm also waiting on a call back from the governor at Stone's prison. I tried to ha– access, I tried to access their records online but I haven't been able to. The governor wasn't available today, but we should get a call back tomorrow.'

'Jesus, Morris.' Read moved to give his colleague a high five and she reciprocated.

'Right? People are exhausting, I don't know how you do it.'

Carter half-laughed. 'You can be back on computers tomorrow if you prefer.'

'Let her chase up her own leads, DS Carter. You might be busy tomorrow.' The intrusion came from the doorway; Archer was slumped against the frame. Carter had no idea how long she'd been listening in on their developments. 'It sounds like it's been a productive day?' She stepped into the room then, closing the gap with the team.

'We believe we've taken some positive steps,' Carter replied.

'Excellent. I want you all to keep me in the loop with these developments wherever you can, providing that isn't a problem for anyone?' She looked from one member of the team to another as she spoke. It could have been a sincere question, Carter thought, but something about it felt more like a challenge. 'Brilliant. In that case, I'd say your work is done for the day.' She turned to leave, but Carter needed to catch his moment.

'I hope you won't mind me asking, ma'am, but, DI Watton...' His question petered out as Archer turned. Her face was set in an expression that suggested she'd been expecting this.

'After the discovery of the van this afternoon, DI Watton and I had some further discussion about her presence in the workplace. We decided that for her safety, primarily, but also for your safety as a team it would be better for her to remain at home for now.'

'She's on leave?' Read blurted and the question was met with a hard kick from Burton.

'Yes, she's on leave.'

'For how long?' Carter asked. His tone was hard-edged.

Archer sighed. 'Indefinitely.'

You decided, Carter thought then, *you decided this was better.* He felt a bitterness rise like bile. The professional in him understood the decision, but his personal feelings for Melanie were stirring something else in him. He tried to swallow down his sincere reaction in favour of a more neutral one. 'Will you be replacing her?'

Archer looked surprised at the suggestion. 'I sincerely hope not. You'll take the lead in her absence, as the next senior member of the team, and DI Watton will be cleared for duty again when this case is put behind us all.'

'But until then–'

'Until then, DS Carter, she's to be kept as far away from these proceedings as possible.'

40

It was nearly seven when Melanie's front doorbell rang out through the silence of the house. On her walk from the kitchen and along the hallway, she'd narrowed down the list of likely suspects: Carter and/or Burton were the frontrunners. She and Archer hadn't left things on especially good terms that afternoon, so it seemed unlikely that her superior would be making an out-of-hours call. As a parting shot – Melanie couldn't help but see it that way – her superior had informed her there would be a patrol car driving past the house every couple of hours, at least. So it could have been a friendly uniformed officer, but as Melanie weighed the possibility up, she landed on it being unlikely – unless something had happened. *God, what if something's happened?*

She'd managed to make herself unreasonably nervous about opening the door by the time she'd arrived at it. She inched it open, peering around slowly to see who the unexpected guest was. But her concerns were quickly washed away by the sight of Hilda. She'd been looking about the space around her when the door had first opened, but now she turned to the nervous Melanie and lifted a grocery bag.

'I hear there's no excuse for us not to have dinner now.'

Melanie's stern expression cracked into a smile. 'You've heard.'

'I've heard.' Hilda stepped forward, bustling her way into the house with a familiarity that Melanie found comforting. 'Your team would not hold up well under torture. Am I okay to go straight through to the kitchen?' she said, already well on her way down the corridor.

'Of course.' Melanie closed the door and swallowed a small laugh as she watched Hilda. 'Make yourself at home.'

Hilda had brought with her a jumble of ingredients that she quickly set about distributing over Melanie's kitchen counter. The hob had never seen more action than a pot of boiling pasta before now, which is what Melanie had been planning to make when she could bring herself to eat.

'I can cook for us?' she offered.

Hilda smirked. 'Pasta with tomato and basil?'

'Or you can cook, whatever.' Melanie tried to sound light-hearted, but the submission had sounded ungrateful, even to her own ears. 'I'm sorry, that came out–'

'Thankless and a bit grumpy, yep.' Hilda was opening drawers and closing them again. 'Peeler?'

'Second drawer over.'

'Ah, the only one I didn't check.' She opened the drawer and pulled out the instrument. 'Go and sit down,' she said without looking back at Melanie. 'I've got a boatload of peeling to do and I'd wager you've got some things to get off your chest.'

In the comfort of the kitchen Melanie felt a surge of something like bravery. She leaned forward and set a single kiss on Hilda's cheek, before she dropped back against the worksurface behind her. 'What are we having?'

'Haggis.' A beat of silence passed between them; too long not to be awkward. Hilda let it roll for a second longer before she looked at Melanie and promptly burst out laughing. 'I'm pulling your leg. Salmon, spinach, vegetables. Now sit down, would you?'

Not for the first time that day, Melanie followed orders. While Hilda shuffled around the space, Melanie relayed the events of the day – starting with Archer.

'You seem more annoyed with her than you do with him,' Hilda noted.

'Him who?'

'Him, the killer.'

'I'm not annoyed with him.'

'I would be.' Hilda opened the oven and put in a tray of peeled vegetables. 'That'll be about forty minutes, I should think. Why aren't you annoyed with him?'

'He's just an idiot with an axe to grind.' But no sooner had Melanie said this, and she wondered at the truth of it. 'He probably said the same about me at one time.'

'You had an axe to grind with him?'

Melanie flicked through her history with Stone; a montage of not-quite-arrests and charges that wouldn't stick. It had become an axe to grind over the months of his law-breaking, but Melanie also thought it was part of her job to pursue men like Stone.

'I gunned for him,' she eventually admitted. 'But I wasn't falsifying claims against him or looking for issues where there weren't any. He was constantly breaking the law, constantly abusing animals. It was only a matter of time before he killed someone.' The comment came out with conviction, but a terrible thought followed it. 'But I'm the person that pushed him to that.' Melanie dropped her head into her hands. 'I'm the one who made all this happen.'

'Tosh.' Hilda turned back to the stove. 'We're responsible for our own shortcomings, Mel, no one forces our hand into anything.'

'But that's just not true. If I'd have let things go then maybe–'

'Balls.' Hilda turned back and gesticulated with a stirring spoon as she spoke. 'Utter balls, Mel. You're a bloody good police officer and this pillock has prompted a crisis of conscience that's made you realise you might be human as well as a copper. If he gets in your head, then he's already done what he set out to do. So, leave the woe is me elsewhere because it doesn't wash with me, woman.'

Melanie lifted her head and flashed a tired smile. 'Thank you.'

'You're quite welcome.' Hilda set the spoon on the counter behind her and came to join Melanie at the table. 'Look,' she grabbed her hand, 'I'm saying all of this because I care about you deeply, but this is a shit situation and you can't afford to lose your nerve.'

'Can I tell you something?'

Hilda's expression changed. 'About the case?'

'About the killer. I didn't ever list it in the files, but I went to see him once, when I wasn't on duty. We'd got wind there was a fight happening and I asked– I asked my team to cover it, and they said I needed to let Stone drop until I had something concrete. So, I went, out of hours, on my own. The fight wasn't happening after all, but Stone was there–'

'Are you about to tell me something illegal?' Hilda interrupted, and Melanie shook her head. 'Then whatever happened, you need to let go.'

'But shouldn't I tell someone that I did that?'

'What, that you acted unprofessionally? That you let a case get to you? So you're human, Mel, big deal, we covered that. You think you're the only detective ever to crack?' Hilda spoke with a confidence that Melanie found reassuring. 'You don't need to tell me or anyone else what happened with Stone that night. You didn't plant evidence; you didn't deck the guy. You acted in a way that's uncharacteristic of you, now, maybe, but you were a junior officer then.'

'Busting Stone got me a promotion though.'

'So the arsehole brought some good. Whoopee.' Hilda returned to her spot by the stove and went back to stirring. 'Now, will we watch something with dinner, or will we be civilised and talk more? Because I can moan about students for months after today…'

The rest of the evening rolled out like the pair were an average couple discussing their day. And Melanie found something comforting in their companionship. Although she drew a line at Hilda staying over; she couldn't decide whether Hilda's offer had been made from desire, pity, or concern – perhaps all three. But Melanie's work life had dictated enough of their time together, and she wanted their shared evenings to be something special, not forced.

'Thank you for the offer though,' she said, four times over on their walk towards the front door, for fear that Hilda mightn't make the offer again. 'Another time, if that's–'

Hilda kissed Melanie square on the mouth, halting her sentence. 'You're overdoing it.'

'Will you let me know you're home safe?'

'It's a short drive and I'm a big woman, but sure.' Hilda stifled a laugh. She opened the door and stepped out into the cool evening. 'You'll lock this up behind me?'

Melanie nearly snorted at Hilda's question. But it quickly dawned on her that Hilda's worries were perhaps more legitimate than her own. 'Of course. Bottom and top.'

The two shared a quick goodbye before Melanie bolted the door closed, as promised. The house was almost too quiet now, without Hilda's booming vocals, and Melanie was reminded again at how much she liked having her companionship. She trod along the corridor back to the kitchen and collected the dirtied dishes from their evening. But no sooner had she turned the tap and her doorbell echoed through the house again. There was a flicker of optimism in her. *Maybe Hilda forgot something*, Melanie reasoned, looking around the kitchen for evidence. Despite finding nothing, she hurried along the hallway without a flicker of the nerves she'd felt earlier. It took longer than usual to open the door on account of the extra locks. She undid the top bolt with one thought: *What if it's Hilda?* But undid the bottom with another: *What if it's not?* She tried to peer through the frosted window of the door for a sign of life behind, but she couldn't see any.

'It's probably Hilda,' she announced, louder than necessary, in case the Hilda she'd imagined standing behind the door would hear her and confirm her suspicions – probably with a laugh. A reply didn't come. But Melanie – unsure whether she was acting on her detective's instincts, or against them – inched open the door anyway...

41

The woman had been found in the centre of a football field on the outskirts of the city. Whoever had left her had chosen a spot beneath the floodlights, ensuring a quick discovery. It was hard to discern the victim's age exactly due to the extensive disfigurements. Waller guessed the damage had been deliberate, either to try to prevent a positive identification – or simply to allow the killer to expel significant ill-feeling on the victim. He'd seen both in his career, but in this case he sincerely hoped it was the former. There had been an ID card at the scene, flung a metre or so away from the cadaver, but Waller wasn't ready to believe it truly belonged to their victim.

'What are you thinking, George?' Archer came to a stop alongside him and stared down at the woman. The build and frame made sense, but Waller had hopes...

'There's every chance it isn't her. I'm not going to know until I've taken samples.' This was the most the pair had spoken for years, yet somehow the poor feelings he'd harboured for Archer had dispersed quickly in the face of this tragedy. 'Have you been able to raise her?'

'I've got uniformed officers on their way.'

'Carter?'

Archer shook her head. 'He's likely to panic.'

'Too bloody right he is, and well within his rights too.' Waller snapped on a glove. 'If you don't call him then I will. It's utter tripe not to have him involved already.' The outburst came without thinking but Archer's raised eyebrow halted a second wave. Waller held his hands up in surrender. 'What do I know? I'm just the schmuk that has to cut her open and see if Melanie falls out.'

The ringtone of Carter's phone pulled him from his half-sleep. He'd been dozing on the sofa – a terrible habit he'd adopted of late – but he snatched at the handset before the noise could wake Emily. He didn't take the time to look at the caller's ID.

'Carter, I'm sorry to call you so late. It's Superintendent Archer. Can you talk?'

Carter fumbled; he felt a knot form in his stomach. 'What's happened?'

'We've found a body. It's over on the Parktown Playing Fields, do you know it?'

'The other side of town, yeah.'

'It was called in an hour or so ago and uniformed officers responded, to make sure that it was a legitimate issue. I was called shortly after.'

Carter felt the same knot tightening with every clipped sentence.

'There was an identification card thrown some distance from the body which was obviously checked on arrival. We haven't been able to verify the card yet, Carter, but – Christ, the card belongs to Watton. It's her ID card for the station.'

'I need to take Emily to my parents' house.' Carter kicked

into action. 'I can be with you in half an hour, maximum, I'll do what I can to make it sooner.'

'We're doing what we can here already, Carter. Waller is on site and he's trying to ID the body. I've called uniformed officers to get to Watton's home but I'm yet to hear anything back from them. I won't turn down an extra pair of hands here, of course, but you need to go there as a matter of urgency. Are you comfortable with that?'

'Fu–Sorry, Christ, yes, ma'am, of course. I'll get to her as soon as I can.' He took a deep pull of air to steady him; he needed to remember who he was talking to. 'Has DC Burton been made aware of the situation, ma'am, or anyone else in the team?'

'No.'

'Can they– should I–' Carter gave up the sentence and started over. 'Do I need to tell them, ma'am? I mean, is this something they should be aware of?'

Archer fell quiet for a moment and Carter thought there might be a plan forming. 'Call Burton. She might be able to get to DI Watton's home before you. If she can't raise her, then she's to come here. I'll contact the rest of the team when we have more information.'

'I understand, ma'am. I'll be with you when I can be.'

'Carter, look, there's something else. The ID card... there was a taxidermy structure left alongside it.' Her inhale was audible through the speaker; Carter could hear the nerves in her. 'The bastard left a stuffed mouse.'

Burton's fist pounded against the wood of the front door and Melanie answered almost immediately. Once her junior was safely inside Melanie bolted the door again.

'Are you okay?' Burton asked, her voice breathless.

'I don't know, Chris, truthfully.' Melanie stepped around her colleague and walked into the living room. 'I tried Carter but I couldn't get through, and it felt dramatic to call Archer for something like this.' She half-laughed. 'I bet she'd bloody love it after the talk we had earlier. She told me I needed to be taking care of myself, taking this more seriously.' She sat on the edge of the sofa and Burton quickly came to join her.

'No one could have known this would happen,' she replied, closing the distance between them.

It wasn't quite a reassuring arm around the shoulder, but Melanie was grateful for the press of a thigh against her own. Despite it being no longer than ten minutes since they'd got off the phone, Melanie had felt the house shift from a safe space to somewhere threatening – somewhere threatened – in that time.

'Should I try Carter again?' Burton broke the silence.

'I don't know, maybe? He's the senior officer, so, I suppose.'

'Okay, well, I'm his partner.' Burton nudged her superior and gave her a tight smile that Melanie thought was meant to be reassuring. 'I'll call him. While I'm doing that, maybe you could get the structure so I can take a look?'

Melanie nodded along and then turned to meet her colleague's stare. 'I used gloves.'

'Good, boss, that's a really good thing.' Burton paused to pull her phone from her pocket, in time for it to hum in her hand. 'Serendipity,' she whispered to herself as she answered the call. 'Carter, I was just– What? No, no you've got that wrong...'

Melanie moved from living room to dining room. The space was largely open plan, but still she'd placed the thing as far away from her as she could. There were two fresh pairs of gloves on the table already; she hadn't known whether her colleague would want to handle the item. But she started to pull apart a pair for herself, snapping them on with a ferocity that made her wince, even though she couldn't feel the discomfort. She'd numbed in the last thirty minutes, which she thought may be a good thing. She stared down the item as though they were in direct opposition to each other, and she half-listened to whispers of Burton's phone call.

'You need to get over here then... Call her and explain, tell her...'

Trish? Melanie wondered. *Who else would he need to call at this time of night?* She enjoyed the intrusion of these thoughts, allowing them to steer her away from the task at hand.

'But how did he even...'

Melanie tucked gloved fingertips around the edge of the structure. It was set on wood, which at least made it easy to carry. Although, for a second time that evening, she was surprised at the weight of the thing as she lifted it from her dining room table. She felt her breath begin to stagger in her chest as she moved with the abandoned creature.

'Carter, I'm sitting right in front of her... I don't know either... No, she isn't dead... Can you just... Okay, okay, I will... Bye.'

'I'm dead?' Numb to even this announcement, Melanie asked the question in a deadpan tone. The animal was deposited on the coffee table now, only inches away from Burton, who seemed fixated with it already. 'What– Did something–' Her sentences broke off, and Melanie back-stepped towards the armchair in the corner of the room. A safe distance, she decided, from the taxidermy.

'And where was this?' Burton asked, glazing over Melanie's half-questions.

'Front doorstep.'

'There was no sign of him at all?'

'Nope. Hilda had only been gone minutes.'

'Have you two spoken?' Burton snapped.

Melanie gave a slow nod. 'She called me to say she was home

safe, which I asked her to do. I haven't said anything about...' She petered out and gestured to the figure. 'I'm dead?'

'Carter will explain when he gets here.' Burton's stare was set on the creature opposite her still. 'I hope.'

Melanie opened her mouth to reply, but she suddenly felt like, for tonight at least, there were very few words left. She leaned back in the chair and tucked her legs up onto the seat beneath her. Taking a quick glance at Burton – who was still enamoured with the latest delivery – Melanie soon found herself staring at it too. It was lying on its side but with its head upright, giving it an alert appearance; the eyes added to the effect. The fur was an ombre of browns, building to a striped pattern across the creature's stomach, but its tail graded into black rather than brown. Its paws were a perfect white still, as though it had never set foot outside. Melanie had assumed this was another one of Halloway's creations. Circumstances aside, she had to admit it was impressive. To begin with, she'd mistaken it for a real-life cat.

42

Carter slammed the desk phone down and filled out the last of his notes from the conversation. Williams had put a rush through on forensics for the van. It had been a tactical decision to clear their plate for forensics on the latest murder victim, Carter suspected, but either way he was grateful. Plus, these latest results made their growing evidence against Stone even more concrete.

From force of habit, Carter looked towards Melanie's office. At this point on a normal morning he'd be going in to give her an update. But the closed door brought home again the reality of their situation – and the urgency of it. Instead of giving the update, he'd been running it. He checked his watch and noted there was only five minutes before he and the team were meant to convene in front of the evidence board for a catch-up. It was more than enough time to get a coffee, Carter thought. But as he stood from his desk Burton kicked open the door to the communal office space, carrying a takeout cup in either hand.

'If one of those is for me then I might promote you,' Carter said as his partner closed in.

She set the cup down on his desk. 'Do you have that kind of power?'

'I'll award myself that kind of power.'

'It's gone to your head already.' Burton laughed, but Carter's expression was a saddened one. 'Oh, Carter, I didn't mean–'

'No, no I know.' Behind Burton he spotted the rest of the team falling into place. 'We should...' he nodded behind her, and then shifted to join Morris, Read and Fairer in front of a fresh evidence board. Carter had requested it as the old one – rammed full of taxidermy structures and hidden messages – wasn't ready for another murder to be added. *Neither am I*, he thought as he stood stock still in front of the team. *I should be sitting down there with them.* 'Okay, I'll kick us off with a few things we already know, but we can see them in stone now.'

'Was that a pun?' Read asked.

Carter remembered all the tense team meetings that Melanie had seen them through; how she'd always allowed for their humour, even tried to bring her own sometimes. He slapped on the same smile he used when he and Emily were watching *Frozen Two* and said, 'Ah, shit. No, but it could have been. I spoke to Williams over in forensics just now and they're finished with the van. It won't come as a huge surprise to anyone, but they found DNA that's a match to Stone in the front of the vehicle, from hair lifted from the head rest. They also managed to pull some clean prints from the steering wheel too. And, for bonus points, there was blood on the steering wheel.'

'Halloway's?' Burton asked.

'Got it in one.'

'So, we can prove that it was the getaway vehicle?'

'Which brings me to my next revelation. The back of the van showed animal hair that likely belongs to foxes and domestic cats, as well feathers and skin shreds similar to that of a bird.'

'Can they be any more specific?' Fairer asked.

'They're working on it but frankly, after the body turned up, matching animals' DNA hasn't been a priority,' Carter admitted.

'Oh, the body. Is this where Read and I step in?'

'The floor is yours, boys. Make sure one of you writes up as you go.' Carter took the seat next to Burton. He felt a wash of relief from looking at the evidence board at this angle again.

'Grace Evans,' Fairer started, as Read scribbled up information behind him. Their victim had been disfigured to the point that she was unrecognisable. Stone had been kind – or clumsy – enough to leave her real identification details in a handbag discarded close by – but Waller had said on discovery that he'd need dental records before he could confirm who the woman really was. 'Thanks to the positive ID, we've managed to find out a fair bit about her. She's thirty-six, lives in the city centre with her partner of twelve years. They weren't married and don't have children. Evans was a financial adviser. She used to work with a larger firm in Leeds but set up on her own when her and her chap, Phillip Tate, moved here. He tells us there was no bad feeling between her and the previous firm. They've moved to a different city entirely too, so there was no chance of Evans making competition for her firm.'

'What about the partner? Any bad feeling with him?' Morris asked.

'Nothing that we've managed to find out about so far. We've spoken to two friends already, but Tate has provided us with contact details for more so that's our job for the remainder of today. The two we've spoken to said the pair were a happy couple, known them for most of the time they've been together and, minor arguments aside, everything seemed to rumble on okay.'

'Has Waller come back with anything on the state we found Evans in yet?'

'Yes, he has. That was a nice alarm call for Read at 6.15 today.'

Fairer turned and nudged his partner who flashed an unimpressed expression.

'Waller called you at six in the morning?' Carter couldn't keep the amusement from his voice, despite trying.

'Yes, boss, yes he did.'

'Wait, why didn't he call me?' Carter asked, his tone changing.

'Would you have liked that wake up?' Burton replied.

'Fair question. As you were, Fairer.'

'Cause of death looks to have been manual strangulation, determined by the type of bruising that had formed around the victim's neck. Waller reported what looked to be thumbprints, not that we can draw any ID from them. But they've contributed to Waller's conclusion on the strangulation ruling. He found ante-mortem bruising on the victim's arm that suggests a struggle, and he also found blood underneath her fingernails to support that.'

'What about the damage to her face?' Carter asked the big question; the one they'd all been dreading the answer to.

'Post mortem. Waller thinks a knife was used to inflict the majority of the damage. There were signs of skin having been cut and lifted to–'

'Okay.' Carter held up a hand. 'Include it in your report.'

Fairer nodded. 'Yep, that's fair.'

'Imagine that at six in the bloody morning,' Read said as he turned to face the room.

'That's us up to date, boss. We haven't heard anything from forensics yet, and I'm guessing Williams didn't pass anything on this morning?'

Carter shook his head. 'They're still working through everything as far as I know, but from all this it sounds like there's a lot to work with, so we can only hope they'll pull some results for us. I know Evans has been sucked into the Stone case but she's a victim in her own right. She still deserves some justice for this.' He tried to keep his tone measured, steady. 'Did Evans' partner provide a picture?'

'Oh, shit, sorry.' Fairer thumbed through his folder before retrieving an image. He handed it across to Read to pin on the board, right aligned from the mess of notes. 'It's clear why Stone chose her, although I'm sad to admit it.'

Read stepped away from the board to give the rest of the team a clear look at the woman. She was happy in the image; the background looked to be a bar, maybe a restaurant. Carter wondered whether she'd been out with friends when the picture was taken, and the thought caused a pull of sadness in him. Her smile was asymmetrical, tucked up to cause a pert dimple in her left cheek. Her hair fell longer than her shoulders, and was a dark brown; there might have been lighter shades, *highlights?* Carter wondered, but he wasn't qualified to tell. He, and the rest of them, studied the image from top to bottom and back again. Although it was clear from the first look what Fairer had meant; Carter could understand Stone's choice as well, in a sickening way. Because in the right lighting, Grace Evans bore a startling similarity to Melanie Watton.

43

He closed the door to Melanie's office behind him. The room felt wrong, somehow alien now without his boss inside. It hadn't been Carter's first choice, but he needed some privacy from the team and this was the least conspicuous place at the moment. Any time one of them left the office, the others would sit up on their haunches, a mob of meerkats looking out for their missing relative – or, more likely, wondering what was being investigated without them. So he'd told Burton he needed a minute to call Trish, and he'd slipped away quietly without causing alarm. But inside the empty office – already stale from three days of being sealed shut – Carter wished that he'd chanced somewhere else. This wouldn't take long, at least; he'd nearly convinced himself she wouldn't answer. It even crossed his mind that Melanie didn't have the phone but someone else might, Archer maybe. Still, he couldn't let go of a sliver of hope.

He pressed the phone to his ear, and held his breath during the long silence that stretched between the connection tone and...

'You've reached DI Melanie Watton. I can't get to the phone right now but–'

'Fuck's sake.'

He'd called Melanie's mobile seventeen times in the last three days. Under any other circumstances, he'd be pulling himself in for questioning. Five calls in it had become obvious that her phone was turned off – although not disconnected – but he'd convinced himself that it was a temporary measure. Since the night of the murder – the night of the home delivery too – he'd spent a mere two hours with his boss, while initial statements were made. Since then Archer had stashed her away somewhere, like a pirate protecting loot. Carter shifted between being too scared to ask what had happened to his boss, and wanting to march into Archer's office and demand an explanation. This morning, it was the latter.

So, he felt a stab of gratitude when a knock came at the door, followed by Morris' nervous expression peering round at him. 'I'm sorry to interrupt, boss.'

Carter slipped his phone back into his pocket. 'No intrusion, it's just family stuff.' The lie came easily to him. So far the team hadn't pressured him for information about their rightful boss, and Carter wanted to keep it that way. The last thing he needed was to openly admit he knew nothing of her whereabouts either. 'What can I do you for?'

'It's more what I can do you for, I hope. I wanted to run through the facial recognition details with you, if you've got a second; and Burton and I have been looking over some vehicle leads as well.'

'Lead the way.' He followed Morris to her desk, where Burton was already positioned. She looked to be clicking through a string of grainy images. But when Morris dropped back into her own seat Burton shifted out of the way, letting her colleague take over again.

'Facial recognition?' Carter asked, nodding at the images.

Morris frowned. 'It isn't an exact science. I'm doing what I can here, but I've outsourced some of this to the technology team. Nell Burgess over there kind of lives and breathes this stuff so I've asked her to pitch in. They've got a handful of images of Stone, including the most recent ones we pulled from CCTV, which is also what we're working from.' From a series of clicks she pulled up a collage of Stone's face, at various points in ageing, starting with his first mugshot and working up to just a week ago. 'We've used these pointers,' she gestured to different spots on Stone's face as she spoke, 'to try to track him through facial recognition software that we're using alongside general CCTV footage. We're looking specifically at the high street and the essential shops. But we're waiting to hear back from petrol stations in the local area, and street views surrounding a number of pubs.'

'Morris, how much material is this pulling?' Carter didn't understand the technology side of things – he'd as much as proved that during their previous cases – but to him this sounded above and beyond.

Morris ran a hand through her ruffled hair and looked back at the screens. 'I just– I can't.' She paused and took a deep exhale. 'I don't know what else I can be doing.' Burton gave her shoulder a quick squeeze and Morris smiled at the gesture. 'It's a lot of material and it'll take time, but...' she petered out, her explanation tangled up in her ragged breathing. Carter sensed tears weren't too far away, so he pulled up a chair and sat level with her.

'We're going to find him.' His tone was level, controlled; even he believed it. Morris opened her mouth to reply but Carter cut her off. 'No. Whatever it is, no. We're going to find him because the boss needs us to.' Morris nodded and gave her superior a tight smile. 'Talk vehicles to me,' he said, trying to steer their concentration into something.

'So, Morris and I were trying to scout through recent reports of vehicles that had been stolen over the last few days,' Burton started, and Morris looked relieved for the respite. 'We went back to the night the van was dumped. We're yet to work out how he got from the farm fields back into town.'

'Unless he walked it,' Morris added.

'But either way, he would have needed a new mode of transportation sharpish. So we looked over reports from that night, and the nights following. We started with vans, on the assumption that he might trade one style for another, but the only van that was reported missing was taken two days later and it had a huge catering logo on the side of it, so, hardly the least conspicuous of things. We've tried narrowing the search for properties on the outskirts of town, which would have been the first he came to if he'd walked back from the dump site, and there were even fewer results to wade through for that. So, we eventually decided to try to combine sources.' Burton leaned back then, as though making physical space for the explanation Morris was about to deliver.

'We're searching for him on traffic cameras. We're still going to look through reports of theft, for both vans and cars that were stolen on the night of the van dump. But we're also liaising with the traffic team to try to utilise their cameras, as well as distributing Stone's image to their street workers and motorway workers.'

'Motorway?' Carter questioned. 'You think he might flee?'

Morris shrugged. 'We think he might do anything.'

'The last thing we're looking into, which is on our list for today–'

'How long is today?' Carter interrupted. 'Just so I'm clear on your workload.'

Burton gave a playful eye roll. 'We're also contacting local car dealerships. Stone has given us a lot to work with since the murder and the...' she trailed off. 'Since DI Watton. It occurred to us that stealing another car might be a step too far in making himself known. But what if he bought one? We've got no idea what his revenue stream is right now.'

'On revenue,' Morris took over. The two were like a double act, and Carter followed one to the other, feeling a swell of respect for the pair of them. They'd only liaised as a team yesterday and somehow, while he'd been ringing through to Melanie's voicemail at intermittent intervals, his whole squad had arrived at these points. *What am I even bringing to this?* Carter wondered, with an all too familiar feeling of self-doubt. 'Read and Fairer haven't heard back from forensics for the Evans murder. But they're spending the day calling through the victim's remaining contacts and then chasing down Stone's family.'

'Chasing them down?' Carter's respect was replaced with alarm. *Are they going rogue?*

'They're planning to discuss it with you,' Burton jumped in. 'Obviously, they won't do anything without your approval.' She was trying to pacify him and, although Carter saw it as an obvious attempt, it still soothed his immediate concerns.

'Okay. Okay, well I'll...' He pointed to where Read and Fairer sat huddled. 'If you need anything though?' Burton and Morris nodded and unison, and Carter left them to their investigations. Somehow, he felt optimistic and utterly deflated all at once...

Carter knew that Melanie always called ahead. So, he also knew he was acting out of protocol by simply turning up outside Archer's office. But he wanted the element of surprise. Or, more accurately, he didn't want to give Archer time enough to come up with an excuse, or a generic line. He tapped his knuckles firmly against the door and waited for his summons to enter, which seemed to take the best part of a minute.

'Come on then.' She already sounded irritated, even from this safe distance. But her expression at least appeared friendly when Carter stepped into the room. 'DS Carter, apologies, you caught me on a phone call then. Seat?' She gestured to the empty chair opposite.

Carter resisted the urge to look around the office. But in his peripheral vision he spotted the changes: the new picture of the dog; the flowers; the muddied boots in the corner. They were touches of Archer he hadn't noticed before. 'Thank you, ma'am. Forgive me for the intrusion.'

'Not at all. I told you, now more than ever you're welcome in this office.'

It was true, Carter thought, she had said that. But he hadn't really believed she'd meant it.

'You've come to talk to me about the case?' she asked.

'In a sense. I want to talk to you about DI Watton.' Archer's expression shifted, but Carter couldn't read the new emotion. 'I've been trying to call her, but I can't get through.'

'That'll be because her phone is off.' Archer spoke matter-of-factly.

'No, I guessed. I haven't left messages. I was nervous of going to the house. I'm not sure why, in truth. In case she didn't want visitors, maybe. I thought – well, it struck me as odd that she hadn't reached out to any of us. At least to see how the case is going.'

'She's under strict instructions not to.'

'Right.'

There was a full and awkward silence in the room then, elbowing its way out.

'DS Carter, you're obviously angling at something and you're making a hash of alluding to whatever it is, so why don't you come out with it.' Although her words were stern, there was something more understanding in her tone that gave Carter the encouragement he needed.

'Where is she?' he asked plainly, before adding, 'Ma'am.'

Archer smiled. 'I can't tell you that, Carter.'

'Is she safe?'

'Of course.'

Carter breathed a light sigh of relief. 'But we can't have contact with her?'

'No. If there's something you need from her then I'm happy to liaise. But it would compromise the investigation, not to mention DI Watton's safety, if you were to have direct contact with her, especially when such great efforts have been made to ensure her protection.'

Carter understood and he didn't want to push further. There was no need for him to know Melanie's whereabouts exactly, and he knew that. But there was still some comfort to be gained – for the team as well as himself, he guessed – in knowing she was at least close by.

'Ma'am, allow me one last shove, but can you tell me whether she's in the city limits?'

Archer's set expression softened. 'God, you really are her DS, aren't you?' The question was said affectionately, although she didn't wait for a response. 'Carter, I'll give you this, but you aren't to ask a single question more on it. Do you agree to that?' He nodded furiously to show his compliance. 'Very well, if it'll help you to know. DI Watton is long gone from this city.'

44

Melanie took her provisions back to the house and unpacked slowly, to make the task last. Even though the place had been empty when she arrived, she'd found herself pestered by the thought that everything somehow had its place – as though the last owner hadn't quite relinquished their life there. Earlier that day she'd spent a long time putting things into cupboards, only to take them out an hour or so later, rehoming them elsewhere. She imagined her baked beans having the same sense of displacement that she felt.

She packed tins of soup into the cupboard next to the microwave for convenience. The milk was in the fridge, the fresh loaf in the bread bin – a kitchen article she hadn't even owned before this. At home she'd only ever stored the bread in the freezer, to try to drag out its lifespan. She leaned back against the sideboard and let a deep sigh fall out. *Who knew bread brought so many options with it?*

The jingle of her alarm tone made her jump out of the moment; any sound felt like an intrusion in the empty space.

'So much to adjust to,' she said aloud, grabbing the mobile.

She laughed then; not a sincere laugh but a sad one. 'Apart from talking to myself. That I've already sorted.'

She'd set an alarm to sound when high tide was an hour away – although it was partly to remind her to make dinner as well. When Archer told her the location of her hideaway, Melanie resolved to try to make the most of the situation, promising herself a walk along the beach every evening. This would be the first time she tried out the theory in practice. Her walk through the town that afternoon had revealed small boats, moored at the opposite end of the beach, and that was her target for the night.

Melanie crossed to the fridge and took out tomatoes. She'd bought them specifically to make home-made sauce. She also took out a clove of garlic and scouted the fridge to make sure there was nothing else she'd need. *I wonder whether Hilda would be proud?* she thought, as she grabbed her phone to double-check details of the recipe. It wasn't often she made pasta one meal at a time; typically she opted for a bulk boil to stash away for a week's worth of dinners. She was midway through keying in her search terms for the recipe when she corrected herself, double-clicked out of the window and threw the phone on the worktop.

'The phone is for me to get in touch with you,' Archer had said when she handed it over. 'Untraceable, keep it that way. No internet, so no online music, and no Carter or Burton.' She'd leaned heavy on the last part of her instruction.

There was a small selection of recipe books fixed on a shelf, faded from years of direct sunlight. Melanie grabbed one, then another and another until she found a recipe that fit her ingredients. She snapped the spine of the book, as though stretching it out from years of underuse, and spread it out in front of her. There were a handful of basic steps that she was midway through reading when she stopped, grabbed the fullest tomato from the bunch, and sank her teeth into it. She held it like an apple, grabbing at the skin and pulling away a chunk.

With juice running down her chin, she waited for a tin of chicken soup to heat through as an alternative dinner plan. When there were seconds left on the timer, she went to take out her fresh bread.

'Bon appétit,' she said, her tone flat, as she tucked a towel around the hot bowl.

The house wasn't unpleasant or uncomfortable, but it wasn't home either. The rooms had a feeling of not being lived in, even though she knew there had been someone here only a month ago.

Places like this were in high demand, so Archer said. 'These are extenuating circumstances, though, everyone understands that.'

'Everyone? Does that include the team?' Melanie had pushed.

'The team aren't to know anything about this, Mel. Otherwise, what would be the point in moving you at all?' Her tone had been firm, so Melanie backed down. 'It's important that you stay out of harm's way. You're a valuable commodity.'

It wasn't quite the sentimental farewell Melanie had needed – only hours after a murderer had left a stuffed animal outside of her home, while a uniformed officer supervised her hurried packing. Burton and Carter had been rushed out, quickly replaced by Archer, and everything from then on had been urgent – secret.

She only managed half the soup before she went back into the kitchen for her phone. She knew Carter and Burton's numbers by heart. But with the case ongoing, she didn't know whether either of them would be at home, or whether they'd be in the throes of work at the station. Somehow she desperately hoped for both things at once.

Against her better judgement, she dialled Carter's number and blocked her own. *He might not even answer a withheld number*, she reasoned. She pressed the phone to her ear and took a deep breath with each ring, all the while hoping this wasn't a terrible mistake. But then if he didn't answer...

'DS Carter.'

Melanie thought she could hear the bustle of the station in the background.

'Edd, it's Mel.'

45

Read stormed into the office, closely followed by his partner. He slammed a slim folder down on his desk and dropped heavily into his seat. 'So much for Stone's bloody family,' he announced.

'Dead-end?' Burton looked over her screen. She'd been watching traffic camera footage since the early hours of the morning, and she was grateful for the break. There hadn't been any sight of Stone, neither in the town centre nor around essential shops. Wherever he was, he was doing his utmost to live outside of a watchable space.

'Spoke to the mother and two of the brothers. None of them even knew Stone was out.'

'How has he orchestrated this without involving them? Like, where does he eat dinner?' Fairer looked perplexed by the idea.

'I know,' Carter chimed in, although he kept his stare fixed on the first of several sheets of paper he needed to look through. 'After a hard day of being a criminal there's nothing I like more than having a nice home to get back to, have my dinner in.' His delivery was deadpan but at least it caused a murmur of amusement around the office.

'What's got your attention?' Burton asked.

Carter spoke to the room in answer. 'Forensics. Blood from under Evans' fingernails matches Stone's DNA, so there's a direct link between the two of them now. We'll have to be mindful of that when we catch him, make sure he's checked for scratches, marks.' Carter deliberately used 'when' rather than 'if'; a trick of the trade from Melanie. 'Fox hair from the back of the van looks to match the specimen left behind at the fire scene, as best as forensics can tell at least.' He skimmed the rest. 'Williams sent these over with a note attached to say they're still exploring other samples, whatever that means, but whatever they find now only strengthens the case. This is enough to tie him to both murders if nothing else.' He turned his attention to Read and Fairer. 'The family didn't give you anything?'

Read widened his eyes and puffed out his cheeks in a show of anguish. 'Nothing apart from a deep sense of disappointment.'

'Our visit was the first they'd heard of Stone being released. Apparently they kept in touch during the early months of his incarceration but after the incident with his brother they all cut contact with him.'

'We asked about hangouts of his. If he couldn't come to family where else might he go? They refused to rat out anyone else in the area.' Read held his hands up in surrender. 'Their words, not mine. They don't want to tie anyone else to what Stone is doing now.'

'How honourable,' Carter replied.

'Read and I have got an invitation to the prison, though, so we'll be heading there later today. Thanks to Morris.'

'You're welcome,' she replied, without looking up from her screen.

'The governor is seeing you this afternoon?' Carter clarified.

'Access all areas apparently,' Fairer said. 'But we can check their visitor logs while we're there to make sure the family aren't blowing smoke about their contact with him. There should be a postal record of everything he received too.'

'Great, that's really great work. Can you see if you can get a copy of the visitor list for Stone? It might be worth having.' Fairer nodded along while he noted down the instruction on a Post-it. 'I have some calls to make and I could do with the quiet for it. Does anyone object to me using the boss' office for the afternoon?' Carter asked, scanning the expressions of his team.

'You're the boss now, right?' Morris chimed in again.

Burton snorted. 'What she means is, no, no one minds. It's yours.'

Carter hadn't told anyone about the phone call from Melanie. It would lead to too many questions; most of which he couldn't answer, and some he didn't want to. She hadn't told him where she was hiding, but they'd talked about the case in more detail than they should have – considering Archer's ban on them discussing it at all. But it was during the conversation that both considered something that had gone previously unturned.

'Have we checked romantic entanglements?' Melanie had asked.

'Is there someone you've got in mind?'

'There aren't any partners in Stone's file, I don't think, and there certainly weren't any at the time. But what if he met someone inside?'

'Another prisoner, you mean?'

'I was more thinking a lonely-hearts situation. You hear about these women visiting male prisoners all the time. What if Stone had a female visitor, and she's helping him orchestrate things on the outside?' Melanie didn't sound entirely sure of the idea even as she said it, but it caught Carter's attention.

'It would make all of this even easier, if he were working with someone we don't know.'

'But they were keeping in touch somehow. So, she must have been visiting, writing letters, both, right up until the time he was released. If she exists, I know.' There was a pause while Carter tapped his boss' suggestion into a fresh note on his iPhone. As though misreading the silence, Melanie added, 'Look it's just an idea, it's not one you have to use.'

'It's a good idea, boss, why wouldn't we? But...' he hesitated. 'You know I can't give you a blow by blow of everything we're doing. I mean, it wouldn't be–'

'Safe, I know.' She sounded exasperated, more emotional than Carter recognised.

'I'm sorry this is happening, Mel.' He took a personal tone rather than a professional one, sensing his boss might need the closeness. 'It won't be forever; I swear that much.'

Melanie had sighed. 'I hope not, Carter. I really bloody hope not.'

He hadn't slept much since their talk. He'd gone back into the office like nothing had happened, went home like nothing had happened, then stared at the ceiling for hours on end. He knew that Melanie could be clutching straws – not to mention breaking the rules of her protection – but it was one of the few ideas they hadn't explored. And as acting lead on the investigation, Carter was determined to explore everything – no matter the dead-ends he found along the way.

By the time he'd arrived at work the morning after their talk, it was clear the avenues the team were looking into were fast running out of fresh materials. Carter needed something to busy himself with, though. While Read and Fairer were liaising with the prison, he decided to go back through as many Stone files as he could stand to read. Best case scenario, he might find a woman tucked away between a forgotten incident report. Worst case, he decided, he'd make himself an expert on his prey.

When he edged into his third hour of reading Stone's notes without a result, Carter began to wonder whether this would be another day wasted. *But what else is there?* When he was three pages off finishing a report for pet theft there came a knock at the door.

'Hello?'

Fairer stuck his head into the room. 'Got a minute?'

'Got a whole thirty of them, I'm about ready for a break.' Carter closed the file. 'Hit me.'

'We're back from the chat with the governor. Interesting woman, doesn't take kindly to small talk, as it turns out.' Carter smiled as his junior started to reorganise the bundle of papers he'd brought in with him. 'According to her, Stone only caused as much trouble as the rest of them. There weren't any outstanding incidents, nor was he especially friendly with anyone on the inside. They have a minor gang problem emerging but, again, nothing that Stone looked to be interested in. But it's the visitor's record that got us excited.'

Carter felt a twist of interest. He leaned forward, giving Fairer his complete attention.

'The governor confirmed there weren't many visitors for Stone in the way of family members, but she could remember a woman. While Read gunned us back I had a quick look through the records to see whether anything, or anyone, jumped out, and there's this.' He lifted a sheet of paper onto the desk and pointed at a name right at the bottom of it. 'Now, I haven't done a head count for how many times her name appears exactly, but it's more than twenty.'

Carter glanced at the name: Yasmin Lacey.

'Where's Read?' Carter looked up.

'Searching our database for her.'

'Brilliant.' Carter stood up. 'We need to see what Morris can do with this name.'

'Another thing, boss,' Fairer added, matching his superior's beeline for the door. 'The prison opens letters before they're passed to the inmates. Apparently, some time back an inmate had a coded letter smuggled into them about a planned escape – that's another story, but because of this chap planning an escape, they're taking copies of the letters too. They're scanned in and stored and–'

'Those letters are on their way, is that where this is going, Fairer?' Carter's fist was wrapped around the door handle, his impatience to leave the room cracking through.

'They should be in our inboxes by now.'

'Fairer,' Carter yanked the door open, 'I could bloody kiss you.'

It wasn't the same as when Melanie said it, but Carter hoped the sentiment was clear.

46

They split into teams. Carter orchestrated a division of labour where he and Burton took control of the letters, while Read and Fairer looked over the visitor's log. The leader role came naturally to him when it needed to. Carter ordered his juniors to be on the look-out for any patterns emerging in the visits: how often? Were there any incidents recorded? When did they start, and how many in total? He and Burton had the disadvantage of only having the letters coming into the prison from Lacey, and not the ones out from Stone, but they readied themselves to look for patterns, topics; what were they spending these hours talking about?

'Okay, and what do I do?' Morris asked, a stern expression set on her face.

'You get on that thing,' Carter gestured to the computer behind his colleague, 'and you find out everything there is to know about Yasmin Lacey. I don't care how you do it. I don't need to know how you do it. Understood?'

Morris raised an eyebrow and smiled. 'Understood.'

Carter and Burton both pulled up copies of the letters at once. They'd decided they should both read them all – 'In case one of us misses something the other picks up on,' Carter had reasoned – so they started picking over the opening correspondence as a pair.

'This is like reading a dodgy dating profile,' Burton announced, her eyes scanning down the screen. '"I've never done anything like this before but I know they're always looking for people to write in..."' She used an unnecessarily high-pitched voice and pranced from side to side as she spoke, as though mimicking a Barbie figure. 'They're always looking for people to write in? What does she think this is?'

'Stay focused, Burton.' But Carter couldn't dispute her point. The opening letter was a strange introduction. It read as though Yasmin Lacey was an innocent woman looking to do a good deed. *Maybe that's how this started for her, though*, Carter thought, as he rolled on to the second letter. They were all dated in the top right corner, and this looked to be just a week on from her opening message. 'Stone must have been using his one free letter a week to write back in the beginning. It must have been love.'

'At first write,' Read said without skipping a beat, but his eyes were fixed to his own task.

Burton started to snap her fingers to grab her colleague's attention. 'Carter, letter four–'

'Woman, how fast do you read?' He crossed to her desk to read over her shoulder.

'Paragraph four, "I've included the self-addressed envelope you asked for," yada, yada. "It's wrong they limit your writing so much," yada, yada. Then she says, "Isn't it a good thing you've found someone?" before she prattles on about looking forward to him writing back. Four letters in she's talking about them having found each other?' She looked up at her superior. 'What does that sound like to you?'

'Like he wooed her from the off.'

'Side bar, as a single man you absolutely shouldn't use that word because it shows your age and then some. But yes.'

'Go back to reading,' Carter said with a smile. 'I want to know more.' He landed hard in his own chair and went back to skimming the letters. Burton was right; everything about these early messages made it sound like a romantic bond from the off. *Had that been what Lacey was looking for?* He'd heard stories about women who went out of their way to have relationships with criminals, but was Yasmin Lacey one of those types? Without knowing more about Stone, it was impossible to guess whether he was smooth-talking enough to have turned an innocent woman into an accomplice. But five letters in, Carter hadn't yet found evidence of anything more than a woman with growing emotions – which wasn't a crime, no matter how misguided it had been.

'Letter nine, "have you been involved with women like this before?" and then letter ten, "it sounds like she really put you through some awful stuff. I'm not surprised it's hard for you to let women in again," but with no mention of names,' Burton relayed.

'Do you think it's Mel?' Carter suggested.

'I didn't, but it could be.' Burton looked back at the screen. 'She doesn't ask for more information, so, whatever Stone told her was enough to make her feel sorry for him, but also not make her ask any more questions.'

'Bastard should've been a con artist rather than a petty thug.' Carter looked back at his own screen and skimmed through to letter nine to look over Burton's found evidence. 'Hang on, she says here, "can you tell I'm nervous still," at the bottom of the page. So, she wasn't fully committed to things by this point, right? Ten letters in and nothing was set in stone.'

Read looked up, bright-eyed as though ready to make a pun but a stare from Carter shot him back down.

'Have you looked at how many letters there are, though?' Burton asked.

Carter clicked from one page to another, and another, and...

The office had been quiet for a longer than average stretch of time when Morris announced she needed a screen break. She cracked her neck, explained that her computer should be left alone to search through databases, and then took coffee orders. Carter had never been more grateful to know that a flat white was on the way. He'd always considered himself a young detective – being only a few years older than most of the team, but still a few years younger than Melanie – but the screen time had worn him out too, and he found himself longing for the luxury of printed documents. He rubbed at his eyes, causing bright flickers under his lids, and he worried that pain was close by.

'Burton, have you got anything for a headache?'

'Wait, wait, I've got something,' Read announced from the opposite side of the room.

Carter stood. 'For a headache?'

'There's a patch of time where their visits stop.' Read was still staring at his paperwork, his fingertips fixed on relevant points in time. Carter and Burton arrived at Read's desk as he explained, 'They have regular visits once a month up until this point, here,' he gestured, 'where they go nearly a full three months without seeing each other.'

'Read is working from the beginning and I'm working from the end. We're hoping to meet in the middle,' Fairer explained. 'But so far I haven't found any breaks like that in their time together. Although there are times when their visits actually increase.'

'Gimme the dates for when their visits stop, would you?' Carter asked and Read reached for a scrap of paper. 'We might be able to skip ahead to their letters around this time, assuming there were any. She might give something away in whatever she wrote to him.'

Read passed over a Post-it. 'The date they stopped and the date they started.'

Carter flashed the note to Burton as he spoke to his juniors. 'Nice work, lads, keep at it.'

Burton turned back to their side of the room and Carter followed. 'If you work back from June, and I'll work forwards from March?' he suggested.

'Got it.'

Minutes later Morris reappeared and trod softly throughout the room, delivering coffees to each desk without a word. Carter considered her a kind of fairy godmother in those moments. He blew hard on the drink, sending droplets over his keyboard, but his attention was fixed on the screen. It looked as though there were blank points in the letters at around the same time, which was a result – although not one that gave them material to work with. He was two sips into his drink when he found the first letter, dated at the end of March, so nearly a full month after Lacey's last visit to the prison.

'Get a load of this, "I saw a different side to you during that visit," this letter starts. "I understand you've been hurt but you can't lash out at people like that."' Carter raised his voice to Read, 'In their last visit did anything happen? No pushing, shoving, shouting?'

Read shook his head. 'There's nothing like that reported in the visits ever.'

'So, you can't lash out at people,' Carter repeated to Burton. 'What's she referring to?'

'Something he's planned?'

Carter scrolled to the next letter, dated another two weeks later. 'Here's a money shot if ever there was one, "you obviously aren't over what happened between the two of you," and "I've been involved with men who hold grudges before and it's never gone well for me but you already knew that."'

'What are we thinking, he introduced the idea of revenge somewhere?'

'But she reacts terribly to it, so, how do they end up hatching something together?'

'Unless they don't,' Burton said, scrolling as she spoke. 'I'm working back from their final letter and she says here, "I know you deserve the chance to explain things properly so of course I'll come," and she finishes the letter by saying "there are two sides to every story and I understand it can take some telling."'

'Shit, I wish we had his letters.' Carter pressed a palm flat against his forehead, imagining it were a cold flannel. 'So, he tells her something that makes her think he's aggressive, we're assuming that, right?'

'From the lash-out comment?'

'Sure. But she reacts poorly to that, to the point that she doesn't even want to see him. Which scuppers his plans of having someone on the outside waiting for him. So, he has to back-pedal, to explain himself better in a way that she'll be sympathetic towards.' Carter peered up over his monitor. 'Fairer, get on to the prison and see whether you can get Stone's purchase history for the tuck shop, would you?' He turned back to Burton. 'There's a lull in letters before the first one, after the lash-out visit, and I don't buy that he only got in touch with her weekly. The tuck shop will at least flag up stamp and envelope purchases.'

'You think he hounded her?'

'There's no way of knowing but I'd bet a fair amount on it.'

'So, he writes a bunch of letters, tries to explain himself, makes it sound like stuff came out in a way it shouldn't have done.'

'She buys it, starts visiting again.' Carter glanced at his screen. 'We need to go through these interim letters with a fine comb to see whether there are any hints for what he was telling her.' Losing patience with the sight of a screen, he added, 'Burton, go ahead and print this bunch. I know the environment needs its trees, but I need a sheet of paper I can highlight.'

His colleague leapt to the task with an enthusiasm that made Carter wonder if she'd also been feeling the screen fatigue – unlike Morris. Carter crossed over to her desk and gave a gentle knock on its surface.

'Can I interrupt?'

'Please.' She gestured to a spare chair nearby. 'How are the letters?'

'Long. How's the internet?'

Morris half-laughed. 'Also long, but I'm getting there.' She tipped her head back to drain the remains of her coffee. 'There are a couple of things that will take a while to get to, so I don't have everything I wanted to find just yet. But we should have the basics: address, relations, dealing with the police, employment history, all of that stuff.'

'And,' Carter lowered his voice, 'what about the non-basics?'

Morris smirked. 'I've no idea what you mean...'

47

After years of dodging prison, it wasn't half as bad as the blokes down the hound had made it out to be. There were always chances for 'improvement'; ways they thought we might make our shitty selves better for the world once we'd been unleashed back into it. Sometimes that meant talking to people; Christ, and talking to each other. It was a lot of touchy-feely for lads who were mostly in there for knocking people about and stealing their unmentionables, but I suppose they needed to tick boxes for what they'd done for us. If we'd wanted to get better we had some chances. The ones who were in there for longer seemed to throw themselves in more. I saw that soon enough. But they mostly had people waiting for them on the outside. I had my family, sure, but only for a while.

'We'll come as often as we can,' Mam said to begin with. It felt a lot like me being out of the house had made her appreciate what I'd been bringing into it. 'Your brothers will come too. And I'll write. Every week. Is there anything you need?' She asked the same question every time she visited but I never could answer. 'That copper's head on a cast-iron platter,' I'd wanted to say time and again but I always bit back on it. You never knew who was listening.

But the visits dropped off soon enough. She had her reasons.

Yas arrived not long after that, though, and suddenly family didn't matter. I had an in to the outside world; someone to give me a jumping off point when I got back into it. Talking to her was easy enough; whether you're doing it through pen and paper or whispering it straight into their ear, women often want to hear the same thing. I'd told her all about my past relationships – of a fashion – and how much emotional baggage I carried round with me from it.

'It often felt like she was just out to get me,' I said across the table during one of our close and cosy chats. 'Anyone ever made you feel like that?'

She looked at me with sad eyes and said, 'Yeah, yeah they really have.'

Our knees knocked under the table and I knew I'd sealed it.

I told her bits and pieces as I thought she needed to know them, never enough for her to leave and find out more on her own. There was one time when I asked whether she knew why I was inside and she said she did; said the charity hadn't approved her letters because of it.

'But I sensed something good in you,' she said and I smiled, almost laughed. 'It sounds terrible what you went through to get here, Roddy. I just think – well, I think it's unfair how she pursued you. Unfair and unprofessional.'

'You're right.' I flashed a thin smile. 'She really shouldn't have come after me.'

And she shouldn't have done, because she should have been street smart enough to know I'd be coming right back at her one day. She might flounce about the place like sliced bread, with her news reports and murder squad and the girlfriend she thinks no one has noticed. But I noticed, all right. She kept everything and gained on that; everything I had went swirling down the drain of a shared prison shower. See, you can't have that kind of a knock on someone's life and not expect something back from it; especially when you're someone like her. Special for all the wrong reasons; there were women before and since, sure, but never anyone quite the same. When I let myself get really lost in her, there were even times when I thought about life after Watton. What gap might she leave, I wondered, and which member of her smug team would do the press conference asking for witnesses, information, help wiping their arses without her. When the right moment took me, I even wondered who'd stand on the podium out the front of the station; who'd make the announcement once they'd found her?

48

The sunlight was cracking through the blinds in Carter's bedroom. It was a lazy shade, as though the sun also didn't want to rise. But still Carter pushed back the duvet and threw himself out with a force enough to wake himself fully.

He hurried through his shower, got dressed and spent longer than he should have loitering in the doorway of Emily's empty bedroom. When things had started to escalate at work he'd asked his parents to take her for a week – 'Maybe longer? I'm sorry, Mum.' They'd waved away his apologies. He let out a gentle sigh while staring at her made bed, and then yanked himself downstairs for coffee. The first he drank standing in the kitchen; the second he filtered into a thermos and packed in his bag for work. The coffee shops wouldn't be open for another hour, and there was no way he was going without.

He managed to skip the usual early morning traffic, arriving at the station an hour before the team were due. They'd spent the previous day reading, highlighting, and comparing notes on Lacey and Stone's time together, and Carter wanted to look over it all once more before Morris' reveals came later in the morning. She'd spent the day before at the computer, grunting at offers for coffee and cursing when a blocker popped up in her plan. Carter knew whatever she'd found needed to be good for the sake of tracking down this new character, but knowing Morris and her technology prowess, it would be better.

Carter scanned himself into the building, climbed the stairs and loitered outside the office door. *Is that...* He pushed his way in, bringing a stop to the chatter. Morris and Burton's heads snapped round in synchronicity.

'You two went home last night, right?'

Burton laughed while Morris answered, 'For a while, we did.'

'Not everyone has cute kids to rush home to.'

Burton was being playful, Carter knew, but he still felt a twist deep in his stomach. He wouldn't be rushing home to Emily until this case was cleared.

'Have you put together a file on Yasmin Lacey, Morris?' He stood at his desk to unpack his belongings, reaching first for the coffee and then for the notes he'd taken home.

'Yep, it's in DI Watton's office,' she answered without thinking. 'Oh.' She caught her mistake and turned to face Carter. 'I'm sorry, I didn't–'

'Force of habit,' Carter interrupted her with a smile. He wouldn't hold the error against her. In the last four days there had been several occasions when he'd gone running to Melanie's office too – only to be reminded. He wandered into the small room behind his desk and returned with a case file that was nearly an inch thick. 'Morris, are you for real?'

'Too much or not enough?' she said, wary.

'Just right.' He leaned on the edge of his desk, coffee in hand. 'Give me the highlights.'

Morris crossed to the evidence board and grabbed a marker. 'Burton, would you be so kind?' Her colleague snatched the pen away and took up a spot in front of the board to note-take. 'Yasmin Lacey is twenty-nine years old, she's never been married nor does she have children. Both parents died in a car accident nearly ten years ago and she doesn't have any siblings. I was able to track down some distant relatives but scouring her social media didn't reveal much contact with them, although they are connected through those channels.'

She paused for breath and to let Burton catch up. 'We've got her last registered address, and no reason to think she's moved elsewhere, not from her online presence at least. We've also got a car that's registered to her, and Burton pinged the details of that over to the traffic team this morning so they can be looking out for it. It saves us the job of staring at footage for hours on end with hope in our hearts,' she said, her tone flat. 'They'll flag up any signs of the number plate on cameras and send the isolated footage to us so we can look over the driver and location, in relation to the case.' She reached over to her desk and picked up a single sheet of paper. 'At the moment she's assisting a florist, but she's previously worked as a sandwich-maker, a barista, and a delivery-woman. None of those jobs lasted for more than around twelve months. I couldn't find any qualifications beyond her GSCEs so it looks as though she became a bit of a drifter once mandatory education wrapped up.'

'How long has she been with the florist?' Carter asked.

'Ten months, near enough, on a part-time basis. She's also been liaising with several charities during that time, one of which is...' She paused for dramatic effect. 'Prison Outreach, a charity established five years ago to work with criminals, on the inside and when they're released. Members of staff are encouraged to meet and greet criminals, incarcerated for relatively minor crimes, they develop a friendship, of sorts, and discuss their options for when they get out. It seems a mighty coincidence, but our working theory is that Lacey must have come across Stone during this work and either accidentally contacted him as part of her postal duties, or contacted him outside of work time.'

'Why would it have been an accident?' Carter jumped in again.

'Because Stone was put away for crimes that are classified as serious by the charity, so members of staff wouldn't have been encouraged to contact him.'

'Plus,' Burton added, 'we looked back over her introductory letter to him, and she didn't mention anything about the charity or her work with them. In fact, a few letters in she comments that she isn't working right now and that's as much as she says.'

'So, what, she took a shine to him and decided to put in extra hours?'

'That's our best guess, really, but the jury is out,' Morris replied.

'So she might not be so innocent?' Carter pulled up a chair and cast a look across the evidence board.

'She might have been misguided, at best. At worst, she knew she was contacting someone who's potentially dangerous and for whatever reason she decided to do it anyway.' Morris shrugged. 'Stranger things have happened when it comes to women contacting inmates. But that really is as juicy as it gets in terms of who she is and what she's done.'

Carter looked from Morris to Burton and back again. 'That's it?'

Morris looked guiltily at the floor.

'It's cute, Morris, but I'm a father of a young daughter.'

'That's true. That sort of stare does nothing on him,' Burton joked.

'In which case...' Morris opened a drawer in her desk and pulled out another handful of papers. 'Phone calls, credit card records.' She waved them like a winning ticket. 'We're waiting on copies of her phone calls from months back, so we can see how often she might have been calling the prison, but these are the more immediate things I've been able to pull. There's only one phone number registered to her right now, so if Stone does have a phone then it isn't something Lacey has arranged for him.'

'A pay-as-you-go would make more sense, I suppose.' Carter nodded along.

'Her credit card records range from the sensible to the slightly absurd, though, so this is where things become more interesting on this front. We can't get itemised billing – or rather, we can, but not for every transaction listed here, and it's something that will take time. She has regular transactions for supermarkets, cosmetic shops, one or two for her local pharmacy–'

'Have we contacted the pharmacy?' Carter interrupted.

Morris glanced at Burton, who answered, 'No, but we can.'

'The more interesting transactions are,' she read aloud from a billing sheet, '£7.30 Fox and Hounds, £9.20 Fox and Hounds, £3.40 Fox and Hounds.'

Carter's eyes widened. 'She's been at our crime scene?'

'Oh, not one crime scene,' Morris continued. '£13.50 to Artists' Hideout. £50 exactly to Imperial Arts. Bonus points, we've got transactions for other pubs in the local area too, some of which were on our original lists to check, so we've set them aside for Read and Fairer to tackle.'

'Wait,' Carter picked up, 'you've found card charges to both the art shop and gallery?'

Morris nodded. 'An even £50 sounds like the kind of money you might set down on a deposit for something, but we really won't know more until the gallery opens.' She checked her watch. 'Which isn't too far off now. Likewise, for the art supply store. We're hoping they might be able to tell us what was sold, from memory if we're lucky, but they might recognise the face if we can get a photograph over to them.'

Carter thought for a minute. 'It's a long shot, but there aren't any charges to Halloway?'

'It is a long shot, but one that Burton and I thought of as well. We looked back over the statements I've been able to pull and there's nothing showing, but it might be that the transactions don't stretch back far enough. Again, we're waiting on details from further back in her payment history, but it might take a little time for the company to respond to that request. Something about customer privacy or some such.' She rolled her eyes.

'This is bloody brilliant work.' Carter looked from one to the other. 'Both of you.'

There was a low creak from somewhere behind the group, as the door to the office opened. Fairer walked in carrying a white plastic bag that looked full to the brim with something, while Read tailed him. But both officers came to an abrupt stop at the sight of the evidence board, now packed with Burton's scrawls, arrows leading from one idea to another.

'How late are we?' Read craned round to look at the clock.

'We brought new leads to the table, chaps,' Burton announced with a notable smugness.

'Yeah, well,' Read spoke through a mouthful of something. He'd wasted no time in delving into the bag Fairer had brought. His one hand was busy shovelling a thick piece of bread crust into his mouth. With the other hand he threw a foiled parcel at Burton. 'We brought sandwiches.' He took another mouthful. 'Walk us through this...'

49

Carter and the team had spent the day chasing Yasmin Lacey around the city. Burton and Morris had scoured the woman's most recent phone calls, cash machine visits – everything they could find. With more information filtering in from different companies over the day to add to their search. Meanwhile, Read and Fairer had taken the task of visiting Lacey's last known address. There were no signs of life, but no signs of disruption either. After ten minutes of banging on the front door and peering in through part-curtained windows, a neighbour had appeared.

'She won't be in at this time of day,' he'd told the officers. 'Never is, anymore. If she comes back at all it'll be this evening but even that might not happen nowadays.' He shrugged. 'Young love, it gets us all I suppose.'

Read caught the man's attention before he could slink back through his own front door. 'I'm sorry, you mentioned young love?'

'She's got a chap, hasn't she?' he replied, as though it was common knowledge, even to the police.

'Is this the chap?' Read asked, flashing a picture of Stone.

'Aye, that's the one.' He shook his head lightly. 'Wouldn't be my choice for her but he seems all right enough, I suppose.'

'But they're not here much?'

'They come and go. Out seeing the world, I suspect.' He looked from Read to Fairer. 'Is there anything I can be doing for you boys?'

'No,' Fairer replied, taking a softer tone than his partner. 'You've been a help already, sir, thank you. If you happen to see Miss Lacey, or the man she's with, might you be able to give us a call?' He took a card from the inside of his jacket pocket and handed it over. 'That'll put you right through to me.'

The neighbour studied the business card. 'DC, eh? Must be something big...' he trailed off as he hobbled back into his own property, shutting the door on Read and Fairer.

'Well, that's a dead-end,' Read said, staring up at the empty house.

'Come on with you.' Fairer nudged his partner. 'They're here somewhere...'

The afternoon hadn't thrown up any alternative addresses that Lacey might be using. Carter had called through to the manager of the offender charity too, to ask about their missing woman, but she hadn't had a bad word to say – nor a particularly useful word either.

'Has Miss Lacey been into the office recently?' Carter pushed.

'No, but she asked for time off.' She giggled. 'Not time off, because she isn't an employee as such, but you catch my meaning. She said she needed a break for a bit.'

'Did she say why?'

'No, but I suspect it's for her well-being. It's more important these days, isn't it?'

I wouldn't know, Carter thought. He was running on black coffee and sheer determination; well-being hadn't had much to do with his nor the team's daily life of late. 'Did she say whether she was planning to go away anywhere, or was she staying in the city, do you know?'

'She didn't say, no. Look, what's this even about? Is she okay?' Her soft tone gave way to something like frustration.

'She's fine as far as we're aware but it's important we contact her. If she happens to get in touch with you for any reason, would you please contact me as a matter of urgency?' Carter tried to stress the point without causing the woman alarm, and it seemed to work, as she agreed he'd be her first phone call if Lacey turned up – but the more dead-ends they ran into, the greater the 'if' looked to Carter.

It somehow felt like admitting defeat, but he'd ordered the team home soon after his phone call with the charity's manager. Morale had dipped over the course of the day – Carter's included. They might have a lot of information to wade through, but wherever Lacey and Stone were hiding out they were doing a fine job of staying off the radar. Carter wondered how Stone had orchestrated such a disappearing act – perfectly set up for when Evans' body would be found, with all DNA matches pointing to him as the culprit. It would have involved meticulous planning, but Stone had already shown himself as a master of that too. How long had this been on the cards for their criminal, Carter wondered. Months, years? Had he been planning this the whole time he was inside?

A string of rhetorical questions accompanied Carter through his journey home. It was another solo evening, so he'd weakened his resolve against takeaways and stopped to get chow mein. *To hell with a beach body*, he thought, realising a trip to the beach any time soon was unlikely.

Carter bolted the front door and carried his dinner into the kitchen. He pulled out his phone and thumbed to downloaded albums, selecting music at random to keep him company. He was used to small feet rushing around, loud laughter and shouting, and the house felt altogether empty without it. Leaving the phone to play out on the work surface, he started to unhook a lid from the metal claws on the food's container. He didn't get as far as grabbing a fork to eat, instead using his fingertips to pull out beansprouts and onions, shovelling them into his mouth while he looked high and low in the fridge for a chilled lager. Carter had just cracked the can open when the music cut out, though, giving way to the hum of a vibration instead. The screen showed a withheld number.

Please be her, he thought, swallowing his last mouthful as the call connected. 'DS Carter speaking.'

'It's me.'

Carter dropped a sigh of relief into the speaker. 'Christ, boss, is it good to hear you.'

'Is everything okay?'

'Everything's fine, it's just been...' Carter didn't know how to finish the sentence without sharing information that he shouldn't. 'It's been a day.'

'You can't say?' Melanie's tone was soft, but her disappointment was clear.

'I shouldn't say.'

'Because of Archer still?'

Carter let out a second sigh but this one bordered on a laugh. 'Archer doesn't even know what's going on. I haven't updated her; she hasn't asked.' He pulled out a chair from the kitchen table and dropped into the seat. 'We don't quite have the same line of communication with her as we do with you, which isn't anyone's fault.'

'No one's listening, Edd,' Melanie reassured him. 'You can whine if you like.'

'The last thing you need is a moan from...' He trailed off and let a beat of silence pass between them. 'The noise in the background, is that – are you by the sea?'

Melanie hesitated. 'You know I can't answer that.'

'If you're by the sea, so help me,' he replied, trying to soften the seriousness between them. 'I bet there's no threat at all, is there? You just needed a break from everyone.'

'My idea of a break doesn't involve check-ins with Archer every other day. All she seems to do is call to make sure I'm alive, and then ask whether I'm enjoying myself. She seems to think I should be making the most of my time in – well, you know.'

'I don't know actually, but that's for the best. She calls every other day?'

'Yep. She said she doesn't want me to feel like I'm in this alone. But it sounds like she should be checking in more often with you. How's everyone doing? Are you all okay, and safe?' Melanie couldn't keep the worry from her voice, and although it was Carter's job to keep her safe and catch her threat now, he was glad to hear the concern; it gave him comfort.

'We're all okay,' he replied. 'We've got leads that we're working, and we have a lot of stuff to wade through. You were right, by the way, about there being a woman involved.' He reasoned the least that Melanie deserved was to know her idea had been a worthy one. 'We've managed to track her down to an address in the city, which she's no longer spending much time at, according to her neighbours. But I've got patrol actively looking for her, plus we've got credit cards and all the rest of it.'

'It sounds like you don't even need me.'

He laughed. 'I wouldn't go that far, boss.'

'Can we talk about why you haven't told Archer everything you're telling me?'

Carter crossed back to where his dinner sat on the work surface and again used his fingers, this time to pull a bundle of noodles into his mouth. He hadn't taken to Archer – but he knew that it was nothing to do with her, specifically. It was more that... 'Well, she's not you, is she? She doesn't have the same bond with us all.' He was still chewing as he spoke. 'Plus, it would be nice to go to her with actual results.'

'You have actual results.'

'See, and that's what I mean, that kind of gentle encouragement, I don't get that from Archer.' Carter knew how childish he sounded, but between losing his superior office, losing his daughter, and losing sleep, he felt entitled to a small outburst. 'I'll tell her, boss, I promise I will, I'd just like to be able to tell her we've found the woman, rather than the promise of the woman. The same goes for Stone.'

'She hasn't said a bad word against the work you're doing.'

Carter grabbed another bundle of food. 'Yeah, but would she?'

'Carter, I'm being serious. Every time she calls, she tells me to enjoy being where I am, and to rest assured I'm in safe hands with you all. Besides, if she were that concerned with the work you're doing then do you not think she'd be actively involved in the investigation, rather than trusting you to run things unsupervised?'

She had a point, but Carter wasn't confident enough to admit it. 'I just want to do what's right by you, boss, that's all this comes down to.'

'Could you spend some time thinking about whether doing right by me, and by this case, might involve reporting details to a superior officer?' she asked, then quickly added, 'Not for guidance, because you're doing everything that I'd do, for what it's worth, but just so she knows.'

Carter swallowed a beansprout whole. 'I've missed you.'

'I know.' There was another thrash of something in the background and Carter felt even more certain that the sea was close by. He was about to push the issue for a second time when Melanie said, 'Can I ask something else? Sort of about the case but almost not?'

Carter snorted. 'Well that was convincing. Sure, fire away.'

'Has anyone spoken to Hilda?'

50

Hilda was red in the face by the time she got back to her office.

'The bloody cheek of some...' she spoke aloud to herself as she dumped her briefcase in her visitor's chair before landing with a thump in her own. She'd been lecturing all morning, and for the second time that semester she had wondered whether teaching was what she really wanted to be doing. 'But I suppose that ship has sailed and hit an iceberg at this point in my life, has it not.' She turned on her computer and, while the machine whirred into life, she pulled her mobile from the top drawer in her desk. The screen showed no missed calls and no new messages; as she'd expected, but she'd hoped otherwise.

Superintendent Archer had been clear about the restrictions around Melanie and contact, but still Hilda had hoped the situation might somehow have resolved itself over the course of her morning in class.

'Because that's how police cases work, isn't it?' she asked herself.

There was a firm knock against her door before Benji, their

postal delivery man, stuck his head around the edge without waiting for permission – as he usually did.

'Anyone here with you, Dr Addair?'

She gestured him into the room. 'Come, you'll be company.'

'I'm just doing the rounds.' He pulled a squat trolley behind him. 'I thought I'd heard you talking away in here.'

'Only to myself.'

He laughed. 'Best conversation you'll have all day, I bet.'

Hilda knew it was meant to be a compliment; she was saddened by the comment though. 'Well, there is that, Benji,' she answered, choosing to leave out the fact that this was likely her last conversation of the day too. She didn't have any more classes pencilled in, nor tutorials. So unless a student turned up on her doorstep – *which they may well*, she thought – she'd be going home alone, without another word passing from her.

'There's the usual letters,' he said, setting a fat bundle of papers in the letter tray on Hilda's desk. 'And where shall I put this?'

Hilda turned from her computer to see what he was referring to. The postman stood with a long cardboard box between his hands; a good twenty inches, if not more, Hilda guessed.

'It's a weight,' he added, 'but maybe it's something nice for you?'

'Nothing that I'm expecting. Could you pop it on bookcase, the lower one?' She nodded behind him to where the furniture stood. 'I'll get to it.'

He followed her instructions and left the parcel flat across a family of books.

'Be seeing you, Dr Addair,' the man said as he backed out of her office.

'That you will, Benji.' Hilda was already skimming emails, waiting for the click of a closed door. When she was alone, she was up and away from her desk to investigate the parcel. The logical part of her knew this wasn't from Melanie, but who else would send something through her office? 'Okay, it might be a leap,' she said, taking a pair of scissors to the sealed ends of the box. 'But a girl can dream.'

She lifted the lid with anticipation and found the contents were covered in patterned tissue: a light blue with a simple stick-bird drawing. There was a small card sitting on top of the tissue, though, showing a seaside illustration.

'Someone's gone to some effort, then,' she said, lifting the lip of the card, with one hand already worrying at the edges of the paper. But the fidget of her fingers stopped as she read the note, written in a scribble she thought she recognised:

OH, I DO LIKE TO BE BESIDE THE SEASIDE...

Archer nodded along with everything Carter said, murmuring or grunting now and then to show her understanding. After his last call with Melanie he'd realised it was time to come clean with his superior officer about their discoveries. He hoped she might offer some guidance on it all – *or maybe a secret way of tracking people through a city*, Carter thought, *that would be fine too*. The only good thing about their midmorning meeting was it had given Morris time to liaise with the traffic officers, who'd reported sightings of Lacey's licence plate number. It was a small lead in the scheme of things, but Morris was working with the footage to see whether she could improve the camera focus on the driver.

'Is it likely to be Lacey?' Archer asked.

'It's impossible to know at this stage, ma'am.'

'I see.' Archer looked to drift off into thought.

'All we know for certain is that sightings of Lacey have been sporadic since the Evans murder. But we can verify that she and Stone have been to the house since then, according to what the neighbour shared with DC Read.'

'Do we have eyes on the house?'

'I don't have a patrol car outside for fear of scaring anyone off, but I do have them monitoring the area. All uniformed officers are aware that Yasmin Lacey is a person of interest regarding the case, though, and of course, everyone knows about Stone.'

She let out a noise that was nearly a laugh. 'Well, yes.' She paused for thought again. 'Do we have any reason to believe Lacey is being held against her will in this scenario?'

Carter shook his head. 'Unfortunately – well, unfortunately for her, I suppose, all we've been able to find so far is evidence to suggest she's complicit. We can't prove she's helped Stone with any of his endeavours, exactly. But we can at least place her credit cards in two of the establishments that were hit as part of Stone's work.'

'And you're checking Halloway's...' She trailed out as Carter started to nod. 'I see. The confirmed sighting of the vehicle in question, what direction did it look to be heading in?'

He knew this question had been coming; if anything, he was surprised it hadn't arrived sooner. Yet there was still a swell of anxiety somewhere in his stomach over it. 'The car was heading out of the city, ma'am. He, or they, could be heading to any number of places. Another major city, or even the coast.' He'd told himself not to react when Morris had said those exact words earlier in the day; he wasn't meant to know where Melanie was, so there shouldn't have been a weighted significance to the idea. But he saw Archer flinch at the mention too, which didn't help his worries. 'Should we be worried he's trying to flee, ma'am?'

'He's managed to evade arrest just fine in the city, so I don't know why he'd feel the need to leave to escape us.' Her tone was hard-edged and judgemental, and Carter's head snapped back a fraction at the sound. She leaned back in her chair and pressed a thumb and fingertip hard against her eyelids. 'Apologies, Carter,' she spoke without looking at him, 'you'll understand this is a fairly stressful situation for us all.' She looked up at him then. 'Even me.'

He laughed. 'Of course, ma'am. You're right, he has managed to evade us up to this point. But now we've got the vehicle details and shortly Morris will be able to confirm further information on the driver, all being well. So, we're making steps.'

'You're quite right, Carter, I know th–'

Carter's shrill ringtone cut through the room. 'I'm so sorry,' he said, fumbling for the device in his pocket. He glanced at the screen. 'It's Hilda Addair, ma'am. I can call her back?'

'I've been meaning to ring her for days. She likely just wants an update on things. If you're happy to...' She trailed off, so Carter pressed to accept the call.

Between the pitch of her voice and the severity of her accent, the woman was difficult to understand. 'Hilda,' he tried, 'Hilda, you need to slow down because I'm only getting... what arrived at the office?' He saw Archer's eyes widen across the desk from him. 'There's no chance it might have been from someone else...' Carter held the phone away from his ear as Hilda answered, her voice rising. 'Hilda, keep calm. I'm going to get over to the office, and I'll bring a uniformed officer with me and... Hilda, go back to that last part,' he asked, still struggling to hear her. 'The note actually says, "Beside the sea"?'

51

Carter hurried the phone back into his pocket and went to fill in the blanks of Hilda's half of the conversation. But Archer pressed a finger flat against her lips to stop him. She held up a sheet of paper for Carter to read: OFFICE BUGGED.

'Hilda doesn't sound too together. Is everything okay, Carter?' She feigned neutrality in her tone, but her expression was pure panic.

'I think there's been a mix-up with something delivered. Christ, I don't know really.' Carter tried to laugh. 'The case is difficult for her, isn't it, with DI Watton being personally involved. She looks to have received something in the post that she wasn't expecting, that's all.'

Archer scribbled while he spoke, then held up a second sheet of paper: LEAVE QUIETLY. 'We'll finish our talk over tea?' She pushed back her chair and Carter matched the gesture. He stood and rushed for the door. 'All of this paperwork can wait until later, can't it,' she said as she tried not to hurry to the open doorway, where Carter was already waiting. She slammed the door shut behind her and dropped herself hard against the wood. 'The fucking bastard.' Her voice was still low. 'I need you to call Morris, or whoever it is that Morris liaises with. Get that office swept, now. We have to assume he knows where Mel is but we're not going to know how much he knows until we can work out when the goddamn thing was planted.'

Carter already had his phone to his ear, waiting for the call to connect. 'Morris, I need you down at Archer's office. There's a bug.' He could hear excited chatter in the background. 'Did I miss something?'

'We've got Stone as the driver of the car. Incredibly clear still from a camera that's clocked him doing ten miles over the speed limit on the motorway.'

'The motorway?' Carter repeated, sending Archer's eyes wide again. 'Which direction?'

'South. We're keeping eyes on him as best as we–'

'Superintendent Archer's office has been bugged, Morris,' Carter interrupted her.

'Shut up,' Morris said away from the speaker, silencing her rowdy colleagues. 'I'll need to get a kit sorted,' she spoke into the receiver again, 'and I'll call the tech team, they have people better equipped for this than me. I'll put an urgent order on it.'

Carter toyed with the idea of telling her what Stone had likely heard. He shook his head. *There's no 'likely' about it, though, is there*, he thought. The message to Hilda had been a message to the entire team. 'Morris, Stone knows where DI Watton is.'

Archer moved as though she might grab the phone, but Carter stepped out of her way. 'Leave Burton and the rest of them to monitor his movements as best as you can, and get down here, would you? I'll need you to liaise with the tech experts when they get here. Please,' Carter took a deep breath before finishing, 'please, stress that an officer's life might be at stake.'

'I'll be two minutes,' she replied, her voice shaking, and Carter disconnected the call.

'You had no right to tell them that,' Archer snapped.

'They deserve to know what's on the line.' He matched her tone, adding, 'Ma'am,' as an afterthought. 'Fear can be a powerful motivator.'

Archer paced the hall, her fingertips pressed hard against her forehead. 'I need to think.'

'Is there any point over the past few days where you've left the space unsupervised?'

She shot him a warning look, but Carter knew it was a fair question. 'I never leave the room without locking the door behind me, not least because of sensitive information like this. There must be a spare key somewhere, of course.'

'We can liaise with the cleaners, the general manager to see when the space was last accessed without your being present. Who else? Come on, ma'am, what are we missing?'

'Carter, I don't leave that office unattended!'

He stepped back, as though putting a safer distance between the two of them. 'I'm trying to protect her as well,' he admitted, speaking to the floor.

Archer pressed her back flat against the door to her office and slid down into a squat. Her head hit the wood with a gentle thud as she tipped it back. 'I stashed her at the bloody seaside as though this might be a holiday for her.'

'She told me.'

Archer's head snapped up. 'She told you?'

'Does it matter now?' Carter raised an eyebrow and Archer looked away. 'Morris will be here any minute and we can leave. Who do we need to be calling? Someone in the police force nearby must know that you've put her there.'

'You're right, Carter, of course you're bloody right.' She stood and struggled to get her phone out of her pocket. 'The chap's card might be in my...' She trailed off, as though realising something. She stashed her phone away and yanked open the door she'd been leaning against, storming back into the room with Carter only a few steps behind. Neither spoke, both all too aware of their eavesdropper. Archer ignored the central spaces though – she didn't go for the phone or the computer, the obvious choices, Carter thought – and instead yanked over a full vase that was sitting on the windowsill. She pulled out the blooming sunflowers and emptied the contents of the vase across the carpet. There was nothing but muddied water, dirty from days of constant sunlight, but when the vase was upside down both officers spotted it at once: a covert listening device, no larger than the average USB stick, taped to the underside of the container.

He could have snatched at it and smashed the thing to pieces. But the flowers, the vase, the bug; it was all evidence. Archer set the vase upside down on the window, leaving the listening device exposed, and gestured for them to step back out of her office.

'How long have the flowers been there?' Carter asked when they were back outside.

'Three, maybe four days.' She began to pace again; Carter hadn't realised she was the type. 'They were delivered by a young woman. Do you have a picture of Yasmin Lacey?'

'Not on me, but we can get one. Ma'am, isn't this what–'

'I'm here.' Morris rushed round the corner and came to an abrupt halt, inches away from Archer who was mid-lap of the hallway. 'Christ, sorry, ma'am,' she panted. 'I'm here, you can both leave. The tech team, they're coming too. They know it's, well, a matter of urgency.'

Carter didn't know whether the panting was the speed at which she'd rushed from one part of the station to another, or the panic at what was happening – both, he suspected. But Morris took up guard outside the door without instruction.

'We managed to isolate the bug in the room. It was taped to

the underside of a vase of flowers that Superintendent Archer believes was delivered three, perhaps even four days ago. She's yet to see a picture of Yasmin Lacey, can you–'

'I'll arrange for one,' Morris interrupted. 'I can also get the desk sergeant to pull the CCTV footage for the last four days, so we'll be able to verify for ourselves whether it was Lacey or not.' She paused for a deep inhale. 'Burton is texting you the details of Stone's travel. I've shown her how to track him using motorway cameras, but we've got no way of tracking him when he leaves the motorway unless he's caught on camera somewhere again.'

Carter flashed a tight smile at his junior. 'Nice work, Morris.'

'Thanks, boss. Bring her home, yeah?' She looked from one superior to another, as though asking for reassurance. But Carter didn't have the confidence in him to give it.

Carter and Archer paced down to the car park together. She had her phone pressed to her ear the entire time, alternating calls between Melanie and their police contact down at the coast.

'Why doesn't anyone answer their phones anymore?' She snatched at the door handle of her car, but her head snapped round at the clunking sound of Carter unlocking his own vehicle. 'I'm driving, DS Carter.'

'Ma'am, with the greatest of respect...' He didn't finish. For the last ten minutes she'd been swearing and cussing and calling one number after the next; if Carter drove, he reasoned she was free to continue with that. Archer thought for a few seconds before rolling her eyes, locking her car and moving across to Carter's. 'Thank you. This isn't a defeat, Carter, we just don't have time to argue.'

While Carter strapped himself in, Archer was contending

with the car's internal navigation system. She keyed in a postcode from heart. 'That's the cottage she's staying at. We can make it there in an hour, easily, if you're not shy with the accelerator.'

'Never have been, ma'am, never have been...'

52

Melanie had left her mobile phone on the kitchen counter at the house. She'd picked it up and put it down three times before deciding against taking it out with her. She was finding it increasingly difficult not to call Carter, not only for updates on the case, but also to reach back into the comforts of home. She'd wanted to ask about Emily, Trish, everything she never asked when they were in a car together. But now wasn't the time, she thought, promising herself that when all this was over she'd make the effort.

She'd woken early after a fitful night of sleep. After hours of being indoors with little to occupy her, she'd walked the beach. She moved at a slow pace, only shifting from sand to concrete when she arrived at a set of steps to climb into the quiet bustle of the accompanying town. The place wasn't exactly busy with tourists. Yet the vendors along the seafront had still unpacked for the day – optimistic for latecomers to the area who might need a bucket and spade, or a bag of marbles to take home with them. Her adventures in the previous days had shown her there was more to the place than clichés, so she weaved through the street-sellers into what passed as the high street. Like any area, the place had become overpopulated with coffee shops and Melanie went through a process of elimination to choose: *That one looks too busy; that one looks too far away*. She settled on a café called The Seagull that looked to have only two other patrons.

Melanie took a free paper from the rack by the door and, noting the sign that said 'Table service', she grabbed a spot by the window. People-watching was one of the few pastimes she could indulge in. Although she appreciated the opportunity to sit and read the news too – rather than making appearances on or in it.

'Kelly, right?'

Melanie nearly didn't answer. Archer had told her that she'd need to be out of harm's way, away from the city. But she hadn't mentioned the new identity until they were unlocking the front door of the hideaway house.

'I don't look like a Kelly,' Melanie had protested.

'No? You sort of do to me,' Archer had replied as she pushed the door open. 'You don't have to be a Kelly if it truly offends you. But I don't know how long you'll be kept alive if you stay as a Melanie.' She'd spoken as though Melanie were a petulant child, rather than a grown woman having her world shifted. It hadn't seemed right to argue with her only link to the world back home, though, so Melanie had bitten her tongue.

Now, she smiled at the young waitress. 'That's right.'

'Welcome to the neighbourhood. I'm Ronnie.' She flashed a smile that seemed rehearsed, which made sense for a waitress in a busy seaside town, Melanie thought. 'Are you settling into the area okay? Everyone being nice enough?'

Melanie admired what she thought was a protective streak in the girl. 'Yes, thank you, everyone's quite nice. I'm enjoying the visit so far.'

'Good, and what can I be getting you here today?'

She ordered a pot of tea and a slice from their Bakewell tray bake, and she skimmed the day's headlines while she waited for the order. There was the familiar clunk and murmur and stir that comes with any coffee shop, plus a strange comfort in the sound as well.

'Here we go,' Ronnie said, minutes later, setting a tray down. 'I completely forgot to say, honestly, I'd forget my head,' she unloaded teacup, saucer and so on, 'Officer Ingram was in earlier, he mentioned he needed a word with you. Been misbehaving already?' The woman winked and Melanie's stomach turned over.

'He didn't say what about?'

'He didn't but he did mention another officer, someone visiting. God, now, what was the name?' She dropped the empty tray to her side and looked toward the ceiling, as though the answer might be pinned there. The more the seconds rolled on, the more Melanie thought she really could take a disliking to Ronnie. 'Carter? That might have been it. A colleague of his. D – I don't know, DC, DS, one or the other, Carter, visiting from the city.' She shrugged. 'Station's only up the road, you could always go and check after. For now, you just enjoy that tray bake.'

Melanie couldn't have cared less about the tray bake, the tea, or the free paper. Her stomach was a cat's cradle. *Why is Carter here? Have they caught Stone?* One thought rolled into another in a way that she couldn't manage or filter. She took a few sips of hot tea to try to steady herself but there was no use. She caught Ronnie and asked for the bill.

'But your tray bake.'

'I'll take that to go,' she said, reasoning there was likely a bin on her travels.

~

Archer and Carter were ten minutes into their journey and neither had said a word. Archer had made one phone call after another though. With Melanie still not answering, and DC Ingram – the officer charged with minding Melanie, Carter had learned – also out of the station, Archer had called in recruits from elsewhere. She'd logged a request for a call back from Ingram's superior – 'Always go over their heads, Carter, never bow out,' she'd said on ending the call – and she'd got in touch with Read and Fairer to give them the postal address for where Melanie was staying. She held the phone close to her mouth but still on loudspeaker, so Carter could be privy to the calls.

'What route are you taking, ma'am?' Read asked and Archer looked to Carter.

'Motorway,' he answered, loud enough for his colleague to hear.

'Fairer has pulled up a route planner and there isn't a huge time difference between motorway and A-road, so we'll take the scenic route in case there's any sign of Stone. Maybe we can head him off.'

Archer shook her head, as though the idea didn't hold water, but said, 'Good thinking, Read, let us know if you need anything.' She ended the call and dropped her head hard against the seat behind her.

'You don't think they'll head him off?'

'Not a chance, Carter. I don't even think we'll head him off.' Carter looked at his speedometer, which was nearing ninety miles an hour. 'It isn't because we're not driving fast enough either, it's because he has a three-day start on us, thanks to me.'

'Ma'am, you can't be–'

'I think you'll find I can, when I'm the one who gave away Melanie's whereabouts.'

'You didn't do it knowingly,' he protested.

'No, it was merely accidental sabotage.' She nearly laughed.

'May I text Burton and ask her to liaise with uniformed officers? We need as many feet on the ground down there and with Ingram not answering the bloody phone, there must be other forces close by that can assist.'

Carter wasn't sure whether she was asking his permission. 'Of course, ma'am.'

'She won't mind a text, is what I mean.'

'Oh, I see.' Carter let out a small huff. 'Some of the hours that Melanie has been known to text, I'm sure a message from a superior officer won't rattle her too much.'

'She's a good officer, isn't she?'

He didn't know whether she meant Burton or Melanie – but it didn't matter. 'One of the best, I think, one of the absolute best.' He pressed his foot a little harder on the pedal.

Bar the loud hum of the engine, the car was quiet for the minutes that followed. So the shrill ring of Archer's mobile made both officers jump.

'It's Ingram,' she said as she answered, hitting loudspeaker again. 'DC Ingram?'

'Superintendent Archer, my apologies, I've heard that you've been after me. I've been out doing the rounds this morning. It's nice, isn't it, to touch base with your people at the start of every day. Plus, the beach–'

'It's idyllic, Ingram, it really is, but that's not why I'm on my way there, unfortunately.'

'Oh, you're coming back down so soon?'

'We have reason to believe DI Watton's location has been disclosed, and the suspect we're currently pursuing is either en route to the area or perhaps even there already. I need you to get over to DI Watton's property as a matter of urgency, as we haven't personally been able to contact her over the day either. We're all quite anxious for her safety, as you can imagine.'

'What a terrible thing. How was the information leaked? If you don't mind me–'

'As a matter of fact, I do mind,' she snapped. 'Now, my colleague and I are probably another thirty minutes away, maybe slightly longer. Could you please get to Watton's property, ensure her safety, and let me know when you've done such?'

'Of course, ma'am, absolutely,' Ingram replied. He sounded startled and Carter was relieved to hear it; that at least meant he was taking this seriously. 'One of your other officers is actually already here, though, and I've attended to his needs regarding the case, ma'am, so there's no need to worry. He'll be securing the property by now, I suspect.'

Archer and Carter exchanged a look. 'I'm sorry, Ingram, what officer is already there?'

Ingram hesitated. 'He identified himself as DS Carter.'

53

The cottage looked undisturbed from the front. There was nothing to suggest the door or the windows had been tampered with; all the locks were in place, with no signs of damage. Melanie scouted the building as though she were working a case and, deciding no one else had entered – from this side, anyway – she unlocked the door and took a cautious step into the hallway. She didn't bolt the entryway behind her; it would help her nerves to know where the clear exits were. But the further she trod along the hall, the more she managed to convince herself the fears were irrational. *If Carter is here, or is coming here, it won't be with bad news*, she thought, peering into the downstairs office space – the first open doorway she came to – before moving along to the kitchen. There were no signs of life in there either. *They've caught him*, she concluded, *they've caught him and Carter is coming to tell me*. She rounded the corner into the living room to satisfy one final shred of anxiety in her. But expecting the room to be empty only made the sight of feet, legs, thighs all the more jarring. She edged in slowly, delaying the reveal, but Melanie knew who was sitting on her sofa long before she saw the man's face.

Roderick Stone looked at his wristwatch and said, 'You took your time.'

Melanie glanced around the room in a hurry. She soon spotted a shower of glass lying across the wooden floor, where the doors that opened out onto the patio had been smashed.

'You'd think Superintendent Archer would put her best officer somewhere safer than this, really, wouldn't you? I practically had a police escort get me here this morning. And not the police escort I'm used to, let me tell you that much, DC Watton.' He laughed and turned to look at her for the first time. 'Sorry, it's DI Watton now, isn't it?'

Melanie shifted her foot back a fraction and Stone dropped his eyes.

'I wouldn't.' He stared at her feet until they were stationary. 'You're only delaying the inevitable by doing that.'

'The inevitable?' Melanie tried to keep her voice steady.

'I found you once,' he stood as he spoke, 'I'll find you again.' He took two small steps forward, not enough to bridge the gap between them. 'Tell me again how you came by that promotion? It wasn't because of little old me, was it?'

Working the Stone case had seen Melanie promoted from detective constable to detective sergeant. But the inspector role she'd gotten all by herself. She had to swallow down the urge to correct him; it wasn't the time, and her fighter instinct needed to back down to a sensible level if she was going to get out of this.

'Why did you come for me?' she asked, braving a step away from him.

'Because I owe you, don't I?' He made it sound obvious, but Melanie's frown pushed him to explain further. 'You took my family, my freedom, a lifestyle I'd become accustomed to. My career wen–'

Melanie snorted and immediately regretted the reaction. 'Career? You were a criminal.'

He took another step then, as though punishing the outburst. 'I was damn good at it.'

'But you got caught, Roderick.'

'Because you were gunning for me!'

'Because it was my job!' She matched his volume.

'And now it's your job to catch killers, isn't it,' he said with another step. 'It's so much harder to get your attention these days, DI Watton. There was a time when I could turn your head without trying, and now, look at the lengths.'

That can't be all this has been about, Melanie thought. 'That's why you killed Norman Halloway, to turn heads?'

Stone looked disgusted at the mention of the name, his lips curling into a sneer. 'All of those animals that people had done away with and he's there,' he paused and jerked his head forward, as though swallowing a gag, 'he's there stuffing them full of fuck knows what, bringing them back to life, selling them for a profit. It was easy to work up the guts to kill him. Did you see the animals he had lined up?' Another step forward. 'If a bloke like me had done that you'd have been shouting your mouth off about rights and cruelty and–'

'Norman Halloway wasn't breaking the law.'

'You never could prove I was,' he snapped back, and Melanie felt his spittle land on her bottom lip. 'You always hated that, didn't you, that's why you came for me?'

Melanie took another step away from him. 'You gave me everything I needed.'

'Do you remember the time you came to see me, DI Watton?'

She wished he'd stop using her title; every time he said it, he made it sound like an insult.

'Vaguely,' she lied. She remembered the evening all too well when she went to track him down, hellbent on bringing him in for anything she could charge him with. But it hadn't worked out that way when she'd found him.

'My mates, they said, "She's got a thing for you, lad."' He took two steps then. 'Bit of a crush, they meant. I always wondered about it a bit myself up until I got out the nick. Then I started seeing you with that woman of yours.' He was close enough for Melanie to feel his breath and the sensation unsettled her. 'You've got a thing for her, haven't you?'

Melanie wasn't sure whether it was Stone's proximity or his mention of Hilda, but she bolted. She could remember leaving her mobile phone in the kitchen, just one room away, so that's where she ran. Stone was close behind, reaching out to grab her jumper but missing by a fraction. Melanie's shoes slipped on the smooth tiles of the kitchen floor, but she steadied herself on the edge of the work surface, using it to guide her into a corner. She looked over everything within grabbing distance, searching for whatever she might be able to use as protection, and her attentions landed on the block of kitchen knives. She seized the closest, paying no attention to which of the bunch might be the sharpest to use.

All the while Stone stayed in the opposite corner, as though enjoying her panic.

Trapped like an animal, Melanie thought, *this is what he liked – still likes.* 'You wanted me cornered?' she asked, the knife at arm's length in front of her.

He laughed. 'We're alone in a house. Wherever you are in here, you're cornered.'

Melanie glanced at the phone next to her, then back to him. 'I could call for help.'

'Go on, then.' He laughed when Melanie hesitated. 'But you won't, because you still want to bring me in yourself, don't you? You still want to be the big I am who catches Roderick Stone. Well, here I am.' He opened his arms wide. 'Are you going to catch me or kill me?' He nodded to the knife and added, 'Because I'm an unarmed man. And it doesn't seem like reasonable force if you go plunging that knife anywhere, does it?'

He was right; it wasn't reasonable force. *Or it isn't if he's unarmed.* Melanie couldn't believe he'd break in without some form of weapon, but could she take the chance that he had? Her mind darted between both possibilities. She could feel the thump of her heart against her innards and noticed the thrum of a vein in her wrist as she tightened her grip around the implement. A wrong move now could cost her her career – or her life.

Their attentions snapped away from each other as Melanie's mobile began to vibrate across the work surface. Both of them stared at the thing, as though it were a creature likely to attack. There wasn't a voicemail function on the SIM card that Archer had arranged for Melanie to take, making the noise an endless distraction.

'Why don't you go ahead and answer that?' Stone said. His tone sounded playful in a way that made Melanie's stomach turn over.

'Hardly anyone knows that number, and everyone who does is in the force. You don't think I'll tell them what's happening here?' she replied, the knife still poised in a way that would allow her to strike if she needed to. 'They'll be coming by now, Stone.'

He gasped and put his hands over his mouth in a theatrical gesture. 'But will they get here in time? Anything could happen between you taking that call and your colleagues arriving. Let me see,' he moved his finger through the air as though counting something Melanie couldn't see, 'I bet it'll be DS Carter. He really looks up to you, you know? Big, bad DI Watton, catching all the crooks.' He laughed. 'I wonder if he'll look up to you after this.' The phone's hum hushed but started again seconds later. 'Go on, answer it. It might be someone calling to say goodbye...'

54

There was a flurry of officers flanked by Archer and Carter, both of whom stormed one room, then another until they found their quarry. Stone was lying flat out on the kitchen floor as though asleep. The only sign that there had been a struggle at all was the smudge of blood on his forehead, that stood out brightly against the pallor of his skin. Carter pressed two fingers to the man's neck, feeling for a pulse; he struggled against the doughy flesh but lost his concentration on the task when a groan emerged – not from Stone, but from the opposite corner of the room. Carter looked up and saw her; bloodied and huddled in a corner, her hands pressed hard against her abdomen.

'Beverley, I've got her!'

He did away with professional formalities as he rushed to his colleague – friend. Carter pulled Melanie close to him and pushed away hair from her forehead, matted there with sweat. Her body was shaking, either from blood loss or shock or both, Carter wondered, as he felt for his mobile phone.

Archer rushed into the room seconds later with her fists

raised, ready for a physical confrontation, but fell to her knees in front of her juniors. 'Mel? Melanie?'

'I've got her, chief,' Carter reassured her. 'Get him.'

'Who gives a shit about him. Give me your phone.'

Archer snatched the handset away and finished the 999 call Carter had been on the cusp of making. 'This is Superintendent Beverley Archer from...' She drifted out of the room, pacing while she spoke to the operator.

'Boss,' Carter tried. 'Hey, come on.' He spoke softly to her, like he did to Emily whenever she was poorly. Melanie clutched her belly, but the blood had seeped through her hands and clothing; the knife was only inches away from her on the floor. Carter resisted the urge to kick it from them; the scene needed to be as close to how they'd found it on arrival. He gave Melanie's shoulders a weak squeeze. 'Hey, you need to stay with me, keep awake, okay? Archer's calling for help.'

Melanie turned her nose against him, resting her face against his chest. Her words were muffled by his stab vest, but he lowered his head to hear her. 'Did I get him?'

He rested his chin lightly on top of her head. 'Yeah, you got him, boss. You did good.'

AFTER

55

Carter took a shaky inhale as he tapped lightly on the door. He didn't wait for permission – as he once would have done – but instead stuck his head round the corner, to see whether she was awake.

Melanie sat upright in the bed with a remote control in her hand. She silenced the television and gestured Carter into the room. 'Never have I ever been quite so glad to see you.'

He closed the distance between them, setting the customary flowers and grapes on the table at the end of the bed. He stood awkwardly for a moment before moving towards his boss. When Melanie put her arms up in an anticipatory gesture, Carter leaned in to give her a hug.

'I'm sorry this is unprofessional,' he said into her neck.

'Don't ruin it.' Melanie let out a noise of discomfort and Carter leapt back. 'Things are sore, that's all, it isn't you.' She adjusted herself. 'So, are you going to give the information willingly or will I have to pull it from you?'

He laughed as he took a seat next to her. 'Well, you didn't kill him.'

'Damn it.' She dropped her head back against the pillow and smiled.

'But it turns out that cracking someone on the head with a bread bin can cause a nasty concussion, so, there's that knowledge to take away from this whole experience.' He shook his head. 'Why a bread bin, boss, of all the things?'

She shrugged. 'It was the closest thing to hand once we started.'

'Once the struggle started, you mean?'

Melanie screwed her eyes shut tight.

'I'm sorry,' he added, 'I shouldn't have–'

'No, no it's fine.' She looked back at him. 'It's kind of wild, Carter, you know?'

'Yeah, I get that.'

'I gave my official statement earlier today. Stone waited until I answered the phone to Archer before he launched himself, wrangled the knife away from me, we struggled. I don't even know...' she drifted off, as though trying to replay what happened. 'I don't even know how he got it. Everything happened so–'

There was another knock at the door and Carter rolled his eyes. 'I know who this is.' He reached over and gave Melanie's hand a squeeze. 'Do you feel up for visitors?'

'It depends on who it is.' She winked.

'Read and Fairer.'

'Then no.'

The two shared a laugh before Carter shouted, 'Come on, then!'

Read and Fairer fell through the door with Burton and Morris close behind. Burton was holding a bouquet of balloons, gathered several inches above her head. Fairer cradled a bunch of flowers that made Carter's earlier offering look feeble.

Meanwhile, Morris stepped over to Melanie's side table and set down a pile of paperbacks.

She rested her hand on the top book. 'These feature nothing that relates to police procedural or detective work, nor do they have any mention of beaches or seaside towns.' She turned back to join the crew but shot around to add, 'Oh! Or violent attacks with knives.'

'That was real subtle, Morris,' Read said as she re-joined them all by the door.

'And what did the last wise detective bring?' Melanie said, raising an eyebrow at Read.

He lifted a plain white carrier into Melanie's eyeline. 'I brought breakfast sandwiches.'

THE END

Printed in Great Britain
by Amazon